Take Me Now

Nancy Jardine

CROOKED
CAT

First Crooked Love Cats Edition
Crooked Cat Publishing Ltd. 2016

Discover us online:
www.crookedcatpublishing.com

Join us on facebook:
www.facebook.com/crookedcatpublishing

*Tweet a photo of yourself holding
this book to @crookedcatbooks
and something nice will happen.*

If I hadn't thoroughly enjoyed a family weekend, which featured a return seaplane trip from Glasgow to Oban (Scotland), coupled with a chartered sail around the Inner Hebrides, I might never have come up with the plot for Take Me Now.

I dedicate this version of Take Me Now to my late brother-in-law, Neil, since the trip was organised for his birthday.

I'm so glad we all had the opportunity to have such a fantastic time together flying over some of the same ground as Aela and Nairn in Take Me Now.

About the Author

Nancy Jardine lives in Aberdeenshire, Scotland. She currently shares a home with her husband, daughter, son-in-law, 3 year old granddaughter and 1 year old grandson. It'll continue to be a busy household till late summer of 2015 when a new home will be completed by the young 'uns, on what was Nancy's former back garden. The loss of that part of the garden won't be missed since there should now be more writing time available! Yet, that's only sort of, because childminding tends to be constant over the day. Writing time snatched, when the 'other granny' takes over the childcare or when 'mum' isn't at work, is precious.

Researching historical particulars is a pleasant and constant preoccupation, and ancestry research is a lovely time-suck. Finding out even more about the black sheep of the family can be shocking —but very entertaining. Nancy regularly blogs and loves to have guests visit to be interviewed, or to share their own posts. Facebooking is a habit she's trying to keep within reasonable bounds! Any time left in a day is for leisure reading and the occasional historical series on TV.

Nancy's published work to date has been two non-fiction history projects and six novels. Three novels are the historical romantic adventures in her Celtic Fervour Series. Her three contemporary romantic mysteries will all come under the Crooked Cat banner during 2015.

Topaz Eyes, a treasure hunt mystery based around a complex family tree was a Finalist for THE PEOPLE'S BOOK PRIZE 2014.

By late spring 2015, she'll also have published The Taexali Game, the first of her Rubidium Time Travel series for a Middle Grade / YA market.

She's gradually working on a number of new novels: Book 4 of her Celtic Fervour Series; a family saga beginning in Victorian Scotland; and Book 2 of her Rubidium Time Travel Series which is a Victorian adventure set in Glasgow, Scotland.

Nancy Jardine can be found at many promotional sites including these:

http://nancyjardine.blogspot.co.uk
http://nancyjardineauthor.com/
Twitter: @nansjar
Facebook: http://on.fb.me/XeQdkG

Amazon Author page for books and to view book trailer videos:
US: http://amzn.to/RJZzZz
UK: http://www.amazon.co.uk/Nancy-Jardine/e/B005IDBIYG/ref=ntt_dp_epwbk_0

Acknowledgements

My thanks go to Stephanie and Laurence Patterson of Crooked Cat Publishing for re-launching this new version of Take Me Now.

I'd also like to take the opportunity to thank Kelly May Illingworth for whizzing through the final edits with me.

Nancy Jardine

Take Me Now

Chapter One

Nairn Malcolm's only hope was chugging into the cove down below.

His fingers clamped onto the wrought-iron railing as he compelled himself to accept reality. Waiting for other candidates wasn't feasible; time was too precious for that. He had to be mobile to ferret out the saboteur who'd caused havoc again that morning, never mind to do his normal work. Yet, even if the person below was suitable, could he involve her in something he knew was dangerous? His conscience smarted as much as his niggling wounds. Cantankerous rumbles from the healthy side of his mouth accompanied another squint at the boat now docking.

Shapely legs clambered from his newest catamaran. Deep-pink stilettos touched down on his floating jetty and found balance as it dipped and swayed, while tangled tresses billowed around her head in the stiff breeze coming in off the water. His irritability burbled at her impractical footwear, his temper worse when a wicked gust of wind blew up her flirty little skirt, a flash of white widening his eyes. His fingers scrunched the railing.

The woman's clothes might pass muster in an office, but they weren't practical for sailing around the islands off the west coast of Scotland on a breezy end-of-June day.

Not in any noticeable hurry, she was chatting happily with Aran, his boatyard manager. Though he couldn't hear their words, their easy conversation belied a long-time friendship as the painter was secured to the mooring hook. He heard the generally taciturn Aran chuckle a second time. How the heck did the woman draw the man out of his usual reticence?

Her echoing laugh annoyed him.

His grumble aired loud enough to startle the tern settling alongside him as he willed himself to be ready for the coming meeting, his eyes closing for a moment to regroup. The dip of the wind turned in his favour whipping words up from the cove, but they only made his bad humour worse.

"Honestly. It's no problem. I'll take it with me."

The loud claim came as Aran answered that he could look after it till later. Look after what? Nairn's one good eye popped open and locked onto her rear as she shrugged into the laden backpack Aran passed up to her from the catamaran.

A backpack?

He shook his head to dispel the peculiar image. Why wasn't she shouldering a jaunty little handbag, or a briefcase? His vision was loopy, but he wasn't imagining the monstrous bag as she straightened up. The dull wallop of a pile driver at the back of his skull had been present all day. Now it pounded even more from the stress this woman produced – and he hadn't met her yet. Who, in their right mind, came to an interview wearing bright pink stilettos, for God's sake, and sported a groaning backpack?

Aela Cameron's agile skip along his undulating floating-jetty was unimpeded by the weighty luggage. When she came to a halt at his boatshed, she peered in the little side window, her Canadian accent clearer when it drifted up to him.

"That's a cool collection. Can I have a peek at his floatplane?"

He watched them vanish inside his boatshed. His mouth pursed at the continued delay. Shifting his body to a better position, he waited. Then waited some more.

A peek?

He could have built a ruddy fishing boat by now. What the hell took them so long? Dilly-dallying wouldn't suit him at all, but he owed his ex-PA, Brian, big time. Brian had worked his ass off to get even one candidate, though he doubted this woman really would have the experience he needed. An awkward shunt moved his aches and pains to the side of the gate. Just out of view, he still overlooked the boatshed.

Finally, they exited the wooden building. Aela Cameron's head whipped up when Aran indicated the climb, his finger pointing to the top of the cliff. Unladylike snorts and comments burst free from her as she tackled the zigzagging wooden stairway built onto the rock face. Part way up, a huge smile lightened her face before she quipped something down to Aran, who lugged a box of supplies. Aran's laughing answer drifted off on the breeze.

A funny woman was she? Nairn shuffled along the wall to prop himself against a stout beech tree. The tumult in his head amplified as he prepared to meet her, his usual control as elusive as the vision he struggled to balance. The greenish gull-plop that landed on his elbow was one more indignity, exemplifying how he felt.

Fresh horse crap. Steaming and hazy…and overheated.

***

Aela huffed but only a little bit.

Nobody had warned her about the climb. The only information given by the appointments agency was that she should present herself at the marina for two p.m. where she'd be met and ferried to the island of Lanera, for an interview with Nairn Malcolm, at his Garvald home.

Aran, the pilot of the catamaran, had been chatty during the journey, though had been circumspect about her prospective employer, the location of his house and of how she would get there once they arrived at the island. Not being bothered over what she considered minor details, she'd told him about her sailing experience as they skirted the Mull of Kintyre on their way north to the island of Lanera.

Now, a few hundred treads up, she was on the top step of the cliff staircase thankful she was fit. The climb with an overloaded backpack, and wearing the ridiculous heels, would have killed some people. She chuckled at the silly image as she unlatched the wrought iron gate set into a high grey granite wall and stepped through onto rough grass. Exhilarated by the scene, she stood transfixed for a couple of moments. It was inevitable, though, that her throaty gurgle sputtered out since she wasn't one to suppress her mirth too often.

"Holy shit, Aran. Would you look at that? Hell's bells and baubles. You said it would be worth it when I got to the top, but you never mentioned it was a cute little castle. Hey, can you hear me down there?"

Aran's amused answer echoed up. "The whole island can probably hear you, Miss Cameron."

So taken was she by the scenery, she didn't lower her volume. "This is my first visit to a real Scottish castle. Jeez. Just look at that dinky turret up there. I could pretend to be the lonely little virgin watching my handsome knight in shining armour gallop in on his trusty steed. I'd drop my token handkerchief for him to scoop up on his lance before he fought death-defying tourneys over my honour."

Her unladylike hollers and arm gestures wouldn't have matched the weeping-willow creature she portrayed, but she was on a roll, her mind's eye taking flight in the magical setting.

Aran's voice floated from just short of the top step, the weight of his large package having slowed his climb. "Your historical references are a wee bit mixed up, Miss Cameron. We were short of that brand of champion up here in the islands. Our heroes were more likely to be uncouth, more hairy, and a lot less chivalrous."

Aela's loud chortles echoed all around as she scanned the rooftop crenellations. "Scrummy. Sounds exactly my type. Bring the hairy ones on, please, and we'll have a big party in that dinky castle."

Fifty yards ahead, the original turreted keep had been renovated, two extensions having been added to make the whole construction form a U-shape. The facade of grey granite had dark wood bordering lots of shining windows, blending harmoniously. The windows, she guessed, had been widened from original gun-looped embrasures since a couple of these thin rectangular openings remained at each end of the centre section on ground floor level.

"This is the greatest start to an interview, Aran. I'm so impressed," she whooped, unable to contain her bubble of pleasure because in no way did the castle resemble the forbidding bleak structures she'd read about in traditional Scottish tales. "Okay. So, what's next on this escapade?"

She turned back as Aran stepped through the gate. Her beaming smile froze, her hand whipping up to slap her chest. "Who the hell are you? Jeez. You scared the crap out of me. The castle comes with its very own ogre?"

She released an indrawn breath. Fairy tales were abandoned as medieval images resurfaced, her heartbeat settling. The vision alongside the wall was so unanticipated there was no way could she suppress a burst of laughter. "Whoa. This is so incredible. I get to meet the battle-scarred champion as well? I love these full re-enactment deals. It's great to meet you, Sir Smash-Em-Up."

An uncomfortable throat-clearing came from Aran as he crossed the stretch of grass.

The stony stare of the other man curtailed any further gusto. Aela belatedly grasped that her glib comments weren't well received. It appeared that Sir Smash-Em-Up's appearance maybe wasn't set up for her enjoyment.

A huge guy stood braced against the tree near the gate. She wasn't small at five feet ten, but this man was at least six and a half feet. He was attention-grabbing in the way a poster for an Accident and Emergency Department would be: downed in an earthquake and a hotchpotch of his parts thrown up in its wake sort of image. Why was he out of his sick-bed if the injuries he seemed to have were genuine?

His plastered right forearm nestled inside the waistband of his sweatpants. That wasn't so odd, but she gulped over the rest of him. The left leg of the black sweatpants had been haphazardly hacked off at crotch level: the sturdy thigh below a mish-mash of scratches, plasters, purple-black bruises and dark leg hair. A rigid white plaster cast stretched from a little above the kneecap all the way down to his toes.

The view above his waist wasn't encouraging either because the short-sleeved black shirt the man wore was open, and flapping in the warm breeze. White gauze was strapped on below his left collar bone, the rest of his chest splattered with deep scratches and Technicolor bruising. The man was a mess, but quite a glorious mess.

"So. You're not an actor." Her statement gained no response.

He never blinked once as she stared, no part of his shuttered face showing any emotion at all. Eyes of an intense blue regarded her, though the left one was barely open. Dark bloody bruising and puffy red inflammation around the eyelid, the swelling and discolouration on the cheekbone below, made his features unbalanced. Thick black hair, tousled like a blood-sticky thatch, drooped above his bruised brow. An angry gash slashed across his forehead, the wound scabbing over but not sufficiently deep to require stitching.

Mmm...definitely an ogre.

The man bore a vague resemblance to the thirty-two year old Nairn Malcolm of the internet photograph she'd managed to search out, but would the blonde limpet in the recent celebrity snapshot want to curl herself around this forbidding wreck of a man? Aela thought not. She wondered if his blank expression was caused by current circumstances or if this was his normal demeanour since he hadn't been smiling in the photograph either.

Though, with the high granite wall as his backdrop, she could easily imagine this man lording it over the castle, ruthlessly challenging any invaders to his domain. He looked the archetypal highland laird, yet what had the guy been doing to get himself in such a state?

"Nairn Malcolm."

Her gaze tracked his hand as it stretched out in salutation, no other part of his body moving since he remained parked against the tree. Maybe the extreme sporting activities the man marketed were a little too extreme? Did she want to be transporting someone who looked like a walking advert for medical insurance? On the other hand, she could see exactly why he needed someone to fly his floatplane for a while. The appointments agency hadn't made any mention of his medical condition and that came as no surprise now that she could see what he was like. They'd probably feared she'd turn tail and run from the daunting prospect of him.

She moved to return his gesture but halted when one undamaged eyebrow twitched in scathing inquiry. Ah. Tendering the wrong hand wasn't a great start, and neither was her right heel sinking into the soft grass. Shit! Other mental curses were quelled as she entangled the fingers of her left hand with his.

"Aela Cameron. Good afternoon, Mr. Malcolm."

His hand was huge. Warm fingers clamped around hers as he pumped briskly, an awkward three times, a fierce grip that tightened her forearm muscles. Wriggling herself free of his clench, she stumbled right out of her stuck-fast shoe and toppled onto the grass, her backpack bearing the brunt of the impact. An upside down tortoise wouldn't have been any more graceless, her legs wallowing in air. Her burst of laughter was repeated when she looked up into the disbelieving gaze of Nairn Malcolm.

"Upon my ass, indeed. Sorry, Mr. Malcolm. I guess it's not good form to reveal the tighty-whities during an interview."

She squirmed her skirt down before attempting to straighten her face because Nairn Malcolm's good eye had almost popped out. Such events rarely fazed her and this one was proving to be the most comical situation she'd been in for a long time. After rolling to bear weight on all fours, she rebalanced the backpack before rising, her amusement subsiding under his continued displeasure. Sure, she'd fallen over, but it didn't deserve such a scurrilous attitude.

"I'm away round to Mariskay," Aran called from the top of the cliff staircase. "Call me when you're ready, Nairn."

Aela registered how long she must have been ogling the

walking wounded since Aran had already been inside the castle with the heavy load he'd been carrying.

"Thanks for the deliveries, Aran." Nairn Malcolm's reply was brief…and toneless.

"Hey! Thanks for delivering me too, Aran. I adored what you can do with that catamaran." She wasn't sure she wanted to be regarded as one of Mr. Malcolm's deliveries, like a pizza order, although she supposed she almost qualified. She reviewed her circumstances while she waited for Sir Smash-Em-Up to say something else, but all he did was maintain that flinty demeanour. It was definitely the strangest beginning to an interview for a job.

The walking wounded grunted, a heartfelt sigh, before he peeled himself from the sturdy tree. As he lurched past the gate, she watched him glimpse the catamaran already whizzing around the cove before he indicated the French doors. Prior to issuing his orders, she was aware of his deep lingering stare at her lips. She didn't blame him. The fuchsia pink really wasn't her norm.

"Miss Cameron. Those doors to the centre of the building lead into the great room. Wait there."

She nodded, attempting to ignore his rudeness. After padding a few steps towards his castle, twirling her pink stilettos from one hand, she glanced back. The strange man grasped the forearm crutch he'd stashed alongside the wall and hauled it into place, his expression one of sheer resignation. The short walk to the castle must loom like an impossible marathon. The whimper when he started on the first of many lurches made her want to rush to his aid, but he'd set down clear instructions.

On entry to the room, she dropped her backpack to the side of the doors before slipping her shoes back on. Awaiting his slow progress, she admired the décor. When endless seconds passed she returned to the French doors where her grin slipped. "Would you look at that dumb ass? Some bed should still have his name on it."

For every pace the man took, he stopped to regain breath before he repositioned the crutch, followed by a reel as he forced his leg cast forward with a lumbering twist. Laughter went on the back burner. How could she find humour in his predicament? The man shouldn't be interviewing at all, at least not until he was less incapacitated. However, if the idiot wanted to interview her then so be it.

The great room was well named, eminently suitable for someone as large as Mr. Malcolm. Comfortable leather sofas and wide armchairs framed a huge stone fireplace, the grate set with hefty logs and traditional peat blocks. Impressive landscape paintings adorned the white walls and added a kaleidoscope of colour. Small bookcases flanked the French doors. She had plenty of time to examine their contents before he listed into the room.

"Guest cloakroom is second door on the left," he rasped, pointing to the internal entrance doors facing them. His face had leached every vestige of colour.

Aela's opinion remained – the numbskull should be resting.

"Office, second right, when you're done."

Whether she wanted to use the amenities or not, it appeared he'd just issued another order she needed to obey if she wanted this job and having made landfall at this cute castle the location appealed a lot, though she willed her mind to remain open regarding its ignorant owner. He didn't like her – but that was okay because liking each other didn't have to come into it. In a contrary way, it made her more determined to get the temporary job.

"Got that, Mr. Malcolm."

After using the facilities, she gave her face a good wash to clear off the salt spray and tidied her hair with her fingers having found most of the pins holding her top knot had vanished to the wind during the boat trip. Rummaging in the pocket of her jacket, she pulled out two pencils and secured her long hair into a new knot. She felt a bit tidier, if not quite business-perfect.

The hallway was impressive, many doors to either side, light and airy but also very silent. Nobody seemed to be around or they were too well trained to come and find out who wandered the corridor. Adjacent to the cloakroom was a cosy little breakfast nook, bright and welcoming, its large window overlooking the well-stocked side garden. A small arch led through to an impressive kitchen, the décor old-style wooden cabinets, interspersed with modern appliances. She was dying to investigate the rest of the castle, though instead headed for the office reckoning she'd given Nairn enough time to get his broken bones settled.

"Here, please!" His order was terse, his scowling focus entirely on his screen.

"So kind. Thank you." She sat opposite him though, as far as she could tell, her sarcasm had fallen on deaf ears.

The man gave sharp intakes of breath each time he moved, looking even worse than he had outside.

"One minute."

His voice was hostile as he fiddled with his computer mouse while peering, one-eyed, at his monitor. Having noticed he'd avoided eye contact since she entered the room Aela's brows drew together, the first flicker of doubt stealing into her mind. Was she wasting her time even if it had been a lark so far? She pulled her gaze away from him and studied the room. The office was large with an efficient setup. The L-shaped desk arrangement he sat behind was mirrored behind her; the second display angled so the desks weren't directly facing each other.

A thin bead of sweat trickled down his left temple and made a track on his battered face, into the heavy growth covering his jaws. He was the most unkempt prospective employer she could ever imagine. So ridiculous after the effort she'd put in to look professional in her charity shop pale grey suit with its too-short flaring skirt, and nipped-in-waist jacket, but the suit, shoes and fuchsia camisole had been the best she could find at such short notice. It had been a difficult call – come dressed for sailing, or wear more typical PA garb.

"This interview might have to be short."

Her smile faded as she nodded back, disappointment warring with irritation, but she made no attempt to speak.

Was the dratted man admitting he was too ill to continue?

"But first give me brief details about flying my floatplane, and then my 525b jet."

He inched two advertising brochures across the desk toward her, information on the two vehicles he'd referred to. The floatplane she'd seen in his boatshed, but she scanned the jet specifications before she lifted her gaze back to him. His skin tone was as grey as the granite walls of his castle, his deep voice like gravel as he brought his good arm across his chest to brace himself more comfortably in the chair. Stupid man. Determined clearing of her throat grabbed his attention, which seemed to have strayed to somewhere to the right of her shoulder.

Talk about his planes? Nothing would please her better. She loved everything about flying. She licked her lips before starting.

"Your floatplane down in the cove is similar…"

Recounting her experience with comparable planes she watched his eyes glaze over, both lids lowering to slits. Surely, he wasn't bored? Her eulogy hadn't been that long. Her information and experience was as relevant as he would get from anyone, male or female.

"Although I haven't flown the last five months while on my world tour, I kept myself updated on all new developments via the internet."

Only the merest disgruntled twitch broke the stern facemask, which she processed as sort-of listening. As she continued, he slid further down in the chair. His head lolled back to lean on the backrest, his breathing settling to an even shorter rhythm which drew her gaze firmly onto his chest. A deep whimper escaped him as he shunted around a bit more and then his eyes closed again, his good hand making the tiniest of gestures she understood to mean carry on.

Why couldn't the damned man make proper eye contact for more than a nanosecond? Even with his one good eye?

He moaned again and pushed his body back up, his head now awkward, hanging beyond the backrest support, his gaze rolling to the ceiling, his eyelids flickering.

"Excuse me! If you're not already too bored to listen, Mr. Malcolm, I'll tell you about your jet." She waited, till a nod indicated she should continue. "Thank you very much, sir." Full of the deepest sarcasm, but she might have been talking to a blank wall because his response was non-existent. "Hey! Are you even listening to me?"

Not a professional tone of voice, Aela knew, but she wasn't used to being ignored. He struggled to open his eyes, looking like a total drunk as his Cyclops-gaze flickered, before his chin flopped down onto his chest.

"Flippin' heck. Look at the state you're in."

Unable to contain herself she jumped to her feet. Kneeling at his side, she lifted his chin into one hand and used the fingertips of her other hand to pry open his good eyelid. Mmm. It looked like a seriously dilated pupil. She let her trembling fingers drop away as she reflected on his condition. Without her chin support, his head wavered to the side.

"Mr. Malcolm."

Her shrill tone jolted his eyes open as she manoeuvred both hands to rest his cheek against her chest. He snuggled right in, his nose against her breasts…and sniffed. Aela stared down at him. The thrumming pulse at her wrist beat against his cheek. His lids flickered, his mouth wriggled and his one good eye…beseeched?

"Boats…"

Chapter Two

"What? You still want me to tell you about bloody boats when you're almost comatose?"

Aela imagined her question sounded as flabbergasted as she felt, yet the guy's expression flickered assent as he swallowed, the muscles of his cheeks pressing into her softness. Looking down into the battered face of the stubborn fool she was supporting she knew she couldn't keep up the deferential interview stuff. "This is absolute crap! You want me to keep talking?"

"Yes."

His growling sigh was accompanied by lolling head shakes, as though he was clearing his head, his pained whimper making her squirm as he whiffed on her silk blouse. He smelled startling so close up; a mixture of aromas assailing her nostrils as she cradled him. Dried blood still lingered on his hair, a hint of some kind of medicinal alcohol wipe and slightly stale sweat was at his brow – but underlying those was the musky male smell of Nairn himself. She released his head slowly down onto the backrest of his chair, the sole protest from him being another tweak of his lip before he murmured, "Love your voice."

Aela felt herself glow. Blushing was something she'd not done for at least a decade.

Returning to her seat gave her a little time to gain composure before she related her knowledge of speedboats and dinghy sailing. Nairn Malcolm's torso squirmed further down in the chair, the heel of his rigid cast scraping the wooden floor as his legs stretched out below the desk. His eyes flickered, though his attempts to focus on her were failing. At least she thought that was what he was attempting till disturbing sounds emanated from his clenched teeth bordered by lips becoming bluer by the second. Rushing her information, she attempted to speed up the interview process, since he was a hint more tuned into her sailing information. "…but I haven't piloted a catamaran as new as the one used to bring me here today. Uncle Harris hasn't upgraded the fleet to those specifications yet."

He stretched forward two fingers, wildly aiming at the keyboard, the words wrenched from his mouth. "Uncle Harris?"

In the face of what now was a complete travesty of an interview her answer snapped. "My uncle, Harris Cameron, owns Cameron Transport Group."

His head dipped as if in recognition, and after taking a deeper breath, he grunted. It was beyond the silly man to breathe normally, but Aela could tell he wasn't acknowledging his limitations. The mumble that followed took all her deciphering powers.

"Good old Harris. Met him. How's 'e doing?" His fingers stabbed at the keys as tense seconds passed.

She waited till his gaze flipped up, though his chin remained down, his head appearing too heavy to lift. "My uncle's very well, thank you."

"How many hours?" His words slurred.

"What the friggin' heck has that got to do with my Uncle Harris!"

She could contain herself no longer. Leaping up she strode a few paces around the room before returning to her chair, her hands clenched at her sides, composure not much better but a grim determination in place. After plunking herself down, she groaned even louder than Mr. Malcolm. What was the man's frazzled brain referring to? The whole interview had become too surreal now, but she wasn't sure what to do about it.

His focus was still on her mouth because she could swear his face was stuck fast, his chin supporting the full weight of his head. His intent stare was making her feel ill-at-ease.

"Your only job?"

His question came at her as though there had been no break in the conversation at all, no little walkabout for her, none of her inappropriate rejoinders. She wondered if the conversation might go better if she were in cloud-cuckoo-land as well. Maybe she should ferret out some of his happy pills and join him? Biting her lip she answered, calm and collected – she hoped.

"Yes, I've only ever worked for Cameron Transport Group."

His fingers randomly jabbed since he didn't look as though he was even seeing the keys. She was getting too used to his pained breaths as he struggled to raise his head from the chair, gave up, and let it slump back against the headrest. His whole torso drooped as his arms slid down to his sides, the weight of the arm cast making him perch at an awkward tilt. Yet the whine escaping sounded gratified.

Peculiar.

His gaze was almost re-focused when it latched onto hers. "Ah. That's much better."

The guy's weak smile stunned since it was the first proper cracking of his austere demeanour and totally changed him. He breathed slow and measured for a few seconds, a little colour returning to his face. "Bret Walker trained me. Bet you didn't know that," he mumbled, naming a colleague at Cameron Airways, the original sector of the transport group. His head cocked to one side, his smile deepening into a slumberous one, his good eye attempting a wink of sorts.

"I know Bret Walker quite well." Her answer was careful since his cyclops expression was quite different from before. The minuscule lift at the edge of his mouth she imagined was an attempt at being agreeable. "Bret's still Cameron Airways best training pilot, but it was my uncle who trained me."

"Wish you'd trained me. Mmm. You're real gor…jus. D'y know…'at?" A lopsided grin broke free as he slid down even further, and his chin settled on his chest again. "…can't have you, though. S'too dange…us." His head wobbled again before his eyes closed.

Aela's gaze widened at the tenor of his out-of-order comment, and the fleeting look that had accompanied it. The stupid man was passing out. He was on another planet! What would he say next though?

"Lovely voice, matches…spectacular…face."

"What did you just say?"

Her concern over this strange man's behaviour increased. Her personal safety didn't make her fearful, but she was beginning to feel responsible for him since it seemed she was alone with him in the castle. However, why she should feel responsible was the biggest mystery ever.

His eyes flicked open again. "Where am I?"

"Your office, Mr. Malcolm."

"Oh. Yeah. Office…speriens?"

His mumble just decipherable, she detailed what she'd undertaken as Office Manager for Cameron Transport Group. It was once again to his closed eyes; though his little nods she interpreted as an indicator that he was listening. He had to be the most stubborn man she'd ever clapped eyes on, yet she had to award him some merit for persistence. His weird determination annoyed her, but she couldn't watch him suffer any longer.

"I need water, Mr. Malcolm," she lied.

One finger flicked towards the mini-services in a corner of the room. A few seconds later she forced his attention when she waved a glass of water at his face, having pulled his chair free of the desk so that she could get in front of him. Sliding his good leg to the side she knelt between his knees and again lifted his chin, her tone low, but stern.

"Look at me, you stupid bastard. I know you're not interviewing for a nursemaid, but you need to swallow some painkillers."

Her commanding tone managed to get through, just sufficient for him to rouse a little.

"If you fall down, you great lummox, I'll find it difficult

18

to get you up, whereas if you'll just resort to the damn painkillers you're too macho to take I might manage to assist you to bed when they've kicked in."

Having disgorged the anger, Aela waited for the fallout. The man's eyelids flickered, his hand a limp wave at a bunch of pencils on his desk. A blister pack of tablets and the original package – a squashed mess of cardboard – were stuffed inside the round pencil canister. She scanned the dose of the pain killers she was familiar with.

"Have you taken any during the last two hours?"

She waited but no answer came. All he seemed capable of was staring at her. Grasping his prickly chin to lift his face up, days' worth of beard growth scratched the soft pads of her fingertips as she repeated her question.

"No." His mutter was so faint she had to lean closer as he repeated it.

"Tongue out!" she demanded.

"Oh…Yeah."

A glassy gaze locked onto hers. She placed two tablets onto his tongue and brought the water to his lips. After he gulped some she replaced the glass and hunkered back down between his legs.

"Look at me!"

Nairn Malcolm blinked his eyes open. "Y're so pretty."

"Cut the inappropriate comments, you silly numbskull."

Again she forced him to make eye contact. His weary pupils locked on, and remained fixed on her.

Her condescending tone she intended, every single syllable of it, her teeth doing a really nice gritting thing that made her feel better about the ridiculous situation she seemed to have got herself into. "Good. That's good, Sir Smash-Em-Bloody-Up, keep looking at me. Now be a good boy, and while we're waiting for the painkillers to kick in I'll tell you my duties as my uncle's main secretary, and then as office manager. After that, you dense prat, you'll know everything you need to know."

She needed him to gather sufficient strength. There was no way she could manhandle a man of his physique if he was unable to even hobble. Her comments were accompanied by invectives quite innovative for a woman who was being interviewed for a job.

His chin slumped, his slit-eyed focus somewhere below the table, but the lopsided smile on his face she found very weird – as weird as the aerial floating movements of his good hand, which at times did manage to stroke her hair. A sort of soothing pat that made her feel...odd? She really hadn't a proper word for how it made her feel, but she hadn't the heart to stop since he seemed to take comfort from what he was doing, though his breathing was worryingly shallow.

"Don'...need'em...p'ncils."

Before she knew what he was about Nairn Malcolm plucked the pencils out of her hair, sending a tousled mess falling round her shoulders.

"Better." His happy sigh was accompanied by the clattering of the pencils onto the wooden floor.

Aela couldn't prevent her grin because the look on his face was incredible – a mixture of satisfaction, drunkenness and...lust? The jolt of his head slamming forward came as quite a surprise, even more so when his lips collided with hers in a bumbled kiss, unable as he was to aim properly, his fingers clutching her breast for support. Or maybe not, since the squeeze was surprisingly firm. The kiss became more rushed...till the grunt of sheer agony vibrating against her lips was enough to wipe the surprise from her face. Pulling away from him, she gentled his shoulders against the chair. Eyes fast shut, and a tight grimace furrowing his cheeks, the idiot made no objection.

"Rain check on that one, sir?" As the words popped out Aela knew that should a job offer transpire another kiss like that one could never happen. The pain killers had to be strong, though, since there was a dramatic change to his breathing, Nairn's whole demeanour relaxing. She was wondering how to get him to do her bidding when his brows whipped into a frown.

"Got to go, Mz...?"

Aela winced because he couldn't even remember her name.

"'Scuse me." Shrugging himself upright with his good leg his whole body tilted.

"Wait a minute, you reckless idiot! Where's your bloody bedroom?" Jumping up she wedged him against the desk, puffing as his whole weight bore down on her, his head plastered against her face.

His mouth quirked upwards, his chuckle tickling her ear. "Y wanna go bed me?"

A disgusted huff passed her lips. "You're the one who needs to be in bed. Just tell me where."

"I like y…" Garbled words mumbled as his mouth settled near her ear lobe. "Like a woman wi' drection, not 'fraid t'ask what y'want."

"Where's your room?" Aela turned her head out of his reach.

His lopsided smile beamed at her as though he hadn't a care in the world. "Yeah. Let's…t'bed."

The ogre had morphed into a sexy wild Highlander, definitely one for the romance books. Her chuckle was a flattened huff into his shoulder as his good arm bumbled around her.

"Look at the state of you, Nairn!"

The sudden voice whipped her head up.

Chapter Three

Aela's gaze flew to the man entering the room.

He chortled as he flanked Nairn from the other side. "Are you taking this lovely lass to bed already, Nairn?"

She felt acute embarrassment flooding her. "I'd like to point out that whatever you think you see isn't really what's happening here."

A loud chuckle was the reply as the older man helped to perch Nairn on the edge of the desk. "Dinna fash yersel, lass! Hold him steady for a bit longer. I've a folding wheelchair outside the door that I've borrowed from Mariskay Medical Centre for the next couple of days. I'll just away and get it in."

Between them they lowered Nairn's almost inert body into it. Aela didn't care who the man was, but the fact he was familiar, and was organised to deal with an invalid, meant he was a welcome intrusion.

"We'll just get Nairn along to the wee downstairs bedroom, lass. Stay with me for I can do with your help."

She trailed the older man as he pushed the wheelchair past the cloakroom she'd used earlier, and beyond the kitchen. Manoeuvring Nairn's almost comatose body wasn't simple, but they got him flat onto the narrow bed with his limbs relatively straight. His mumbled words were unintelligible, his body as lax as one can be with two plaster casts. Trying to lift his head off the pillow he failed, his grunt of acceptance accompanied by a drunken grin. The happy pills worked spot-on.

"G'night, Aela. Meet Ruaridh." Nairn's good arm waved in the air as though introducing them.

"Hold him at the shoulders," Ruaridh instructed. "The

shirt won't matter, but we'll ditch his sweatpants."

Remove his pants? She thought of the healthy…flesh that would be exposed. Ruaridh, thank heavens, was untying Nairn's waistband cord and didn't notice. She had fantasised often enough about a stunning guy peeling off his pants, but hadn't imagined an older guy in the picture as well.

Now, as instructed, she held Nairn steady at the shoulders to prevent jarring of his ribs as Ruaridh first whipped apart the Velcro on Nairn's single trek sandal and dropped it to the floor. When he eased the soft cotton sweatpants past Nairn's hips she gulped. No underwear.

"Ah. You might want to look away, lass." Again the older guy chuckled like mad.

Aela knew she was a bit slow in closing her eyes, but what the hell! Curiosity killed more than cats.

"Mmm. Lovely. Y're hands…like velvet."

Nairn's murmurs were quite audible as his good hand groped out. A feeble blue gaze flickered and latched onto her bent head.

"You're…" A hint of understanding flashed across his face as he realised she was not the one stripping him.

"Ruaridh?"

"Aye! It's me."

A pathetic weak grin was the best Nairn could manage, yet his words ploughed on. "Ruaridh? In't she gorgeous?"

"Just ignore his ramblings, lass," Ruaridh mouthed.

It was clear Ruaridh was taking great delight in the situation.

"Go to sleep, Nairn."

Ruaridh winked at her as he dragged a light cover across Nairn's prostrate body and motioned her outside. His creased face grinned as he held out his hand. "I'm Nairn's father, Ruaridh Malcolm. I wondered how long he'd hold out, but he was determined to do this interview. I'm pleased to meet you although it's clear I should have come back much sooner. I apologise for that and for any embarrassment I might have caused there. You are?"

"Aela Cameron."

Her fingers were engulfed almost as much as when she'd shaken Nairn's hand, his father not quite so tall, but still well over six feet.

"So, Nairn's employed you?"

Aela had no idea how much Ruaridh might know about his son's business, so her reply was cautious.

"Not exactly. My experience with planes and boats, I think, was favourable." She knew that might be a bit of an exaggeration, given Nairn Malcolm's lack of reaction.

"Sounds good, lass." Ruaridh's smile was encouraging. "Was your office experience acceptable, as well?"

Ruaridh, without doubt, knew about all the jobs, so Aela decided not to fudge her reply. "Sorry. Can't answer. I pulled the plug on the interview before your son could assess my office skills."

Although she strove to be professional her mouth twitched, the twinkling of his grey eyes just too much. Succumbing, a guilty smile split her face.

"You called a halt to the interview? Wish I'd been spying in the window and had seen that."

Since the interview hadn't been completed, Ruaridh deemed it necessary for her to remain on Lanera till the following day when Nairn could continue. "Will that be a problem?"

"No problem. Is there a hotel you recommend?" She was happy to remain on Lanera for a few days, her backpack having everything she needed.

"Och no, lass. No need to look for that. The office apartment will do just fine."

A self-contained one-bedroom suite, with a tiny efficiency kitchen, was down the hall from the office, in the opposite wing from the small bedroom Nairn was using.

"Make yourself at home, lass. I'll have a meal ready at seven o'clock and I'll see to Nairn. That'll give you time to walk around the grounds before dinner, or wander down to the harbour at Mariskay."

Aela needed little persuasion. Shucking off the suit, she

changed into jeans, grabbed a light sweater, and donned her habitual walking boots – glad to be away from her potential employer for a while.

Mariskay was fascinating, the village carved into a small curved inlet, yet bigger than she'd envisaged. An interesting range of shops, bars and restaurants catered to locals and tourists alike. At present, it was full of people sunning themselves on benches surrounding the horse-shoe bay, listening to raucous cawing of the hovering gulls and sweeping terns, and inhaling the sea-salt smell permeating the warm air from the bladderwrack that littered the pebbled white sand.

The harbour moored a variety of boats: some commercial fishing craft, others purely for pleasure. The catamaran that had picked her up earlier was berthed beside a large boatyard. As she got closer, Aran walked out with a number of other men, bidding each other goodbye.

"You got the job, then, Aela?" Aran asked.

"Not quite. I'm continuing the interview tomorrow."

A wry grin split Aran's face. "Ah! I'm guessing the stupid bugger collapsed on you?"

"Mr. Malcolm wasn't able to complete the interview in one session."

"He asked you to stay on for another day?" Aran sounded amazed.

"Not Nairn. Ruaridh asked me to remain till tomorrow."

"Right. Ought to have guessed that. Nairn should never have left the hospital yesterday. His plastered limbs are a painful bloody nuisance, and the rib fractures are hampering his breathing this time, but it's his concussion disorientation that's his main problem. The consultants didn't want to release him, yet he would have it I brought him home so he could get back to work. Hates being tied down."

Aela didn't find that difficult to imagine. The concussion explained his almost comatose state. A real numbskull! Yet the way Aran referred to this time made it clear Nairn Malcolm was no stranger to serious injury.

"Would you like a tour of the boatyard?"

She jumped at the chance as Aran pulled out his cell phone.

"Give me a second while I explain to the wife."

When he'd finished, she hastened to apologise. "Won't your wife mind you shepherding me around the boatyard?"

"Och, no. She's Ruaridh's secretary, but clocks off early to be home for our two young school kids. She knew you were interviewing today, so this time is as good as any."

The luxury craft being built in the boatyard were impressive – small fishing vessels, a yacht, speedboat, and a few catamarans. There was another area for producing dinghies, jet-skis and kayaks. As Aran explained some technical details Aela would have loved to find out more, wanted a shot in all of them, but glancing at her watch put the scuppers on that. "Hell's bells and buckets! I'm having dinner with them at seven. Sorry, got to run, but thanks for the tour, Aran."

His offer to drive her up to the castle she declined. "No need if I go now."

Aran explained that she could head back a quicker way via the shoreline to the cove, only possible during the current low tide.

"Oh, that's brilliant. I'll nip round that way." Her thanks drifted back as she sprinted along the quayside, waving goodbye to Aran.

Rounding from Mariskay Bay she became aware of how quickly the landscape changed, the terrain rising steeply to form the high bluff. The vegetation of ferns, bushes and trees grew thick above the shoreline, protecting and concealing the top rise, the reason she'd been unable to see the castle from the water earlier that day. Ten minutes later she'd picked her way around the narrow strip of silvery sand and rocks to the cove.

Skipping up the staircase, wearing boots and bearing no backpack, was a doddle. Not winded at all, the sight of the castle was once again stunning. Regardless of her experience with its disquieting owner, the building was enthralling. Back inside via the great room she headed straight to the kitchen calling softly, not wanting to disturb Nairn Malcolm if he was still asleep.

"Punctual as well as beautiful, lass. That'll go down well with my very exacting son, Miss Cameron. Nairn's a master of time and hates wasting any, which explains why he's so frustrated at being laid up just now. The food's ready, and we can eat as soon as you like. Nairn's still out cold so it'll be just the two of us."

Over mouth-watering seafood paella, Ruaridh explained Nairn's debilitated state. Brian, Nairn's recent PA, had spent the previous Friday on Lanera bidding farewell to colleagues at the boatyard. "On Saturday morning, Aran ferried them down to Glasgow with Nairn's motorbike on board. Brian headed for his flight to London, and Nairn rode off to conduct business nearby."

"His motorbike was on board?" She grinned imagining the tricky transfer of a motorbike on and off the catamaran.

"Easy to do, lass. Nairn built a special ramp and a clamp for the bike. Sometimes he takes the bike and is ferried from Oban, on the mainland, back and forth to Lanera."

"Why didn't he fly the floatplane?"

"The simple answer is Nairn likes using all his toys. The business venue was about 10 miles from the marina in Glasgow so it seemed convenient to take the bike."

"Seemed convenient?"

"You can see from the state of him that his bike wasn't a safe choice on Saturday. Nairn's accident occurred on the famous Loch Lomond road, when his bike malfunctioned."

"So it was nothing to do with an extreme sport?"

"Nothing sporting about it at all!"

She winced at his change of tone.

"I'm thankful there was no collision with any oncoming vehicle. His injuries aren't minor, but neither are they as life-threatening as they could have been."

Since it was only Tuesday she couldn't prevent her frown, scarcely crediting Nairn Malcolm had ferried her here three days after the accident. "Jeez! Guy got a death wish or something, interviewing so soon?"

"Och no, lass. But my Nairn's a stubborn cuss."

"Why couldn't he wait till he could hold a meeting without collapsing?"

The food piled in as Ruaridh answered in fits and starts. "Wouldn't wait any longer. Too much going on for him to be confined to base, and he's interviewed for two weeks already for the PA job- before the accident. Hasn't found anyone willing to come up to Lanera for days at a time."

"Why wouldn't they want to escape London and come to this pretty little island?" Amazement widened her gaze.

"Not everyone thinks this place beautiful in the depths of winter. You're seeing it in good weather just now." Ruaridh's ironic tone wasn't lost on her, neither was his vibrating chuckle.

"Mr. Malcolm, I'm from British Columbia. Do you think the sun always shines there?"

Ruaridh was no stranger to Vancouver and neither, she learned, was Nairn. As he cleared away their main course Ruaridh related visits they'd made. A toffee dessert and a selection of Scottish cheese followed, and at his urging Aela had both.

"You can cope," Ruaridh laughed when she protested about the fattening aspects.

"Are you saying it won't add layers to my hips, Mr. Malcolm?" She felt very much at home with Ruaridh who reminded her of her Uncle Harris.

"You're not one of those willowy-thin types my son often squires around. I like to see a lass with a healthy appetite."

Aela wondered if he was referring to someone in particular, someone different from the tiny doll-like blonde she'd seen clinging to Nairn's arms in the newspaper rag.

Refusing her offer to help tidy up Ruaridh popped the remaining paella onto a covered plate. For Nairn.

Hours passed as they chatted, Nairn remaining fast asleep when checked on. Sipping coffee laced with Glayva liqueur she told Ruaridh of her plan to meet with anyone related to her great-grandfather who had emigrated from the island of Mull.

"So that's why you requested a short-term contract, and why you'd already organised a work permit and visa?"

She laughed at his expression since he seemed impressed.

"Exactly. I'm well-planned. After I finished university, I was too desperate to get back to work to take the ubiquitous year out. There were too many new planes to fly since Uncle Harris had upgraded the fleet, and at that time too many of his newly acquired boats to play with since he'd expanded into other transport forms. Don't know where the time went, but January of this year, you know those New Year resolutions nobody ever sticks to? It was now or never, I told myself. Ruts be damned; big changes were on the cards."

"I don't get the impression ruts are your usual style." Ruaridh's eyes twinkled back at her.

"I managed to plan six months travel, but I'm starting an M.B.A. course at the University of British Columbia, beginning September 1st. Since it's the end of June already, I've not got long to make contact with any of my great-grandfather's family."

"You didn't expect a contract flying a floatplane?"

"Shit, no! I expected a filing job. The appointments consultant was flabbergasted when she read Mr. Malcolm's requests for a PA, and for a pilot-cum-driver. She'd already remarked on my flying credentials during our earlier email contact."

"Call me Ruaridh, and I'll call you Aela, if you don't mind, lass? Saves the confusion of there being two of us called Mr. Malcolm."

"Be glad to, Ruaridh. Tell me to piddle off, if you like, but I'd love to know how you're so familiar with your son's business."

Ruaridh's answer was candid. "I was sole-owner of Gale Breakers till eight years ago when the business took a nose-dive. Not often a guy has his son pull him out, but that's what my Nairn did. He'd recently amassed a chunk of money, so he invested. Now it's half his, half mine. I run the operation here with Aran as our boatyard manager. Nairn does the globetrotting for client meetings, as well as travelling for his other companies."

By nine o'clock Nairn still hadn't wakened.

"I'm heading home, lass. I'll be back the morn, sometime after seven."

Chapter Four

"You don't live in the castle?"

Aela was staggered by Ruaridh's statement.

"Och, no, lass. I'm away back to my own bed. My house is down in Mariskay."

"What if he wakes up?" She wasn't inclined to panic, her first aid certificate covered a few scenarios, but not welding together limbs that needed re-pinning.

"He'll be fine. He only passed out because he tried to do too damn much. It'll take a couple of weeks for his ribs to feel good, but he's a determined lad, and he'll work around his problems. Always has and always will." Ruaridh made for the back door, Aela in tow. "He'll likely sleep for hours, and when he wakes up he'll find the food I've left for him."

She wasn't sure about Ruaridh leaving her alone with a man she didn't know, a man who had made a pass at her during the charade of an interview. One good thing though? Out-running him would be a piece of cake.

"I'll set the alarms on the way out. Here's my home and mobile phone numbers just in case you need them, though I'm confident you'll manage." Ruaridh's wink was blatant.

"But you're leaving your son with a stranger, I could rob him blind!" Words failed her.

"You could, but I don't think you will. You've told me enough, lass, for me to know my son's in capable hands. You'll be fine." Ruaridh left with another wink.

Staying in new accommodation was something she'd grown used to over the last five months. A few of the places during her world trek had been a tad threatening, but this beautiful castle was wonderful, so the situation didn't overly bother her.

At first.

After Ruaridh's departure she watched a film but was so restless she couldn't for the life of her have given details when it was over. She'd popped out into the hallway a number of times, but there had been no indications Nairn had wakened: no noise in the kitchen, office, or in the great room. Sleep would be impossible without knowing how he was, yet she didn't want to alarm him if he was already awake. Her noisy treads along the corridor made her confident he would at least be alerted to the presence of another person in the house.

He lay as though dead to the world.

Aela pushed away the dreadful thought…then it slammed back. Was he still breathing? It was more than six hours since they'd laid him down on the bed. The last thing she wanted was to be alone in a strange castle with a corpse. Way too imaginative. All she wanted was a job for a few weeks, but the darned man needed to be still alive.

"Mr. Malcolm," she whispered as she bent over, her hand tentative on his forehead.

His arm shrugged off the thin bedcover.

"Mmm…"

Aela tried not to breathe too loudly. His breathing was shallow though it didn't seem too pained. Battered as he was Nairn Malcolm was compellingly masculine, yet at present also vulnerable. She grinned. She could do anything with him, within reason of course, till he woke up and realised what might be happening. She didn't mind him like this when he was unaware of her.

An unexpected yank at her camisole pitched her down on top of him. His lips curled up before she made contact, and promptly squashed him. A gigantic moan blasted her eardrum, his body jerking in agony. Talk about hitting a man when he was down? Slipping completely from his grasp, Aela vowed she'd not touch him again.

"Not tonight, Casanova!" Her whisper echoed as she left the room.

Walking back past the kitchen, she left him a brief note

on the easy-wipe board that hung near the refrigerator, and then went to bed determined to sleep.

***

A sense of wellbeing flooded Nairn as he woke up, the remnants of an arousing dream still hovering behind his closed eyelids. Trying a deep breath, pain slashed across his torso. Ah. Still there, though not nearly as bad as it had been the day before. He moved his head from side to side and waited. The persistent headache and concussion wooziness seemed to have gone.

In progressive stages, he opened his eyes and found moonlight filtering into the room since the curtains hadn't been drawn across the small window. Reckoning it must be the wee small hours he flicked on the lamp beside the bed. The clock read one-twenty a.m. Amazing. He'd no memory of coming to bed.

Shutting his eyes again he forced recall of the previous day. It'd been such a bloody awful morning. What with his staggering around like somebody smashed, and then the news of the friggin' maniac wrecking the morning at his London headquarters. His buildings security needed a huge ruddy shake-up if it was so simple for someone to access the energy systems and shut them down. Just like it had been too easy to instigate the other incidents, but he had engaged a company to do a full security audit...hadn't he? Starting Wednesday. Was that today? He wasn't sure. He felt he'd had a good sleep but was convinced it hadn't been any longer than a few hours. His good hand rubbed across the fuzz at his chin. There was a good growth there, but he wasn't exactly Rip Van Winkle. He hazarded a laugh. Life was more like a friggin' nightmare than a fairy tale.

Ah.

The afternoon.

That was even hazier.

Aela Cameron had come to be interviewed. Nebulous details flashed around. He vaguely remembered asking her questions and finding the answers she'd given panned out, regarding her qualifications. He was fairly sure he remembered being fixated on her lips...though maybe that was just in the erotic dream he'd had? Was the woman he'd dreamt about Aela Cameron – Aela of the lava black hair, cocoa brown eyes and weird pink lips?

Bloody hell!

Had what he dreamt taken place? With a woman who had come to interview for a job? Nairn groaned, his pain entirely unrelated to his broken body. Now well awake, he looked around the tiny room.

A wheelchair sat beside the bed, an object of his derision the morning before when Ruaridh had suggested it, but since it was the only transport he could operate himself he reckoned he might as well try it. One-handed he wheeled himself to the nearest bathroom. A few minutes later, left-handed-splashed-water was a token gesture to cleanliness. Then he headed for some food since his stomach rebelled, loud and clear.

The dents he made in his hallway walls he ignored as he entered the kitchen, the first real humour for days breaking free. The wheelchair was infinitely better than the one-crutch-lurch he'd been trying to perfect earlier. Fumbling the paella into the microwave, he waited for it to reheat as he nibbled on the side-salad and bread Ruaridh had left for him. He'd consumed every last scrap of food and had scarfed a mug of coffee before the note written on the wipe-board drew his attention.

I'm staying over in the office apartment. If you need anything, let me know – Aela Cameron.

Nairn's invectives were explicit. Why the hell was the woman staying the night? He tried to remember the end of the interview – but couldn't. Damn. Had he given her a job as pilot, captain, driver...? Had he employed her as his PA as well? Surely he should remember?

Wheeling himself to the office apartment, he found the

entry door wide open. Deliberate? He imagined so because it had a lock should it be required. The wheelchair hissed as he crossed the sitting room carpet and entered the open bedroom door.

Double-damn again.

It wasn't Sleeping Beauty of the golden hair lying in the bed, but the occupant was a dead ringer for Snow White and even more like Cher of the Sultry Voice.

His memory hadn't failed him. Long dark hair spilled across the pillow in ripples, an ethereal shine reflecting in the moonlight since she hadn't closed the blinds. Her pale face was mesmerising, her eyelashes a black curve below each eye. She lay in total relaxation on her back, her mouth closed. Her chest rose almost imperceptibly, outlined under thin material. She was the woman he'd dreamed about though she'd been annoyed at him – about on par with the way he'd felt about her too, at times. She'd derided his battered body: he'd felt gutted by her dismissive treatment.

When the hell had he seen white panties?

His groan escaped before he could muffle it. He couldn't employ her. His wheeled exit was silent, glad the woman hadn't wakened.

The end of the afternoon remained unclear. Someone had removed his sweatpants and put him to bed. He hoped to hell it was Ruaridh because it would be too humiliating if it'd been Aela Cameron. He wasn't averse to women removing his clothes, but only when he was able to do something about it.

Resolute he could do nothing till the morning, he entered his office, booted up his computer and went to work, needing to get to grips with everything that had been neglected during the previous three days.

The phone bleeped. He debated not answering, yet knew it would just increase the stack of calls still to be attended to. He lifted the receiver, listened, and then made an arrangement to make contact later when his PA was available. Because the call had originated in South America the response was routine – given time differences, though who the PA would be Nairn didn't yet know. He started on the stack of e-mails awaiting his attention.

A couple of hours later he was relieved to find the concussion headache and wooziness hadn't returned. His concentration should have been good, yet a vision of Aela Cameron kept intruding. Her hair an ebony river he wanted to thread his fingers through as she bent between his knees. Startled, he'd a memory of her doing exactly that very thing, but when? What the hell had he done?

His professional conscience cringed.

Forcing recall of the interview, he remembered asking her to tell him about his floatplane and jet. He remembered thinking her Uncle Harris had given her a cushy job, a nice wee sinecure, because she was his niece. However, she'd been very snippy when he'd asked how many hours a week she'd worked. Now he couldn't recollect her answer. The image of deep pink lips popped into his head, yet during the interview the pink had vanished. He'd been annoyed that his battered face had merited a wipe-off of the lip gloss but it was so unprofessional to fixate on a candidate's lips. He also had a niggling feeling that he'd spoken way out of turn, even if he'd no recall of the exact words.

His father had put him to bed.

Only partial relief came with the memory since Nairn now suspected it wasn't only Ruaridh who'd got him there. Serious damage control seemed to be hovering on his horizon.

His ribs ached like fury. Knowing it was stupid to push himself too much, he collected his tub of pain killers and headed for bed. He considered turning right instead of left as he wheeled out of the office but Aela Cameron would still be asleep. As he rolled along the corridor, multiple questions bugged him. His swearing was ripe as he wheeled into the small bedroom.

**

Six thirty-five?

Aela peered at the clock again, memories of the evening before slamming in. She had intended to check on Nairn during the night, but it was well past the time for that.

Bacon was crackling and crisping under the grill. She was finishing the last of a stack of pancakes, having found some maple syrup in one of the well-stocked cupboards, when she became aware of someone entering the kitchen.

"Well, isn't this a sight for sore eyes, lass." Ruaridh's voice boomed in the near silence. "It's about time someone as beautiful as you made something smelling so good in this kitchen."

"What? No blonde bunnies cooking for your son?" The tart comment slipped out.

Ruaridh's chuckle was infectious. "Och, no, Aela. Nairn's blonde bunnies wouldn't have a clue about which end of a wooden spoon to use."

She gurgled along with him as he came over to the cooker and inspected her gelling pancakes, the current batch blowing bubbles, just ready for turning.

"Nairn's lady-friends aren't Scottish island mentality. They're more inclined to baking themselves in the sun at his Corsican villa than whipping up a batch of pancakes."

Mentally filing away the snippet of information, she avoided further banter about Nairn's women friends. "Well, this is no culinary feast, but there's plenty if you haven't eaten yet."

"You're tactful, too," Ruaridh praised before he asked for an update on Nairn.

Aela's hearty laugh pealed out. "Nope. I'm not too good at tact, but I know when to keep my mouth shut which isn't exactly the same thing. It's just the two of us again. Your son sure likes the land of nod."

Bacon slices and a stack of pancakes were placed in front of Ruaridh before she sat down with a full plate for herself. His chuckling continued as he complimented her on her cooking initiative.

"I hope you don't mind me doing this. You did say to make myself at home, and making breakfast seemed fair since you cooked for me last night."

Ruaridh answered around a mouthful of syrupy pancake. "No problem at all, lass. Glad to have you on board."

***

"On board what?" Nairn's question had their heads whipping around. It was obvious neither Aela Cameron nor Ruaridh had heard the whisper of the wheelchair, but his enquiry interrupted their conversation.

"On board the company flagship, of course. Morning, Nairn. I see the long sleep improved your temper."

His father continued to eat, his mumbles coming around mouthfuls of bacon, his sarcastic wisecrack accompanied by a wink first for Aela, and then one for him. A reaction typical of Ruaridh. What the hell did he mean? Company flagship? He must have given the woman a job, but he remembered not a blasted thing about it, and now his father and Aela Cameron were tucking into food at his kitchen table. He snagged Aela's gaze. Her molasses-rich eyes were twinkling, but not at him. Ruaridh was the source of her good spirits.

"Good morning, Miss Cameron." Turning to Ruaridh he ensured his voice was saccharine sweet. "Morning, father."

"Oh, my word, lass. Do you hear that?" Ruaridh laid his hand theatrically over his heart. "Somebody in this room must have got out of the wrong side of the bed."

Aela Cameron laughed again. The woman was far too flippant. Something about disrespect niggled at Nairn. He was sure he'd felt it the day before, as well as finding her too inclined to laugh at the state he was in. None of the banter shared with Ruaridh made him feel any better. Even the cosy sight of them sitting at his table aggravated him. It had been his father's hearty laugh and a gentler tinkle of female amusement that had wakened him. Though he couldn't hear what they'd been saying, it was obvious Ruaridh and Aela were getting along very well.

With a scrubbed face and still drying hair hanging

straight down her back – a black shimmer trailing almost to her waist – the woman was striking. No doubt she'd ensnared Ruaridh's attention from the sound of the charm oozing out of his father. The thought of his old man flirting with Aela Cameron held no appeal. At fifty-seven, Ruaridh was very popular with the local ladies even though he'd never shown signs of wanting to remarry after the divorce to Nairn's mother more than a decade ago. Yet Nairn knew Ruaridh was more than capable of acquiring a new woman, or wife, if he were to choose.

"Would you like breakfast, Mr. Malcolm? I've made plenty."

She'd made herself at home in his kitchen? Bloody hell! Had he given her a job as his cook as well? She'd soon learn he cooked for himself when he was home, though, maybe not right now since his injuries were a damned nuisance. He swallowed his pride, with difficulty.

"I would. Thank you, Miss Cameron."

Aela jumped up and removed a chair to make room for his wheelchair, her movements efficient.

"So you're making use of the chariot then? Just think, Nairn, with a bit of practice you'll be doing wheelies on the quay side, and you'll have forgotten your stookies." Ruaridh's chuckled comments were interspersed by pauses, as he mowed his way through his plateful.

Nairn made no initial comment, Aela cutting pancakes and bacon into small pieces before placing the plate in front of him. Did she think he was incapable of feeding himself? Annoyance stirred again as he focused on his father's remarks and grins but much as he tried, he couldn't quite suppress the twitch at his mouth because his father often managed to make awkward situations light hearted. "Thanks for fetching it. Wheeling around, strangely enough, is much easier on the ribs."

"All joking aside, how do you feel this morning, Nairn?" Ruaridh flicked open the syrup bottle, added some to the residue of his pancakes then waved it, asking a silent question.

After receiving a liberal sprinkling of tawny maple syrup over his breakfast, Nairn picked up his fork with his less than expert left hand. "The headache and disorientation have finally gone, thank God." He deliberately sought out Aela's eyes. Eyes he thought were maybe hiding something? "Miss Cameron will be delighted to know, like a good boy, I'll take the painkillers on a regular basis till the ribs heal and not be stupidly macho about it."

He watched Aela suppress a grin, didn't break a smile himself, but he remembered more of her barbed words of the previous afternoon – because what he'd just stated was a sanitised version. There was no hint of remorse or embarrassment in her expression as she attacked her stack of pancakes with enthusiasm. He'd expected his comment to ruffle her, but there wasn't a hint of discomfort showing.

A bit of pancake was shuffled around before he managed to spear it properly. He just caught Aela Cameron's full blown beam in his peripheral vision as he lifted the fork to his mouth. She was laughing at him again, looking as though she knew something he didn't, but he'd turn the tables on that soon enough. Only good manners prevented him from throwing her right out on her ass. Out of his kitchen. Out of his castle. He gulped over a mouthful. Out of his jobs. Out of reach of…Ruaridh…who was behaving as though Aela Cameron belonged at his table, as if she'd been a fixture for ages.

Ruaridh must have asked the woman to stay overnight.

The sweetness of the syrupy pancake was suddenly sickening. What had happened before she'd gone to bed in the apartment? The pile of pancake and bacon pieces slowly found their way to his mouth as he deliberated how to achieve her expulsion, because the woman was a thorn in his already aching flesh. He laid down his fork to fumble for the napkin Aela had set beside his plate and used it to mop the sweat from his brow. The room was so damned hot now he wished he'd not squirmed his way into his towelling robe. Maybe he was running a temperature? When he looked at his table companions it seemed he was the only

40

one to feel the excessive heat.

The meal progressed, Ruaridh and Aela dominating the conversation. Ruaridh chattered about sights to see down in the town of Mariskay; Aela responded she'd been delighted with her short foray down to the harbour. Nairn found Aela's voice husky – not a figment of his imagination, and just what he remembered from his erotic early-morning dream. Replies he gave were minimal as he concentrated on attacking his food, making sure it reached his mouth and not the floor.

"No, lass, I'll tidy up." Ruaridh intervened as Aela started to clear the table when all three of them had finished. "Nairn will want to formalise your job, now."

"Formalise her job?" His comment spat out along with a bit of pancake. He tried to interpret the statement as Ruaridh continued to stack the dishes.

"Aela needs to get started on the backlog of your calls as soon as possible, Nairn. You know how your inquiries build up."

"Your timely reminder is duly noted, Father. Since you're so up to date with my business, maybe you should be the one to formalise Miss Cameron's job?" He knew Ruaridh's sigh was for effect…and as a blatant prod since his father's expression and body-language indicated he was being obtuse.

"Nairn. Appropriate documents weren't ready yesterday. You only dealt in the verbal. Do I have to remind you that you were not *compos mentis*? Aela needs to sign her contract."

"Her contract?" Nairn stared, a tense silence lingering. Ruaridh muttered as he stacked the dishwasher. He glared at Ruaridh's obdurate back because his father was up to something, though he didn't know what.

Aela, he was gratified to see, gaped at both of them.

He blasted his father to hell and damnation along with a few curses well-aimed at himself as he acknowledged what must be done to salvage the mess he appeared to have made. Wheeling himself out of the kitchen, he snapped, "Miss

Cameron. Come to the office, please."

Aela didn't immediately follow him. He could hear her tight voice speaking with Ruaridh as he bowled along the corridor.

"We'll have to discuss the details again, the salary quoted and such," he grunted when she entered the office.

Her face was stormy as she clumped in, looking ready to do battle. He felt just as wild. He couldn't believe he hadn't documented anything useful on the file he'd opened for the interview the day before. He was usually meticulous about details. Apart from some poorly spelled comments that he'd listed on her flying and boating experience, there was an all too revealing sentence stating she could drive any transport he had, but first those pink lips could learn to drive him.

Unable to believe he'd written it, he deleted it.

"Mr. Malcolm." Aela stomped up to his desk forcing him to raise his head. "Before we go any further, may I just make clear what happened here yesterday afternoon?"

He heard the resolute tone and noted her grim determination. Was she going to lord it over him that he'd been, to all intents and purposes, insensible – like a drunk – during the interview? Were demands starting? Had he also made verbal sexual overtures like the written comment, even though she'd given no indications of it in the kitchen?

After a momentary closing of his eyes, he braced himself for the retribution it seemed he'd merited before waving her into the seat, wincing when she didn't take up his offer. She forced his eye contact, her gaze spitting fire. Balled fists bracketed her hips. Her words zapped out like pinging little pellets.

"Mr. Malcolm. We didn't get to the point where we discussed terms. I'm not even sure you were able to process any of my experience in my uncle's Head Office. You were, to be frank, incapable of making any friggin' decisions."

Nairn was confused. She was so damned snappy she had to be telling the truth. He watched her take a couple of deep breaths, her eyes flicking closed then opening to reveal sepia haloed pupils. Then her unwavering resolute tone and steadfast gaze didn't falter at all, her voice calming a little as she clarified.

"Mr. Malcolm, you did not get around to offering me a job. None of your jobs for that matter, regardless of what your father says. I don't know what the hell Ruaridh is up to, but I won't be party to it. I can't stand here and pretend otherwise."

He waited for her to continue. He hadn't given her a job? What the hell *was* Ruaridh up to? Waving her into the seat again, he braced himself. Momentary relief flooded when she plopped into the chair, since her towering stance had been too much for his poor head to contend with. Concussion disorientation hadn't returned: it was bad conscience that currently plagued him. It was twisted, he knew it, but seeing that Aela Cameron was discomfited pleased him, though he guessed it shouldn't. Those fabulous eyes of hers were now distressed. Sort of resigned.

"My experience in flying similar planes to yours, and driving the other vehicles you use, appeared favourable but…"

Aela's voice almost dried up before she continued, her gaze unwavering, her mouth whiffing as though making a momentous decision. He liked her more for it, though he was unsure why.

She resumed. "I haven't been a PA before, although I was my uncle's main secretary, when I wasn't out flying."

"Your uncle?" He regretted his slight hesitation. It let her know he didn't have a clue what she was talking about.

One side of her mouth turned up. "Harris Cameron. Cameron Airways? I told you about him yesterday."

"Harris?" After a moment he nodded back. Nairn studied the woman opposite who was clearly uncomfortable with the current situation. Her face was uptight with what could either be blazing anger, or complete frustration. He couldn't decide which. "Yes. I do remember. I can recall some of your office experience now, Miss Cameron, even though you think I heard nothing."

She'd soundly berated him for continuing to interview

when he was so ill. Did she really say some of the things he now recalled? Ribald comments that would have been in keeping with the company in an airport hangar. Locations she'd said she was well used to. She was proving to be a woman who neither shilly-shallied, nor beat about the bush regarding her principles. A woman of courage to be telling him how it had been, and not Ruaridh's devious version. As she waited for him to continue he enjoyed recall of more inspired comments, suppressing the grin that wanted to escape. "The events of the day are filtering back in, Miss Cameron. The real version. Thank you for that."

Aela's taut expression lifted, a grateful smile making her appear happier at not being party to what he now realised was solely Ruaridh's machinations.

Could he employ her?

He needed her skills; he'd no-one else to interview, and procrastination wasn't viable. He had to be on the move to sort out the mess his life was in. Brian's replacement was past critical, too. One finger typing with his weaker hand was useless.

He'd more than a niggling feeling he'd overstepped the boundaries of employer-employee liaison the previous day, which could have resulted in a sexual harassment case, but Aela hadn't hinted at anything. Nothing at all. In some ways the woman seemed perfect, a paragon, yet…maybe too perfect? Could she have another agenda for ignoring infringements he'd made? Was she interested in getting the job to remain in Ruaridh's orbit?

No way was his father engaging in a flirtation with this woman. He'd deal with Ruaridh because it was evident there'd been no scruples over foisting Aela on him by deceitful means. If it was because Ruaridh wanted to keep Aela close so he could get to know her better, his father would soon find out that wasn't going to happen. His father was as much a company member as he was. He would engage Aela as his temporary employee, but he'd make sure neither he, nor his father, had any personal dealings with the woman.

44

"I'll just confirm some particulars with you, Miss Cameron."

For the next hour, he asked questions about her flying experience, her boat handling and the office duties she'd experience of. Aela was confident with the answers he needed: succinct and knowledgeable. It was the interview that should have happened the day before and showed, without doubt, Aela Cameron did have the experience her paperwork indicated. Her answers demonstrated a spirited degree of gumption. Nairn hesitated no longer. Squashing down misgivings about possible danger he cleared his throat.

"Miss Cameron. I'd like to offer you the position, on a temporary basis."

Chapter Five

"Which job, and how temporary are you talking, Mr. Malcolm?"

Aela looked for positive signs in his offer because he didn't look particularly pleased. No frowns, but there had been something tentative about his throat-clearing and his use of the word *position* that had put her on guard. The awkwardness of it didn't match well with the thorough interview techniques he'd just used – techniques she'd admired a lot. The man was such a conundrum now. He seemed like a totally different guy from the day before. The difference in his focus was remarkable but then, Ruaridh had warned her that Nairn was like that. She wanted the job even more now that she'd seen Nairn the businessman, rather than the comatose idiot. But she was no pushover; she needed to be sure about what he was offering.

After a moment Nairn nodded. "Four weeks for the jobs of PA and chauffeur of all vehicles I might require to travel in, with an additional clause of any other help required due to my mobility problems."

Down to business. His deadpan expression was annoying but she made her manner brisk, her nod of agreement efficient. "Four weeks of being your PA and driver of your vehicles shouldn't be a problem."

The remuneration package was staggering. Blithely quoting an amount for the PA job, commensurate with her business degree, he added substantial amounts for the other tasks, taking into account her expertise with vehicles beyond the typical chauffeur.

"I might spend a few days here, on Lanera, at first, but you do realise I'll want you on call twenty-four-seven?"

That was quite a concept.

His gaze dropped to his monitor, ignoring her, as he completed the details. "Live-in of course, food provided, with some time off – but that will be dictated by circumstances."

Aela readily agreed. Live-in status meant she'd bank the bulk of the earnings to use in her first student year. Her smile widened. "Won't be a problem either, Mr. Malcolm. I've no specific plans for the coming weeks, and no personal demands on my leisure time."

Nairn's jaw tightened as he nodded, but the tiniest twitch at the edge of his mouth gave her pause for thought. Was he still doubtful of her expertise...or was it something else? For some weird reason she already felt tuned in sufficiently to know there was something about his decision that made him uncomfortable.

But she wasn't. She wanted all his jobs.

"Right then, I'll expect you to transport me in the..." He reeled off a list of his vehicles. "I've a yacht berthed on Corsica, but I doubt I'll be using that soon. My charter service pilots any long haul flights since I don't usually do the flying myself beyond western European destinations. I work with my PA on longer haul flights."

It was exhilarating listening, but she halted him mid-flow. "Whoa there! Please stop, Mr. Malcolm. Although I've flown in a two-seater helicopter, and have had some lessons, I don't have a current licence for that."

"Miss Cameron, I'm not contemplating folding myself into my helicopter with two plaster casts."

Nairn's voice sounded almost whimsical. It was the first flicker of humour that had broken through his deadpan expression for the last long while.

"When would you be able to start?"

"Right now."

His brows rose. He seemed unconvinced. "I expected you'd need to go back to Glasgow, or someplace, and collect some things."

"I really do mean immediately, Mr. Malcolm. All my

current belongings are in my backpack that's travelled with me these last five months. My possessions back in Vancouver aren't relevant."

"Let's get started then," Nairn declared after some contract forms had been signed. "I've already lost too much time."

Looking down at her shorts and cotton shirt made Aela smile since it was not what she'd envisaged wearing to work. "Should I change into office gear?"

"Your suit of yesterday? You can ask me that when I'm wearing this, Miss Cameron?" He pulled the edges of his short black robe together. "No need for formality here on Lanera, not even when we visit the boatyard, so casual clothes are fine."

There was a deliberate clearing of his throat. She noted his gaze was everywhere but on her. Short shorts and dressing gowns were a little on the too casual side – though the idea made her want to grin. She hoped she managed to suppress it, yet a sneaky little muscle kept twitching regardless. Fortunately Nairn's focus was again out the window when he continued.

"I never expected Brian, my ex-PA, to wear business clothing here so why should you be any different?"

An hour and a half later Aela's head was dancing a Highland Fling because she was by then conversant with how many small individual businesses Nairn owned, why he used so many vehicles, and why he needed a PA to co-ordinate his schedules.

Lanwater Whitecap, the diving school on Lanera, started while he was still at university in Edinburgh, had quickly expanded to become a fully-equipped water sports centre offering a range of water-craft courses and experiences. The success of it led to his building other similar facilities around the globe.

"That's how Lanwater Whitecap became the name of the chain," Nairn clarified.

She hadn't found references to Lanwater Whitecap while doing her quick internet research so her notes were copious.

48

Nairn explained his first profits from Lanwater Whitecap had been invested in Ruaridh's boatyard allowing them to diversify from traditional yachts and fishing vessels. Gale Breakers had metaphorically risen from the waves and had started to produce luxury craft, very marketable in the present climate.

"Gale Breakers. Good name!" she muttered as she scribbled.

Noting down what seemed most pertinent she was unaware she was parroting him. She wasn't just enjoying the necessary background particulars; she was also appreciating the dissipation of tension that had dominated their earlier interaction. Relaxed they weren't, not quite; though Nairn seemed a lot less tense than at first. However, his occasional glances were a little worrying, she was pretty sure his thoughts were elsewhere before he wiped them clear.

"I do initial consultations for the expensive yachts and vessels we produce, at venues of the client's choice, hence the need to travel so much. Ruaridh handles other negotiations here on Lanera."

"Okay, got Gale Breakers." Aela's mumble came after the last details were rattled off by Nairn.

Another of Nairn's companies used worldwide locations for providing extreme sporting experiences. Water based ones: white water rafting; river tubing; canyoning and different kinds of bungee jumping.

"Adrenalinn Adventuring?" she asked, remembering the name from her initial searches.

Nairn nodded. An attempt to steeple his fingers failed and mild curses ensued when his arm cast slipped off the edge of the desk. His grumpy moans about ineptitude made her smile. It was gratifying to know that the guy could laugh at himself, and loosen up a bit.

"I'm impressed, Miss Cameron. How did you know that?"

Her answer was nonchalant. "A little internet research before coming to Lanera yesterday. Your companies have nice names, and sell exciting merchandise."

Nairn's tight smile acknowledged his appreciation of her compliment as she continued to jot.

"Adrenalinn Adventuring also provide land based experiences like tank driving; dirt buggies; quad biking; sphereing; bogshoeing…"

"Whoa! Hold on a minute." The peremptory, pleading tone she used halted his flow. She'd devised her own system for note-taking, but his lecture was stretching it to the absolute limit. Smiling up at him, an apologetic grin broke free. "Got my notes in a tangle. Can you back track, please?"

"Do you always take such thorough notes, Miss Cameron?"

Aela looked to see if he was teasing her, since his infinitesimal change of tone implied it. He made proper eye contact with her. How disconcerting! There was just something there he wasn't quite masking. It took a moment to rally her thoughts, enough to answer him, for the man unsettled her equilibrium.

"Initially, till I've got the basics," she said, changing her pencil during the lull. "Okay, so those last pursuits? Did you say sphereing?

"Rolling down a hill in a large plastic ball like a hamster," Nairn drolly supplied. A hint of a smile broke free, a marginal twinkle in…both of his eyes.

The man was definitely thawing.

"I know that as zorbing. Tried it in New Zealand. Fantastic fun."

"I expect you had lots of experiences on this world trip of yours, Miss Cameron."

Nairn's husky tones rippled down her backbone.

"Oh, I did, sir." She decided she wasn't going to rise to his cryptic bait. "On my trip I experienced things I wouldn't have done at home, all equally exciting. But I've never heard of, or tried…bogshoeing?"

Their gazes connected for a couple of edgy moments before Nairn's throat cleared loudly. "Bogshoeing? Er…

50

Bogshoeing is one of the activities customers can do at some of our subsidiary Northern European bases. Bogshoeing is like wearing snowshoes but on bogs. In Estonia."

"Okay. I could maybe do that since I can snowshoe, but I've never been to any of the Baltic countries. I guess they're pretty beautiful? Huh?"

"Very beautiful."

Nairn suddenly seemed fixated on the far side of the room.

"Maybe you could explain about these subsidiary bases, Mr. Malcolm?"

Nairn continued as though the conversation hadn't faltered. "Some European destinations are not completely owned by me, but I hold the highest investment."

"Got that." She scribbled, keeping her head down. "And? What else?"

Nairn continued as though she'd not interrupted. "All my companies are based at my London headquarters."

Her well-worn pencil was changed for another super-sharp one before she asked her next tentative question. "So…sir. I've got notes now on all these companies."

"Yes?"

"Is that it, then?"

"Is what it?" Nairn sounded confused, as if he was losing track of the conversation.

Aela's little huff drew back his full attention. His good eye was clouding over, the other defocusing too – as far as she could tell – because it was struggling to open. The idiot was exhausted again.

"Have you fingers in any other pies, Mr. Malcolm? Not that I think you need any more, you understand."

Nairn actually laughed at her enquiry. "Sorry to disappoint you, Miss Cameron, but I do have other current business concerns."

"Jeez!" Nairn was not meant to hear her tiny undertone, but she knew he did for his laugh rumbled even more.

"I've recently become a provider."

"A provider? What the friggin' heck is that?" She wondered what she'd got herself into. She'd be out in a trice if she found anything underhand about it. Nairn's full blown laugh at her less than professional question made her wary of his humour, but she was glad to find the banter between them blew any residual tension to the four winds.

"That's what I call it."

She waited patiently for more details, pencil poised over the paper…or maybe not so patient for she twirled it back and forth between her fingers.

"My most recent venture completed an order to supply all the small craft and equipment – as one package – for the water sports centre of a brand new Malaysian hotel. It's one of a series of hotels at present being built in the South China Sea."

Her eyes widened as she processed just how many different craft she'd seen at some of the beach hotels she'd experience of. Her throat cleared and her breath whiffed out in a puff of conjecture. "Small venture, huh? I'm taking a wild guess here. Gale Breakers didn't supply all the craft?"

"No. Gale Breakers only manufactured a little of what was needed. I negotiated a good price with the other manufacturers and put a proposal to the hotel as a complete package."

Aela grinned; relieved his explanation of the word provider was legitimate. "So is that venture all done and dusted, then?"

"I'm afraid not, Miss Cameron. It appears they like me so much they want more."

Nairn's smile was as wide as he could manage, but his muscle spasm went undisguised as the bruising stretched. She empathised when his eyes flinched since she could see he was determined to control his reactions. The poor bloodied man was absolutely…enjoyable. "More, huh? I wonder why they like you."

His mismatched eyes crinkled again. "In fact, because of that success, I've already bid for another hotel chain who heard about my competence." He didn't sound as though he was bragging…just self-confident.

"Competence, is it? You've got a big back to pat, Mr. Malcolm, but I get the point. So you like this providing so much you're a sucker for punishment, and you're looking for more?"

Nairn grinned again, his arms cradling his ribs as he nodded.

Aela returned the smile. "And what do you call this providing company of yours? Twenty Five and a Half Hours a Day Enterprises?"

A hearty laugh rang out, though she regretted her facetiousness on witnessing the agony slashing across his face. It took him a moment to get his breath back, determination to complete the conversation very clear – his good hand splayed open in a warning gesture to confirm it. She waited, sensing he was building up to something she wouldn't want to miss. "Sorry to disappoint you again, Miss Cameron. I was in a hurry to name it, couldn't dredge up any great ideas so I called it…" His expression was apologetic. "Malcolm Enterprises."

"You never did!" She was aghast, her censure blatant, an upbraiding tone peppering her response. "Mr. Malcolm. That won't do at all. It's just so dreary."

"Point taken." All Nairn could manage was a faint chuckle. His fingers soothed the ache in his ribs, and again she regretted her outspoken nature. The guy hurt, and she made it even worse. She determined to be more careful of his condition – later – but for now, she wasn't quite finished. Not when he was so approachable.

"One more question, sir." Aela leaned towards him and boldly clasped his good hand, humour not even suppressed. "It's a really big question."

"Fire away, Miss Cameron."

Chapter Six

"Do you expect me to be an insomniac, too?" Her question was accompanied by a full blown grin.

Aela Cameron was full of sass. Nairn knew he definitely liked the woman as she picked up her pad and pencil again.

"Just to finish, to be sure I've got your whole empire, Mr. Malcolm, can you bear with a few more questions."

"Yes?"

Nairn hadn't had such fun for ages. He couldn't remember when he'd been so diverted.

"All your enterprises are coordinated at your London office and warehouses, except for the boatyard here on Lanera?"

"Not quite."

He watched her throat gulp, her eyes momentarily close and her pencil poise once again. He waited. Teasing this woman had great benefits – enjoyment for starters – and the anticipation of her next response. She didn't disappoint. Her smile, when she looked up at him with fallacious, fluttering eyelashes, was barefaced.

"So, you're going to tell me. No. Hmm. Let me guess…" Her fingernail tapped her teeth as she deliberated. "You also have offices in Paris, Rome and New York." She finished on a flourish, her expression a wide beam, and waited for him to clarify.

"Yes, to one of those three. Am I so predictable already?" He couldn't contain his mirth although laughing was killing him.

"Tell me it's Paris? The city of romance," Aela begged. "Can you believe I never made Paris on my travels? I'm so ashamed of myself. Of never experiencing the romance of the Eiffel Tower, or seeing the Seine, the Rive Gauche, or going to any of the raunchy cabarets."

"Sorry to disappoint you, Miss Cameron." Formality of names was meant to create distance, but it was a dismal failure when his lopsided grin sneaked out again. "It's New York. I've a very small office working out of New York which deals with bookings and orders for my North and South American venues."

Aela's smile enlarged and she actually whooped. "Way to go! I've never been to New York either. Fancy that."

Her face sobered as she made another scribble before jerking her head up, a polite enquiry hovering, now the very picture of efficiency. "So, again I'll ask, is that it? The extent of your vast empire?"

"I think so, Miss Cameron." He sobered too, remembering he was supposed to be employing the woman to do an efficient job; he wasn't employing her as his entertainment for the week. Her beaming smile and energised eyes appeared captivated, though, so he couldn't resist a little more repartee. "The prospect of coordinating all my enterprises, and transporting me, isn't too daunting?"

"Hardly!" Aela looked ready to rush out that very minute. "Can't wait. I'm desperate to get you going places."

He was desperate to get going too, though not in the same manner as she was indicating. Back to business, he detailed the most pressing work to be attended to. "Contact my insurance company – details in the cabinet over there – and get yourself immediate cover on all vehicles."

Aela strolled off to find the information as he bent his head and forced himself to immerse in work that needed one hundred per cent concentration.

After a while, his rib ache really bothered him. Wimping out wouldn't get the work caught up, but his body wasn't cooperating. Aela's intent gaze was upon him, just a little bit of the mothering hen lurking there – however, the bulk was of cynical censure.

"Mr. Malcolm, you're a numbskull again. Your grey pallor has reappeared, and you've been rubbing your temples for the last five minutes."

"Are you always so frank, Miss Cameron?"

Though he kept his face bland Nairn enjoyed her pert attitude, enjoyed it a lot. Aela didn't even try to hide her cheeky grin.

"Sure, I am. You might be paying me a wheen o'dollars, but it's not nearly enough for me to be a toady…sir!" He couldn't take his eyes off her no-nonsense walk as she approached him. "Degenerating into the blithering ass of yesterday isn't the answer. Would you like something? Maybe a drink of water, or coffee?"

She was right about the headache returning, though she didn't realise that she herself added to his discomfort.

"Coffee would be fine, please."

He drank his coffee and watched Aela's little sips, her focus intent on the advertising brochures he'd given her. The chime of his mobile phone as it bleeped an incoming text disturbed his stares. It was a message he'd been expecting for a while. After scanning it, he wrestled himself into the wheelchair. "I'm going to rest for a while, Miss Cameron, before the great lummox that I am can't walk, or work properly."

Seeing his barb had reached the mark he should have felt pleased, yet he felt irked, especially when her delighted laughter echoed around the room. "Tackle the enquiries on the answering machine while I'm away, please."

One-handed, he propelled the wheelchair out of the room…

***

Aela muttered some hearty curses at the busy phone lines. Embroiled in the complexities of one particular inquiry Nairn's re-entry to the office stunned her so much she jumped up, her pencil pinging from her grip. Baggy safari pants, one leg unzipped to above the knee, revealed none of the tantalising hairy legs she'd seen the day before.

Not an improvement.

56

She'd begun to get used to the muscular thighs, but it was marginally better attire for the office – she supposed. A short sleeved green shirt, with one button done up, covered his chest. She hadn't realised that her feet had propelled her towards him till her hand cupped his jaw, appreciating the smoothness she found there. "Look at you! You've got no stubble." When she realised her comment had blasted out, her hand rapidly retreated.

"Thank you, Miss Cameron! I'll take it as a compliment." Nairn's tone was so polite. "Courtesy of a neat little battery razor Ruaridh just brought for me which I can wield around my bruising with my left hand."

The imp inside Aela wouldn't be quelled as she stared straight into his deepening blue eyes. "Guess your usual is one of those frightening cutlasses twice a day, sir?"

Nairn's eyelids flickered. Drat! The sexy wild highlander returned before he wheeled away from her and hauled himself into his office chair. She couldn't help noticing that his bruises were more colourful, though the swelling around his injured eye was receding rapidly.

"Ruaridh's coming back to make us lunch. If you're not too hungry, I said one o'clock would be fine?"

His dull tone indicated none of the easy camaraderie from before. Mentally noting it she aped his manner thinking maybe his absence from the office, the shaving and changes of clothing, had taxed him more than rested him. Detached was okay.

No, in fact, detached was better. Her nod was professional as she brought him up to speed regarding phone calls. A grunt of acceptance and a terse dip she realised indicated his approval, so she resolved not to be put off by his cool responses. "Brian called. His father's still poorly, is responding well to his medication, and glad his wanderlust son has eventually returned."

That got her some attention. She liked that much better because she wasn't used to being ignored. She waited for clarification, continuing only after his cynical smile had faded. A sober expression was again the order of the day.

"Brian will remain available if you need to contact him at his father's business number, or on his cell."

"Good."

She ignored his brief response. "Brian was very helpful. He's given me handy hints on how to apply myself as your PA, and how to access all the relevant files."

Now she got the full force of his concentration.

"He was extremely organised, Miss Cameron, as I expect you to be. If his father hadn't had an unexpected heart attack then Brian would still be working for me. He had to go home and take up the reins of his father's small engineering business."

Nairn's gibe seeped in though she refused to be cowed. Holding his snippy-blue gaze, her update was frosty. "Brian also informed me of the handover period which is no longer going to take place. You can rest assured I'll do my best, Mr. Malcolm, in all capacities, though there may be times when I'll require patience to get up to speed with your business transactions."

Reaching for her already well-filled notepad, she flicked to the page with the relevant number for Brian's father's business and jogged it over on a sticky note. Nairn's fumbling fingers touched her hand as he grasped it from her, but she was set on disregarding the sensation she got every time they made any sort of physical contact. A slight strain descended as she sauntered back to her desk and tackled more of her in-tray till Ruaridh beckoned them through to the breakfast nook for lunch.

The platter of stacked sandwiches was devoured quickly, as Ruaridh encouraged her to talk about her recent travels. They compared venues visited by both of them, yet the strained atmosphere between father and son continued to be a trial. Aela couldn't understand it. Ruaridh made friendly approaches – Nairn rebuffed the good humoured attempts his father made to include him. She wasn't enamoured by some of the unsociable looks Nairn sent Ruaridh's way, some when his father was looking and others when he wasn't.

"No, Ruaridh. I've never visited the Pyramids at Giza, far less Karnak, as you well know. That little thing called client meetings ran on too long, if you remember. I didn't even get out of Cairo, unlike others of the party who literally jumped onto ship and went off up and down the Nile entertaining the client's wife for days."

Aela winced. She wasn't convinced Nairn Malcolm was a nice person. His continual snapping at Ruaridh seemed to bear out a nasty streak in him. The meal was over for Nairn though when he bowled over to the door.

"Take a break, Miss Cameron, before you return to the office. Thanks for lunch, Father."

It was already obvious to her that Nairn only used the word Father when he was being super-sarcastic.

Mid-afternoon a sound interrupted them – a loud clanging that reverberated for a few seconds.

"That's the front doorbell. Go check, please." Nairn barely looked up from his set of figures.

Rhona, a nurse from the health centre had arrived to re-dress Nairn's chest wound, the local doctor having done it the morning before.

"Good afternoon, Nairn. It's been a while since I've had to sort you out with anything."

Aela learned Rhona had known Nairn since he was a young lad.

"No need to go out, Miss Cameron, you're not going to see anything untoward," Rhona stated as she proceeded to lay out the necessary medical requirements.

She gulped because she'd seen plenty of his untoward already. But hey! She'd quite like to see more – even though he was the prime contender for the Grump of the Afternoon medal. She looked over at Nairn, but he seemed focused on Rhona, his polite enquiry about her family answered as the nurse did her job.

The wound was healing nicely, Rhona declared, but after checking his pulse she tut-tutted, it was far too fast. Was he taking the pain killers regularly?

She watched Nairn's eyes sweep towards her, his gaze

challenging. "Yes, I'm taking them on a regular basis, Rhona. I'm not such a stupid macho idiot I don't know what's good for me."

Aela was furious with herself. She'd never before been inclined to blush about anything, yet this man had made it happen at least twice already. She bent her head back to her keyboard and attempted to ignore the proceedings in the room. Yet every belaboured breath of his provoked the very reaction she wanted to throttle as Rhona tended to his other minor scrapes and cuts.

"And how are you coping with washing and dressing, Nairn? Since you can't have a proper shower, that is?" Rhona asked as she jotted down notes.

An extremely stressed silence followed. Nairn's throat cleared. He sounded a bit nervous, his gruff answer so quiet it was almost indiscernible. "Ruaridh's been helping me. Done a bit of shopping for things to make life easier."

"Really?" Rhona's response was accompanied by a full bodied chuckle. "Nairn, lad, I've known you for years. I know exactly how independent you are. And how long do you expect Ruaridh to help you?"

Aela was knocked for six when the woman turned to her.

"As his PA I'm holding you responsible, Miss Cameron, for this man's personal hygiene. I know just what he'll damage if he tries to do everything by himself. He'll either stink for days – weeks even – or he'll break his good leg trying to wash himself in the shower."

"I'll hold Miss Cameron to that as well, Rhona. You can be sure of it." Nairn's bold stare was relentless as his battered mouth quirked up.

She thought she might keel over. Then she remembered she'd never fainted in her life.

Rhona's irrepressible humour lingered long after she vacated the room.

Aela couldn't face Nairn. There'd been no sense in telling Rhona she'd just met him, and it certainly wasn't her job to wash her employer. Heavens! What a thought. All those unbruised bits? She busied herself with the enquiry she was working on, but the embarrassed feeling refused to dissipate. It was still there ages later. Ages while she'd avoided even asking any questions. Or looking at him.

"I'm going for a rest." Nairn wheeled himself out of the room.

His abrupt exit stumped Aela since he'd been in the middle of a complex set of figures he said were urgent for the following day. She tried to judge his mood, and failed. He hadn't been angry with Rhona, had even seemed to accept her humour with good grace, yet what had brought about his unexpected decision to remove himself? Had it been because she'd ignored him for the last long while? She could already tell he was a man of moods. She ploughed on with her stack of work.

Nairn returned a short while later but was in no hurry to talk. His rest had been far too brief for a recuperating body, so no wonder he was cranky. She wasn't fussed, though, since small talk never interested her, and she'd more than plenty to do. In his absence, she'd decided it was the only way that she'd cope with being in his employ for four weeks.

Hours passed.

"It's well after six, Miss Cameron." Nairn's declaration came as she typed up the final sentence of the urgent report; figures completed for it after his return to the office. "Do your first bit of chauffeuring and take us both to Mariskay. We'll find somewhere for dinner."

She wanted to try the local restaurants. Sometime, yes, but right that instant Nairn wasn't ready for such an outing. He was far too green around the gills and had been noticeably placing his good arm across his chest as he worked at his desk. Though how not to offend, since he sounded quite peremptory?

Polishing up tact, she persuaded him there was plenty to use in the kitchen, and that she was capable of making a meal for them. Her foray earlier at breakfast made her certain of it.

Nairn's reply was tight. "I've organised my housekeeper,

Kirsty, to be available from tomorrow for feeding us, but if you're sure about cooking tonight, then, thank you."

"Should I make dinner for Ruaridh, too?" Her inquiry was tentative, not sure if his father would be dining with them.

"Ruaridh? Why the hell would he be eating with us?"

Nairn's snarl indicated she shouldn't even have asked, his blue gaze a merciless inquest but she wasn't going to be browbeaten by his bad temper. "It's a good enough enquiry, sir! Seeing as how your father ate here last night, and at breakfast this morning, and lunch."

Nairn's use of her name was grittily direct. "Miss Cameron. My father and I lead separate lives. It's not normal for him to be around the castle and, as of lunchtime, I can guarantee it won't be a regular occurrence in the future either. I don't need his fussing."

The glowering ogre was back again. Biting back the response she wanted to make she turned for the door. "You've made that perfectly clear, Mr. Malcolm. I'll let you know when the food's ready."

She stomped to the kitchen to see what she could rustle up for dinner, berating herself for getting annoyed with the insufferable man. She would maintain her professional polite attitude. She drilled it into herself as she opened and closed cupboards looking for something to produce a quick meal, wondering how to annoy him just a little bit like his tone had scalded her. Maybe there was something she could add, like a little arsenic? Nothing that would kill him of course – just something to make him feel a little bad for a while?

Jeez! She was disgusted with her thoughts because the man was already a debilitated wreck. How could she even joke about making him worse?

A short while later she invited him through to eat, her manner calm. "I neglected to ask if you have any special dietary requirements, but since this is your kitchen I rustled around in the cupboards and reckoned I could give you anything."

The short break from each other's presence seemed to have done the trick since Nairn's snappiness had vanished, congeniality clipped into place. "You're correct, Miss Cameron. You can give me anything."

Drawing in a deep breath Aela concentrated on her task. The last thing she needed was to burn herself – literally or metaphorically. She removed plates from the warming oven then skilfully ladled food from the wok. Hot and cold. That was what Nairn Malcolm was and she was already fed up.

Contrarily, though, lukewarm was also unappealing.

Chapter Seven

Nairn's failure was spectacular.

He tried to imagine his previous girlfriends in his kitchen as he watched Aela move around but drew a complete blank. None of the women he'd associated with in recent years were in any way domestic, as far as he knew. They'd never made him an impromptu meal since none of them had ever been to the island. When he was at Garvald Castle he came alone, and cooked for himself.

The smell of food was enticing, though not nearly as enticing as the smell of Aela herself when she placed a plate in front of him. Her light scent, vanilla or something similar, had been tantalising whenever she'd come near him. The whole damned day.

"Please." He answered her silent gesture with the soy sauce bottle.

Aela liberally sprinkled it on both meals then sat next to him. Spearing up her first mouthful, she indicated they should tuck-in while the food was hot.

"Thank you, Miss Cameron," he mumbled between mouthfuls. "Very tasty."

He slurped around the noodles he speared up with a regular tined fork, because there was no way he was going to embarrass himself by failing with the chopsticks Aela handed to him as an option, utensils he would have handled competently before his accident.

Four weeks of bumbling around in this woman's presence now sounded more of a torture than his physical hurts.

The noodles should have glided down his throat. They didn't. Every single strand choked him.

Karma sucked. With the state he was in, any presentable woman would put him on edge. He'd probably knock her out with one of the casts if he went anywhere near her. The image posed too many opportunities since he'd be wearing the damn casts for longer than 4 weeks. The scenario was probably a lawsuit waiting to happen. Doggedly forking up more of the stir-fry, he avoided looking at her. The woman was bad for his sanity but thoughts ran on regardless...

**

The meal was strung with anxiety. Aela was aware of how much Nairn had to concentrate on eating with his left hand; aware of his almost permanent study of his plate and of how he avoided her eyes, yet no matter he seemed indifferent to her, she was aware of his obdurate strength. Somehow, she managed to keep the meal going with small talk, uncontroversial small talk, till they'd finished and she started to tidy up.

"I'd help clear away, Miss Cameron, but I'll be more of a hindrance than a help. When you're done here though, I'll show you how to set the alarm system by the back door."

A short while later she followed him beyond the bedroom he was sleeping in to the back door where she'd bid Ruaridh goodnight the evening before. Nairn demonstrated how to set and clear the alarm. "If you're not planning to be out this evening we can set it just now?"

A positive answer seemed like the response he sought from the tilt of his eyes, but agreement was easy since she had no intention of wandering. Rain had begun to fall during the late afternoon, and it was now even heavier than before.

Although Nairn wasn't expecting her to do any more work that night, she opted to clear some of the backlog of recorded phone messages. He also settled back to work talking only when she needed clarification on something, his gazes being a constant assessment. At times something flared in them, not banked quickly enough. His dominating presence across the room intruded, though, as she learned how to respond to the multitude of inquiries till just after nine-thirty. She'd long since come to the conclusion Nairn ought to be lying down but was dogged about carrying on because she was still working. Eventually she thumped her way through closing down her computer, all the while muttering and mumbling.

"You know something, Nairn Malcolm? Yesterday I called you some real nice names. Today I've been very polite up till now, but I'm going to add another few. Don't worry, though. They're in my head this time since you're now my friggin' boss. I can see your butt has glued itself to that chair. Mine hasn't. I'm through being a masochist for the evening, sir."

Nairn's head lifted the tiniest bit to look at her, his unfathomable expression annoying as he waited for her to finish. Her sarcasm wasn't ruffling him, not even the slightest.

Stomping across to his desk she forced him to raise his head to make proper eye contact. "You're one of those infuriating guys who don't leave their seat in the movies till the very last credit has rolled, aren't you? Even when it's been the crappiest film you've ever seen! Savour the last drop of pain, won't you?"

Since Nairn did nothing but stare at her, she added a little more. "My pillow has a nice dent waiting for me to lay my tired little head down on it. I strongly suggest you do that, too. You're way past needing it. Good night, sir."

Though she didn't look back, she wasn't confident her irritated flounce had made any impact.

***

Nairn watched her disappear knowing his words were unlikely to be heard since she'd already rounded the doorjamb.

"Good night to you, too, Miss Cameron."

Way past needing it? She was so right. He was beyond

shattered; the biggest glutton for punishment since he hadn't wanted to slope off to bed. Avoiding playing the wimp in front of Aela Cameron was proving to be a nightmare.

He manoeuvred himself into the wheelchair and wheeled past her work station. An organised series of sticky notes paraded themselves down the edge of her otherwise tidy desk. His mouth quirked up in admiration at the prompts because although their conversations had been fraught with tension, and their eye contact had been full of deliberate avoidance tactics, she'd relentlessly rooted out details she needed to know to make progress with whatever she'd been working on. The sticky notes indicated her strategies for not forgetting, or losing information.

What the hell?

Next to the phone was a sticky note with both Ruaridh's home and cell numbers on it. Sudden anger made him want to rip it to shreds. Had Ruaridh visited her while he'd tried to rest earlier that day? His hand thumped the desk dislodging some of the notes. Gritting his teeth, his swearing resourceful, he sorted them all back in order before taking himself off to his temporary bedroom.

***

Aela didn't allow the drizzle of rain to stop her from exploring the next morning after she'd breakfasted in her apartment. A fitful sleep, disturbed by dreams of a totally healed Nairn, resulted in a need of fresh air to clear her sluggish system. Finding the alarm already disengaged her reckoning was that Ruaridh had paid another early visit. That was a brilliant thought since he could deal with any hygiene requirements Nairn might have. She wasn't going to even think about washing Nairn Malcolm. No way!

Wandering outside she explored the area surrounding the castle, located the helicopter hangar, the garage block, and further on some stables where she found Nairn kept half a dozen horses. So, her sexy wild highlander did have a trusty steed. He'd not mentioned that form of transport. A hearty laugh erupted when her active imagination envisaged a scene where she shared a horse with him in his present state. Without plaster casts and injuries would be another matter entirely.

"Come anytime and I'll find tack for you. Nairn won't be riding for a while, but that's no reason for you not to. Our bookings for the locals aren't too heavy just now so there's likely to be a spare mount." Angus, the young head groom, issued his invitation, deliberate in informing her he lived alone in the cottage next to the stable block.

Aela fended off his playful tactics. Although he seemed very nice, she wasn't interested. Nonetheless, riding really appealed because she'd ridden often as a child, though less so in recent years.

Short of eight-thirty she was back in the castle. It wasn't a surprise to find Nairn already working, typing one-handed at a marginally faster rate than the day before. Start positive she thought, entering the room. "Good morning. How are you doing?"

Her polite enquiry earned a genuine smile that warmed down to her toenails; it seemed the ogre was in hiding. Encouraging, yet she wondered what the heck had gone wrong the previous afternoon to change his mood so much. And how long would his present mood last?

"Much better, Miss Cameron." Nairn continued to smile. "You found the apartment comfortable?"

"Absolutely. The bed's a dream."

An economy with the truth. He didn't need to know he'd featured highly in her dreams. Nairn's reply was muffled as he shunted a piece of paper on the desk, a purposeful focus on his monitor rather than on her, but she noticed the smile had already slipped. No scowl, just back to the bland look.

Covertly studying him, she could see he'd attempted some sort of hair wash because his thick black hair was still damp. Thankfully all blood traces seemed now removed from the glistening strands, his whole person looking cleaner than the previous morning. Again, he wore combats the present pair flapping open at the knee on his plastered leg. His short-sleeved shirt was actually buttoned in three places, though where it gaped at his waist the bruising was already ageing to a greenish hue, the purple-black diminishing. His facial bruising was similar: the swelling around his eye and cheek barely visible.

Settling into her chair she attacked the stack of paperwork he'd already deposited on her in-tray. Due to methodical note-taking the day before, few questions needed clarification as she waded through the pile. More than an hour sped past. When Nairn eventually spoke she was so involved with complicated correspondence that his brusque voice jolted her. He was awkwardly cradling his phone to his shoulder, keeping the caller on hold.

"Miss Cameron? Please call Richard, my housekeeper in London. Ask him to have my suit trousers and jackets altered to accommodate my casts, or have new ones made if necessary. No matter the cost it has to be without delay."

She found the number and introduced herself.

"Can you measure the circumferences of his casts for me?"

Richard's question, she knew, was reasonable; but the measuring would not be impersonal.

When Nairn completed his current call she relayed Richard's request.

"Check the drafting table in the corner. You should find a tape in the drawer." Nairn turned his office chair around ready for her to comply and measure, seemingly not wanting any time wasted over it.

Feeding the tape around his lower leg at strategic places she took the necessary measurements, unsure of how much she welcomed the sensation of being at his feet. Nairn's laboured breathing above her didn't make it any easier. Taking his arm measurements was trickier since she needed to be even closer, her movements jittery. Manoeuvring the arm cast she was so conscious of him, only managing to record the measurements by avoiding eye-contact. His muscular physique wasn't the only overpowering thing she was aware of though; there was a strong fruity aroma that somehow didn't match Nairn's personality. Her eyes lifted to his for explanation.

His small grin was of...mischievous delight?

She returned to her desk and was absorbing details from a memo when yet another call shattered the peace.

"Someone asking for you personally, sir," she informed Nairn as she transferred it to his line.

"Mhari!" His delighted laugh drifted across to her. "How are you?

The soft resonance in his tone discomfited Aela though all he'd done was greet the caller. They'd shared a room for hours now, and he'd been on the phone often – but she'd never heard these teasing tones.

"Well, not quite, though how did you know?"

Yet another laugh burst from him.

"Of course I wanted you yesterday! You've no idea. Oh yes, Mhari, your personal treatment's in urgent need."

Personal treatment? She didn't want to listen to any more, but the confines of the room made it impossible for her not to hear his noisy conversation.

"Yes. So clever of you, Mhari. My bedroom needs are a priority right now!"

Jeez! That was way too much to hear. Aela surged up and left the room. It was none of her business what Nairn said to female acquaintances.

On her return a few minutes later the call had ended, Nairn's mood heartier if the beaming smile coming her way was a measure of his frame of mind. Grunting her way into her chair she attacked her keyboard, and ignored him.

After the appetising lunch Kirsty had prepared, and some surprisingly pleasant conversation between the three of them, Nairn declared he would rest and wheeled himself out of the kitchen.

"Have you had a look around the castle, Miss Cameron?"

"Call me Aela, please. Miss Cameron is far too stodgy."

Aela laughed at Kirsty's expression when the housekeeper learned that although she had already stayed two nights she'd only been in a few of the ground floor rooms.

"I'll give you a wee guided tour then, Nairn won't mind a bit."

A look at the whole castle followed which to her utter delight included an indoor swimming pool and gym area, located further along the same wing as the office apartment. The renovations to Garvald Castle were superb, no expense having been spared in the rebuild. The décor was spectacular yet not very personalised. The exceptions being the great room, the office, and the master bedroom suite on the first level, where, she imagined, Nairn's preferences had been catered to. It looked as though he wouldn't be occupying the upper floors for a while, though, for the spiral staircase was presently insurmountable. From Kirsty she learned Nairn's small downstairs bedroom had been intended for occasional domestic help.

The master bedroom suite was fabulous. Extending across the complete first level of the original square keep its darkest navy was highlighted with soft dove grey; cool, yet classy. A massive canopy bed, festooned with piles of soft cushions made her want to experience its comfort. Images of Nairn occupying it flashed up but they were firmly squashed. Then her wayward brain recollected the earlier phone call. She categorically did not want to imagine some female called Mhari occupying the room.

A huge custom built shower cabinet with multiple massaging shower jets meant his en-suite bathroom was luxury personified. Determined to lock Nairn into a little pocket of her conscious mind labelled temporary employer she settled into her afternoon work back down in the office. He returned looking well-rested, and they segued into comfortable working harmony.

The phone rang.

"It's Robert Colby. Your security guard." Aela transferred the call feeling that there was something odd about the request. "Giving you the heads up, he sounds pretty miffed. There's a problem with equipment in the London warehouse. Needs to speak to you personally."

Chapter Eight

"What now?"

Nairn was instantly alert. Robert Colby wouldn't call about something trivial. A few seconds later his good hand thumped the desk startling Aela on the other side of the room. Her gaze locked onto his, her concern discernible.

"I'm going to nail the bastard's ass to the wall when I find out who's doing this! Yes, Robert. Alert the police, now, and cordon off the whole area. Let me know as soon as the cops arrive, and get me a police contact name!"

After issuing further instructions he finished the call so furious he could barely think.

"Can I do anything for you, Mr. Malcolm?"

Aela's question sounded cautious as she walked towards him, yet her gait was determined. He liked that about her, but it was difficult to answer. He cursed, all the while assessing how much she needed to know, since she was now in the line of fire too.

Diving gear for the Malaysian resort had one particular valve malfunctioning. On first glance that might seem a manufacturing fault, but he knew better. To ensure equipment was dispatch-ready there was always a double-check system in place before delivery of all goods. The equipment in question had been received from the manufacturer just eight days before, and had been through a thorough check on arrival at his warehouse. If the goods-in check had been inefficient it was easy to verify which technician had recorded on it. Or, someone had gained recent access to the tanks. He veered towards the latter, in view of recent happenings. Security cameras throughout the warehouses would indicate if there had been unauthorised individuals wandering around, though scrutiny of the tapes would take time.

Valve repairs were necessary, incurring possible delays. Nairn couldn't countenance that because his orders always arrived on time. Much worse, though, was the potential for disaster if final checks hadn't been effective. If the faults hadn't been detected holidaymakers using faulty gear could have experienced dire consequences: injury, or even death. Horrendous thoughts.

The lethal element had reared its ugly head again. Till now he'd conducted internal enquiries, but that couldn't continue – the authorities had to be alerted.

Belatedly he realised Aela was waiting for an answer to her reasonable request. She had to go. He couldn't risk her being exposed to any harm. Taking as deep a breath as his lungs would allow, he thought of how to do it, since he'd no grounds to fire her. She'd done nothing to breach the contracts they'd signed the day before, her efficiency unquestionable.

"Sit here!" He tried to moderate his tone but knew he'd failed when her eyebrows flinched and her concerned expression faltered, replaced by a steely glint of resistance. After another gasp he tried again. "Please."

Aela's slide into the opposite seat was reluctant, her mouth a discontented line. What the heck had he been thinking the day before when he'd drawn her into this mire of mishaps? But he had. Engaging full eye contact with her he made sure there would be no misconception.

"You sure you want to work for me?"

He noticed no hesitation at all. "I'm sure."

"Bet you'll change your mind when you hear what I'm about to say." He watched her expression become more wary as she contemplated his words. "You might have declined my offer if I hadn't been such a bloody deceiver. My bike spill was no accident. I'm convinced it was a deliberate and malicious manoeuvre, designed to injure me, or maybe even kill me."

***

Aela was shocked by Nairn's revelation as his attention momentarily strayed to the nearby window.

"There have been incidents during the past couple of weeks which have harmed my business in some way or another. And I didn't tell you about them either. I'll understand if you walk out this door right now and go back to where you've come from, or wherever you want to be. It's what you need to do."

Nairn sounded furious, his body so rigid with tension she could see the muscles twitching at his neck, the effort to speak an enormous task. "I will, of course, lay on any transport you might need, pay you for your efforts these last two days and a retainer for the month you would have worked."

"No."

Nairn's gaze whipped back. "No?"

She was resolute. She didn't need to think about it. There was no way she was going to turn her back – even if it meant courting danger. "No, I don't want to terminate my employment with you. Whatever has happened doesn't change my mind. I'll deal with anything that comes."

She knew in her gut if this man had not been incapacitated by his present injuries he'd not be so frustrated, or be so vulnerable.

"Aela! Miss Cameron." His voice was thready, and hoarse, as he entreated. "I can't guarantee your safety. You can see I can't even guarantee my own. Someone is causing malicious incidents which have escalated to a potentially lethal extent."

Nairn's terminology wasn't exactly encouraging, but she was determined. "I'm not one to run from adversity. I've been in hazardous situations before and survived."

"Have you ever faced down a saboteur?"

She watched a muscle spasm in his neck, his teeth clenching as his fist tapped a furious drumming on the desk. "No, I haven't, though I've been in potentially deadly

74

conditions which could have downed my aircraft." Sensing she'd need to exert a good bit more persuasion to reassure him she scooted her chair forward and edged closer. So tense he could barely breathe, Nairn's skin tone was ashen amongst all the other hues. "Tell me about the incidents."

She laid both of her palms over his left hand which still sat fisted at the place he'd just thumped. Ignoring the initial heat, she unfurled his fingers and stroked them free of the stress gripping them, flattening them on the desk, keeping them in place with her own. "I'm a good listener. This phone call is about the most recent of a string of catastrophes, you say?"

Nairn nodded, his gaze fixed on their linked hands, the pressure of his grip dissipating with her gentle strokes. As he related details of the current incident, she hoped she kept her dismay from showing. She'd been an innocent holidaymaker hiring similar diving gear not so long ago. Potentially evil situation.

Nairn backtracked. "The first incident happened thirteen days ago. Insignificant at first, it appeared to be lax processing. It annoyed me, but the perplexing thing was no one seemed responsible."

"Somebody good at keeping below the radar?"

"Precisely. And has managed to continue."

Nairn's hand clenched again under her fingers. She continued her unobtrusive massage.

"A batch of kayaks, ordered for a new water sports centre in Ireland, was built here at the boatyard. It's normal to dispatch Gale Breaker craft direct to the customer." Satisfied she was tuning in, he continued. "The last quality control was being enacted when dispatch realised something was odd. The new paddles, and neoprene spraydecks, had been purposely deleted from the order."

"Deleted?"

"We never send out new kayaks without paddles, though the spraydecks were on special request."

He sounded so disgusted she almost smiled but guessed the rest of the story wasn't so trivial. She picked up the threads. "But no one seemed responsible for zapping the order?"

"Bang on. A thorough check of pending orders followed, and a number of them had had deletions, or irresponsible changes made to them. We dealt with a second similar incident though again without knowledge of who'd initiated it. Then a small fire occurred in an area near the main dispatch doors of the London warehouses. A litter bin housing used alcohol wipe cloths had been set alight but that was dealt with by an alert store man who tackled the fire with a nearby extinguisher before the main sprinkler system kicked in."

"The fire authorities were called?"

"No." Nairn shook his head, a rueful expression clouding his face. "The fire was recorded in the incident log, but as it was found and dealt immediately with no further action was taken."

"Is that usual?" She was struggling with the concept that something might have been overlooked by that tactic.

"It certainly won't ever be usual again, Aela."

Nairn's tone was resolute; seemingly unaware he was using her first name. She put it down to his agitation over the situation. He was also unaware he was gripping her fingers so tight she thought he'd cut off her circulation, yet she wasn't pulling away – she welcomed the pain, hoping she could absorb some of Nairn's. When Nairn realised his grip was too firm his apology sought her understanding.

Forcing herself to listen, she convinced herself she was just giving him the reassurance of an interested colleague. Nothing else.

"I only found out about the fire the day after it had happened, when I returned from a publicity event on Corsica. By then it had been internally investigated by my security people, their conclusion being someone had accidentally chucked a lit cigarette in it. The workers have to go outside those doors if they're smokers."

"Could it have been an accident? If, say it was raining, or windy, and someone was smoking at the open door rather than all the way outside, and in too much of a hurry to get back to work?"

"Maybe." His breathing became more even as colour seeped back into his cheeks. "We've thought of all possibilities. Of course nobody owned up, and the cameras revealed nothing."

"The next incident?" She dreaded to ask but sensed there were more to come from Nairn's taut grimace.

"Two days later a nasty virus was planted on our main intranet at the London office." Nairn slid his hand from her grasp to rifle through his thick hair, slicking it back from his forehead. She missed the contact immediately. "It was intercepted by the virus checker, though not quickly enough to avoid all damage. It wrecked some software we use for ordering systems, and deleted other information."

"You fixed that?" She held her now redundant hands in her lap.

"Absolutely, though again it took time. The whole network was down for a day till it was resolved, and some customer orders for the previous twenty four hours had to be re-entered."

Aela was no detective, but she considered the information she'd been given. "So the saboteur is maybe someone who works in your head office, or your warehouses; someone who can come and go with ease? Someone who wanted to cause minor disruption?" Her last question was hesitant for the incidents seemed to be increasing in severity.

"You'd think so on the basis of those niggles, since that's what those initial ones were. They caused me time and money, but I've no idea who has such a grouse against me that they'd want to do this." Nairn again rifled his hair and cupped the back of his tense neck, unconsciously massaging the tight muscles there. She realised she was desperate to jump up and do it for him.

"Have you had unpleasant dealings with an employee in recent weeks, someone you've had to get rid of?"

His swearing was vehement. "I've thought of that, and so

did Brian. Brian's the latest employee to leave, though I'm damned sure it wasn't him."

"You can rule him out?"

Nairn looked appalled at her seeming suspicion. He groped for her hand, and pulled her close again, as though he couldn't do without the connection, his gaze intent. "Brian was with me on Corsica the day the fire was started, so I think that rules him out."

"I agree. Unless he paid someone to do it?" Nairn's negative gestures wiped out the possibility. "Okay. You trust Brian."

"Definitely. He had no motive for doing any of this."

She cringed at her next thought, releasing her fingers from his grasp though leaving her hand close by. She made sure she'd his full attention before speaking again. "You're not going to like this question, but as a virtual stranger I have to ask it. Would you have pissed off some girlfriend to the degree she'd hound you like this?"

Her question was reasonable. Nairn looked startled though, his eyes narrowing as if the idea had never occurred to him. "I'm not aware of a previous lover being so unhappy she'd resort to anything like this. I've not had any long, or meaningful, relationships in years. Recent dates, or affairs, have been fleeting. I'm always on the move."

"Mmm…"

It was easy to see how his constant business needs would make that the case. She thought some more, her next probe careful to catch his response.

"I don't suppose a previous girlfriend would have easy access to your office, or warehouse anyway – except if she was a co-worker? Have you dated…?" His hand flashing up stopped her. "You're going to tell me you don't have relationships with employees?"

"Never!"

"Okay."

Her new tack was marginally different. "Have you been harassed by any employees who've wanted more from you, and didn't get it?"

Aela was treading in deep water and she knew it. She could easily understand female employees wanting to be his lover.

Chapter Nine

"What do you mean?" Nairn's brow furrowed again.

"Jeez, Nairn. Look in the mirror. You're a good looking man." Aela's cheeky smile broke free when he gulped. "Okay, so hold back on the mirror right this minute, but you get my drift. There must have been plenty of women who wanted you to be more than their employer."

His hand again raked his hairline, his eyes wincing at his inadvertent skid over the bump and deep laceration across his brow, a tinge of deepened colour flushing his cheeks. "Yes, Miss Cameron. I've been the target of women who've wanted to be more than my secretary, or PA, but I haven't given any of them one single signal they were likely to succeed."

"Okay. Keep your hair on." She refused to be cowed by his indignant tone as she continued her train of thought, still unconvinced by his statement. Her ardour cooled when Nairn's expression resumed a blank stare. "I'm just covering as many angles I can think of."

A tense silence accompanied their individual thoughts till Nairn's swearing burst free. When she didn't even flinch at the obscenities, he continued. "Anyway, my little mishap on Saturday puts the cat-among-the-pigeons on the jilted girlfriend theory."

"How so?" she questioned, still ruminating over the details she'd heard so far.

"The saboteur wasn't only in my head office and the warehouses, but was also here on Lanera."

"Able to tamper with your bike?"

"Exactly!"

"Ruaridh told me you took your motorbike because you

hadn't ridden it for a while?"

"Yes." Nairn looked confused by her change of direction.

"I assume you always do a thorough check before taking it out?"

"Of course. I did that before I left the garage here at the castle."

"What caused your accident?"

"Initial investigation proved damage had been done to the brake discs."

Aela digested his information, gnawing her bottom lip. She caught Nairn hastily withdraw his gaze as though he wanted to escape the room...the conversation...her? "Was your bike out of your sight on Saturday?"

Nairn seemed surprised by her question. "Sure, during the day. I drove it from the marina to the client venue. It was in the hotel underground car park for hours while we thrashed though details of the request."

"Could the bike have been tampered with during that time?"

"I suppose so. I'd no problem driving it ten miles to the hotel, but it could also have been tampered with on Lanera before I left the island. The repair garage still has to establish if the malfunction happened where it did because the time lapse matched. They're working on tests to prove how long it would have taken for the damage to manifest itself."

"Who knew you were going to a client meeting?"

"Brian, Ruaridh, Aran...and Marsha."

Marsha? The woman of the sexy phone call had been called Mhari, not Marsha. Yet she'd read the name Marsha somewhere. "Why would Marsha know of your movements?"

"Marsha Hilborne's my Office Administrator in London. She isn't in the office this week. She worked both Saturday and Sunday during the last two weekends so she's now having days off in lieu."

"Okay." She nodded her grasp of the situation.

"Since Brian was quitting on Friday, Marsha was primed

to handle my appointments calendar and any correspondence coming into head office for me on Saturday and Sunday."

"Was that normal procedure?"

Nairn appeared distracted by her question. "Not really. Brian would normally have been with me during client meetings, and would have dealt with any urgent calls, or e-mails. It was rare both of us were out of contact for any length of time."

"So Marsha was on alert and knew you'd be unavailable during your Saturday meeting?"

"Yes." Nairn's interest was evident in his concentrated gaze that never strayed from her.

Aela tapped a pen on the desk beside her. "If Marsha knew your venue then other people probably knew as well. When were the details of your meeting settled on?"

Nairn paused to recall, breaking eye contact as he scanned out the window. "It would have been firmed up on the call Brian handled last Tuesday. There was no reason in between to change the details since by then we knew Brian was going to spend his last working day, Friday, here on Lanera and he'd be going back to London on Saturday."

"Is your appointments diary just electronic?" A frown developed as her pencil tapped. "Or, is it also on paper?"

"Only on my computer and on Brian's – now yours."

"So Marsha was given access to that file." She segued into ferret mode, determined to root out some answers. "Can you confirm she was, in person, at headquarters on Saturday?" Nairn nodded. "Then someone else must also have had access to the file prior to Saturday."

Nairn appeared to consider her line of inquiry. She was beginning to like the hint of something else lurking there-maybe some admiration? She wasn't sure, but it didn't matter because they were back to being less tense.

"You're thinking somebody had sufficient forewarning to be at the Glasgow hotel venue and awaited my arrival. Then tampered with the brakes?"

"Or, they came to the island on the Friday." She felt her

82

smile faltering as some doubt flickered in his eyes. "That's all I can think of at the moment."

Silence descended for a few moments as Nairn contemplated the possibilities. "How did you come to those conclusions?"

"Basic facts. No prior prejudices, no misleading information."

"Nothing to do with good deduction skills, I suppose?"

His lazy smile warmed her and almost broke her train of thought. "How did this person know you would use your motorbike? Where were you when you made that decision?"

"At the boatyard with Brian while he made his last farewells. We arranged our Saturday morning pick-up with Aran. That's when I decided to take the bike instead of ordering a taxi to meet me at the marina, and it saved Aran waiting for my return."

Aela had another sensitive question to ask since she'd liked Aran very much the day he'd ferried her to the island, and could only think good thoughts about him. "Is there any way Aran could be a suspect? Would he ever have any reason to be in London at your headquarters?"

Nairn looked appalled. "Never. Aran worked with my father long before I left for university. He helped me start up Lanwater Whitecap here on Lanera. Managed it for me when I was elsewhere. He's a mainstay on the island, and he's never any reason to be in the London offices. He's no motive to do any of this."

His thrashing arm-cast sent a tub of pencils and pens crashing to the floor, Aela quick to soothe as she gathered the fallen ones. "I'm sorry. Hey, I definitely liked what I saw of him, but I'm trying to help you. I can't do it unless I ask these questions, even if they are awkward and seem inane."

Nairn's apology was instant. He grasped her hand when she'd tidied up the pen tub, and pulled her in alongside him. Her chair whizzed into place, her leg nestled next to his, sharing far too much body heat for one small point of contact. Nairn absently stroked her fingers.

Their conclusion was someone had to have overheard his conversation with Aran and Brian – because that's when he'd given instructions for the bike ramp to be readied for use. It was always stored in the boatyard since there was no way he could get the motorbike up and down the cove.

"So, I'm guessing your accident was the end of these incidents? Till today, that is?"

Nairn's head tilted to the ceiling, a momentary closing of his eyes before he answered. "Unfortunately, no. On Tuesday morning, a power failure shut down my whole complex in London for more than four hours till the energy company found the problem. They got it up and running again just before you arrived at the castle."

"Damaging to a lot of your business." She nudged him with her leg giving an encouraging display of sympathy.

"You can imagine how much of an interruption that was. Most personnel were sent home, leaving only a skeleton staff. Just as well mobile phones are used by almost everyone, though by mid-day I'd fielded so many questions for office personnel my head was reeling." Nairn's eyes popped open, caught her glance, and he grinned – an apologetic rueful quirk of his lips. "You know just how much I was reeling on Tuesday."

Aela couldn't deny it. What a ruddy awful time he'd been having, and she'd been so dismissive about him being a prat. She was now the one who felt chagrined; ready to beat the hell out of the perpetrator on Nairn's behalf.

A jangling of the phone jolted them out of their mutual remembering.

"Thanks, Robert. Yes, I'll speak to Detective Woods now." There was a slight pause before Nairn replied. "Yes, I'm Nairn Malcolm."

Unsure if she should vacate the room Aela slipped from the chair, but Nairn's plastered arm flaps indicated she should listen in as he gestured the speakerphone.

"Our expert tells me that particular valve has been tampered with, sir, on all of the tanks. Now, your security guard has mentioned other incidents of a suspicious nature during the last week?"

She listened as Nairn related everything that had happened, including his own accident that no-one in the London office knew about. "Detective Woods. I'm sure you can appreciate why I don't want anyone in my London offices to know about my accident, not even Robert at present."

Detective Woods cleared his throat. "Do you have any suspicions about the integrity of your security guard, sir?"

Nairn was quick to dispel the notion. "None at all. I'd just prefer no one knows yet. Yes, detective, I did have a consultation from that security consultant yesterday."

"Was the nature of the visit with a view to improving your security measures, Mr. Malcolm?"

The detective's tone indicated that the event was a little too late. Nairn's sigh before answering confirmed that he, too, was thinking along the same lines. "Yes. He's gone off to get a quote together for upgraded cameras and a few other implementations to improve the monitoring of personnel movements, but I don't expect completion for a couple of days."

"As you wish, Mr. Malcolm. In the meantime, we'll say nothing of your own mishap. We have employees still to interview and I'll report on that as soon as I can." Detective Woods then explained he'd liaise with the Glasgow City Centre Police Office regarding Nairn's accident. Aela jotted down the relevant contact numbers for both police stations.

After the call, she made coffee before resuming their earlier speculation over who might be a suspect. Her next question was sensitively phrased. "Could anyone else on Lanera have a grudge to settle? Someone who comes and goes to the London base?"

Nairn made no hesitation. "Nobody ever goes down to London from Lanera. Not even Ruaridh. He's entrenched on the island, and happy to be so."

"Okay." She changed the subject back to the bike. "Could someone have accessed your bike before Saturday morning?"

Nairn couldn't deny it might have been possible, but the garage alarm system was operating as normal, so there'd been no reason for him to suspect anything untoward.

"Well, it sounds most likely that somebody tampered with the bike at the hotel in Glasgow."

Nairn readily concurred. Scooting her chair all the way around the desk, she sat closer again, her knees almost touching his thigh.

"What motive would anyone have for putting you out of action? Or causing such pandemonium your business integrity would be questionable?"

Nairn said he'd thought of that aspect. "Or, do you mean something aside from me losing business?"

"No."

She gnawed on her bottom lip. "Let's stick with loss of business. What are your most lucrative propositions at present? What would you be reluctant to lose, or muck up?"

Nairn's gaze appeared riveted on her lips, his answer slow to materialise. "I've already told you this Malaysian deal is a big money venture. The first order was successful, and I'm now supplying for a second. Being a chain of hotels, they could put huge amounts of future business my way. That's why this gas tank meddling has to be dealt with rapidly."

"Anything else?"

Nairn explained other commitments. "Gale Breakers has a prestige order for Prince Khalid. It's an expensive yacht, though it's more the cachet of getting orders like his that's important; good business is often generated by word of mouth."

Aela agreed since her Uncle Harris's business often had huge boosts from people of note using their services. Yet, neither of those two contracts sounded like the underlying cause of the incidents. "Have you potential business that's very competitive, that other companies might want so desperately they'd resort to corporate espionage?"

"Espionage? Nobody's tried to steal from me." Nairn laughed.

"Well, okay, maybe espionage isn't quite the word. Corporate sabotage or serious delaying tactics."

He mentioned a proposed meeting for the following week, in the Caribbean, that he'd probably have to abandon due to his condition. "An upgrade of craft for a newly formed consortium of hotels. They're presently serviced by different American firms, but the intention is to have a corporate image regarding water sports facilities."

"So, if you can't go next week, a competitor could win the bid instead of you?"

He suspected at least three other companies were bidding and told her that although he would present a good package it was no dead cert he'd get the work. Another silence pervaded, yet it was a comfortable one as Aela wondered what the saboteur's motive was. The respect building between them the last while was still there...but a certain reserve had returned. She sensed a different sort of pressure was creeping in, and it was grasping Nairn in an invisible stranglehold.

He next called the Glasgow City Centre Police Office and was informed that Lanera police officers would visit the castle later that evening. Without even touching him, she felt waves of agitation gripping him by the time the call was over.

Chapter Ten

"Still want to continue?"

Nairn felt nauseated, though it had nothing to do with his physical ailments. Bad conscience churned his gut as he stared at the beautiful woman he'd embroiled in his troubles.

Aela's glare, he guessed, mirrored his own as she faced him down. "I don't go back on my word, Nairn Malcolm – not ever."

"Get the Range Rover. We'll see how Prince Khalid's order's progressing."

His bark might have been heard down in Mariskay and deafened even himself. It was a pathetic excuse, but he had to get out of the castle. Frustration mounted. He hated being inactive, hated being injured, and most of all hated he could do little to protect his new employee should even more incidents occur.

He forced a compromise. Going down to the boatyard might jog some memory of the previous Friday.

"How do I access the car?" Aela got up and approached the door.

He watched her turn as she awaited his answer, her cool not ruffled in the slightest by the potential danger he put her in. Her professionalism had been exemplary. He ordered: she carried out. Hell! The woman had been his sounding board for hours, been supportive, her theories astute. Her soothing massage had kept him calm and rational. He enjoyed her presence and found he didn't want anything to hurt her.

Wheeling out into the corridor, he barrelled along till just short of the mud room where he indicated a large watercolour on the wood panelled wall. Behind was a container storing numerous keys. "Top level, first left, there should be a spare key for this back door…" He reeled off the relevant keys, finishing with the garage and security gate remotes. Aela listened, selected the necessary keys and pocketed them. "The key for the boatshed is top row first right. You're not likely to need it yet, but at least you'll know where it is." Having fired out the information, he wheeled out to the garage. "You can use any of the cars for personal use, though at present the only one I'm going to fold into just now is the Range Rover."

As she towed behind him, she blithely remarked she didn't expect she'd use either of the two high performance vehicles to travel a few miles to Mariskay, but she'd like to use them to explore the island…if she ever had time off.

Nairn ignored her jibe, in no mood to respond to her banter. He couldn't quite ignore her, though, when she shunted the passenger seat back as far as it would go and reclined it.

"Your carriage awaits, sir. Fold yourself in while I fold this down," she joked. The wheelchair was soon plopped into the boot.

At the boatyard, Aela trekked alongside the wheelchair since he insisted on wheeling himself. She was greeted in far too familiar a manner by some of the younger males, who all seemed to have valid reasons for being introduced to her, and shake hands with her. He could barely contain his aggression when yet another man hovered.

"How's progress on this one, Aela?" Aran asked as they stood by Prince Khalid's order.

"Is this a trick question?" She was grinning but Nairn didn't get the joke.

"Not at all." Aran snorted as she climbed into the hull.

Nairn listened to their repartee from the wheelchair where he sat feeling like a rat in a trap. A moment later her eager voice floated out.

"You've added a marine GPS Chartplotter and an autopilot system." Her head popped out of the hatch as she climbed back out. "Has it been water tested yet?

Aran spoke of the full trials which wouldn't happen for a couple of days, other internal fitments needing to be added first. Nairn's mood was sour as he noted Aela's interaction with Aran who appeared impressed by her knowledge and interest. How could she know those systems had been added by just looking at the interior? They'd made a couple of phone calls during the morning regarding the order, but failing that it must be she knew much more about boats than he first thought.

Or – and he liked this thought much less – had she been down here already visiting Aran?

Or Ruaridh? God forbid!

Had he been wrong to almost bare his soul to this woman? Could he trust her with his problems? She turned her charm on everyone, becoming their best friend in a matter of moments.

He'd earlier thought her concern had been personal. Maybe he was totally deluded? Yet being suspicious of everyone's motives didn't sit well with him either; he hated mistrust.

"Get the car please, Miss Cameron."

***

Aela wondered what the hell had got up Nairn's butt as she drove back to the castle, the tense silence able to be cut with a blunt knife. She was miffed again with his tendency to black moods.

"You've done enough today. Take a break. I'll see you at dinner."

His attitude as he exited the car was dismissive, as though he couldn't stand her company any longer. It rankled. "Not sure what your problem is, sir, but you look like a piece of...dog's dirt. I suggest you have a nice lie down while I go and do something interesting. After I put the car away, of course."

Her words accompanied a simpering-sweet smile. The

grunt she heard as Nairn lurched out of the door didn't mask his rude comment about cheeky, insubordinate bloody women. Her laugh echoed around the courtyard as she whipped the folding wheelchair back into use and set it beside him.

"Sweet dreams, your eminence." Her cheeky chauffeur salute was obviously not appreciated as Nairn's good fingers twitched in a rude gesture as he slid into the wheelchair.

The pool was one place domineering Nairn Malcolm wouldn't be visiting for a while. The water was a beautiful temperature, just right for fast laps and then a more leisurely swim before she splashed water onto the sauna coals and relaxed in the steamy haze. It'd been ages since she'd had a sauna – her backpacking holiday hadn't included places so luxurious.

Tranquil elegance surrounded her, the lush hydro-planting maintained by the pool attendant. Soothing to the nerves, it was heaven to be away from Nairn's bad temper; his indifference; and also his occasional affability of the afternoon. Away from his attraction. For a while.

"I've set the dining room, Miss Cameron," Kirsty informed her as she arrived at the kitchen door. "Mr. Malcolm's already there waiting for you."

"Sorry. I didn't realise I was late."

"Och, no. You're bang on time."

Although Kirsty had chopped the beef into small chunks, Aela noticed Nairn found it difficult to saw through his pastry left-handed, his sour look not much better than earlier.

"I'll cut it before you mangle it to a pulp. My fault, sir. Kirsty chose the menu for me, said I couldn't be here without tasting her traditional steak pie."

As she drew his plate closer, a grudging thank you reached her ears. It was expected since she'd already gleaned he hated to be defeated by anything. She avoided any inadvertent brushes of fingers or arms.

A strained meal followed where they discussed Nairn's plans for the coming week.

"Take the rest of the evening off. You've already put in plenty of hours, and the police will be here soon," Nairn declared after their coffee.

His terse dismissal grated, but he was the boss. She knew she shouldn't feel rejected.

"In that case, I'll go walkabout."

She wasn't sure whether to feel glad or miffed by his abrasive attitude but she was becoming all too aware the dratted man's attraction was increasing, not diminishing as it should be due to his mercurial moods. It was obvious he wasn't feeling the same pull because he wanted rid of her, now barely tolerating her when she was in the same room.

The wander down to Mariskay was ideal. Since it was a warm June evening, there were plenty of patrons of the harbour bars sitting at outside tables, enjoying the evening sunshine. Aela found a space, ordered a glass of wine and contemplated what a strange situation she'd got herself into. Within minutes a couple of the younger boat-builders she'd met earlier in the day strolled past and expressed delight in keeping her company.

The next hours were the most relaxed she'd been for days, although she was careful to be confidential when Nairn's name cropped up. It was evident that though he didn't tolerate fools gladly he was admired in the local community for generating economy.

Jamie was full of praise for her new boss. "Aye, Nairn wis born and raised here. Did a Mechanical Engineering Degree in Edinburgh, tho', and then went tae Harvard Business School, but he nipped back to see Ruaridh and checked on Lanwater Whitecap during his long holidays."

As the evening progressed more information was uncovered since both of the men had other relatives who'd been employed by Nairn.

"Och, ye'd never have credited it, Aela. Four years ago Garvald Castle was jist a ruined shell wi'nae roof. Nairn brought much needed work fir craftsmen on the isle when he bought it and restored it tae how ye see the day." Colm was then happy to tell her about the boatyard's current financial viability, which gave the young locals some reassurance they'd have jobs in the near future.

She filed away the information as useful to her temporary job: nothing to do with her desire to know everything she could about her well-respected, workaholic, annoying boss. She returned to Garvald Castle warmed by the wine and the congenial company.

The door to Nairn's bedroom was shut tight as she walked past. The office was empty, but at her desk she found a brief, impartial message – the police had called. She went to bed feeling very much the outsider, someone in the know, yet barely involved.

Professional politeness ruled from first greetings the next day. Sometimes Aela looked up to find Nairn's gaze on her then he would open an unnecessary conversation. His eyes betrayed something else before he veiled them – though she did wonder if she read more into his regard because it was what she was beginning to want. Yet contrarily also didn't want.

She berated herself for being fascinated by him. What qualities were there to like about the guy? He could be unfeeling, was a moody unpredictable sod at times, a workaholic…yet the inescapable fact was his rugged good looks and half mangled face warmed her inside. The ogre of Garvald Castle was the most stubborn, single-minded person she'd ever met, his self-discipline astonishing, but she wasn't sure if she admired him, or was just overpowered by those traits.

She determined to maintain the status quo for a few weeks, though, and suppress any feelings beyond liking the man. Soon she'd be home in Vancouver, and Nairn Malcolm would just be someone else she'd met on her travels.

That notion didn't cheer her.

"Your wound's healing very nicely," Rhona declared later when she popped in. "I'm done with you if someone tends to it on Sunday. A quick sterilising and a clean dressing is all you'll need; the stitches are already dissolving. You're managing your personal hygiene then, Nairn?" The nurse's inquiry was deliberate, her statement falling into an unnatural tense silence. "You don't smell bad, but the fragrance is pretty strong. Just use one or two, Nairn. No need to have Ruaridh buy up the whole island stock of baby wipes."

Rhona's chuckle reverberated long after she left.

So that's what the smell was. Aela's lips twitched though she didn't dare laugh outright for Nairn looked…so purple!

Baby wipes? Who else would have thought of using them as a temporary measure? Ruaridh had said his independent son would find ways to overcome his current circumstances, and it would appear he had. She gave him full marks for ingenuity: the wipes more successful than his hacking off the unwanted material of his sweatpants on the day she'd arrived.

She grinned at the memory for she sensed the frustration that must have dogged Nairn when presented with a pair of pants he couldn't get on, since she now knew his other clothes were up the insurmountable spiral staircase in the master bedroom wardrobes.

Their time in the office was profitable, tandem working even more successful than the previous day, but by late afternoon Nairn's disposition was back to remote. His rest had been short in the early afternoon, so he probably felt more pain than he admitted to.

Or, maybe his mood was due to the fact the police had come up with nothing conclusive. His London employees had been questioned, security tapes were being investigated. Tapes from the Glasgow hotel car park had also been requisitioned but were still under investigation. What could she do about his mood changes? She was his temporary employee- nothing more. She told herself for the umpteenth time, she shouldn't forget the fact.

Dinner, however, was agreeable. Nairn's inquiries about her background growing up in Vancouver showed interest, and she in turn learned about his early years on Lanera before going off to University.

Astonishment grabbed her when he dismissed her afterwards because she thought they'd been getting on fine. She would have been happy to spend the evening with him just hanging around the castle and was disappointed no end that she wasn't.

A little while later, she was enjoying the evening sunshine outside a different bar from the previous evening when Ruaridh joined her.

"Hello, lass!" His greeting cheered as though it was a happening every day of the week. "How are things progressing up at the castle? Has Nairn driven you mad yet?"

"He's getting closer." Aela laughed at Ruaridh's humour and far too coincidental arrival. "He's trying, though I don't know him well enough for it to happen yet. I need to know people very well before I get caught in such a trap."

"You'll know him soon, lass, because my son's very predictable. I've just been to see him. He's given me my marching orders too, and claims he doesn't need my assistance."

"Rhona told him to cut back on the baby wipes, so you won't have to go and buy any more of them." Nairn's discomfiture made her chortle.

Ruaridh agreed Nairn would have been mortally offended that they knew what he'd been using but divulged the pack of baby wipes held much more than fiddly cleansing pads for women.

Her giggle was infectious and set Ruaridh grinning as well. "Oh, he'd be stinking now, rather than use them, Ruaridh."

After a pleasant few hours learning about Lanera and its history she set off back to the castle with Ruaridh in tow. Although it wasn't quite dark at eleven p.m. – it being almost the longest day of the year – there was no way he was going to let her walk home alone, even though she told him she'd done it the night before. He didn't come in when they reached the castle door, but he did bid her a raucous goodnight.

When Aela reached the downstairs bedroom, Nairn accosted her, blocking her way.

"I see you've managed to attract an admirer already?"

His acerbic jibe bit her to the quick.

"Yes, I guess I have, sir. For your information it was your father." Anger was building. She noted the annoyed eyes sparking at her and got even more exasperated, unable to control her hurtful responses. "We met in Mariskay, and, being the gentleman he is, he walked me home. What's your problem anyway? You told me you didn't want me tonight." She glared at the tense set of his shoulders as he hunched over the crutch. "You're not in the wheelchair?"

"Glad you noticed. I don't need it any more."

The sound of the crutch clattering to the floor indicated how wrong he was.

Both of Nairn's hands slapped forward pressing her to the wall as he slipped into a tilt, the rough edge on the arm cast stabbing into Aela's upper arm.

"Nairn!" Giving thanks that she was strong, she managed to right him again before they both headed to the floor in a crumpled heap.

He looked at her arm in horror and at the rough edges of his plaster cast, his apology a whisper to the ceiling. A trickle of blood seeped from one of the scratches.

"It's nothing. Let me help you in to bed."

"I'm fine." He hobbled away.

It took minutes for her heart to stop pounding and her mind to gain control as she assessed what had happened. The whole episode had been so unforeseen and so rapid she wondered if she'd imagined it. Why was he so angry? She'd squealed her head off, for sure, but it had been to make him aware of where the cast was gouging her. She wasn't annoyed that he'd almost fallen.

***

Inside the bedroom Nairn slumped against the wall. What the hell was he thinking? His bloody arm cast had made her bleed. Being confined to the castle and not knowing what she'd been doing had frustrated him no end.

Was his father really pursuing her? He knew Ruaridh's voice too well not to have recognised who had walked her back to the castle.

A persistent niggle continued – could Aela like his father more than him? A horrific thought made his stomach tighten beyond belief. Aela a potential step-mother? Never in this lifetime was that going to happen.

Chapter Eleven

Aela woke in a bit of a snit.

The encounter with Nairn had taken on different scenarios in her fitful dreams.

It was unfortunate the morning had dawned almost as dismal as her mood. The weather was overcast with grey, brooding skies and a constant drizzle. Rain didn't normally bother her, but it seemed all too depressing for words. Since Nairn had told her at dinner the night before he wouldn't need her much over the weekend, since he claimed he was going to do what the doctor ordered and rest up more, the time was virtually her own till summoned.

Sipping a glass of orange juice in her tiny kitchen, she decided exercise would lift her spirits. The temptation to saddle up and explore was strong because she felt like fleeing the castle, but it wouldn't be fun with the mist shrouding the area, she'd see very little and then disappointment would set in.

The pool.

An unbelievable treat to use on a whim. Lapping till she was tired and hungry, she headed for the railing to exit the water just as Nairn entered, propped upon his crutch. Her fingers fumbled on the metal grip, her knees trembling as she climbed out. In spite of her misgivings, yet again, Nairn managed to make her grin like a Cheshire cat.

Black plastic garbage bags were an awkward wrap around his casts, kept in place by rubber bands, and he wore only boxer shorts. White silk.

Hells teeth!

They were virtually see-through in the pool lighting. Aela closed her eyes and said a little prayer – though whether it was for the strength to avoid looking at his powerful body, or to bask in its glory, she wasn't too sure. Snatching up the towel from the lounger she wrapped it around herself.

"Good morning. I hope it's all right for me to use the pool?"

Nairn, it seemed, couldn't take his eyes off her. The skimpy bikini she wore was rendered invisible as he stared. "Of course you can use the pool. I can't swim for a while, though I'm going to indulge in the briefest of saunas. Even I'm balking at the poncy smell dogging me."

"I'm going to breakfast after I shower. Would you like some?"

Nairn looked far too mesmerised by the beads of water running down between her breasts to answer her question. "Mmm…I haven't had…some…not…yet." His gaze eventually looked up. "What were your plans?"

"A traditional Scottish breakfast?" she suggested, attempting a distraction with humour. "No tartan but Kirsty's dead set on me having haggis and black pudding. My little refrigerator is groaning with the stuff. I don't eat that kind of breakfast on a week day but, since today's Saturday, perhaps you'll join me?"

"In the apartment?" His throat clearing was so loud she couldn't fail to hear it. His gaze slipped away to look at the water before he answered. "How about we assemble our resources in the main kitchen instead, although you'll have to accept I'll just be the onlooker." Glittering blue eyes locked onto hers, a whimsical smile lifting the corner of his lip.

Aela moved towards the door to exit the pool suite, but he blocked the way. "I owe you an apology for last night, Miss Cameron." His eyes sought her forgiveness yet the banked heat was unambiguous.

"No! You don't, sir. It was an accident." Determination stiffened her shoulders as she brought her gaze back up to face him, the small smile she produced she hoped displayed no offence. "Could have happened to anyone."

Twenty minutes later both were dried and dressed and in the kitchen – at least Aela was dressed. His wheelchair a thing of the past, Nairn hobbled around in the ubiquitous bath robe. It was tied securely at his waist, which was unfortunate since Aela couldn't see which boxers he was wearing. Her small groan was accompanied with a reluctant smile as she tucked such thoughts away. None of that.

Together they decided what to include in their hot calorie-laden breakfast.

"Yes, fruit." Her smile was adamant. "Peaches, mango and strawberries."

"Sure…okay." Nairn teased. "Hey, I like fruit. Just not on the same plate as my eggs, haggis and black pudding."

Aela grinned. "It's a good balance. Live dangerously."

"You don't think I'm doing that already? Looking like this?" Nairn's eyebrows almost hit the ceiling, his chortle amazingly endearing.

"Okay!" she beamed. "Sorry. Poor choice of words."

The words may have been too close to the bone yet they did lighten the mood. They were comfortable with each other as she assembled their meal, though Nairn got in her way rather a lot as he attempted to set the table, the best sort-of-help he could manage. The occasional brushing together of their bodies she put down to his awkward movements – though she knew it was a lie. She could have moved more quickly. So why wasn't she doing it?

They managed to have a decent conversation with him asking about her decision to travel the world and her future university plans. In turn, she learned about his time at his Edinburgh University and then his year afterwards at Harvard Business School.

"Whoa! Harvard. I'm so impressed. Nothing but the best finishing school, Mr. Malcolm."

"I never quite thought of it as such, Miss Cameron, but you're bang on the button." Nairn smiled. "My choice of Harvard was on purpose since it would improve my future business developments."

"Only the best on your CV?" she quipped.

"Never needed a CV. I've always been my own boss."

Her peal of laughter echoed around the kitchen. "I can see the prestige of having a Harvard qualification, though couldn't you have done your MBA in the UK? Somewhere with the same kudos?"

"Calling me a snob, Miss Cameron?"

"Would I dare?"

Her laugh faltered when his features sharpened. Nairn looked as though he wasn't going to reply at first. His good fingers drummed a short rhythm on the table as an enigmatic smile bathed his face. Aela waited, and waited. Then, a decision having been made, he carried on. "I needed to get the hell out of Scotland at the time, all the way out of Europe."

She couldn't imagine what would have made it so important for him to ship out. He'd set up his diving school on Lanera with a legacy from his maternal grandmother before then. What would make him want to leave the country?

"The United States was far enough away for me to leave behind the trauma of my parents' divorce."

"Ah! Not an amicable separation?

"Is there ever?" Nairn huffed, a rueful look flashing across to her. He paused a while before continuing, his words measured. "The Ruaridh you see now is a much more relaxed version than the one of years ago. Caitlinn, my mother, never liked staying on Lanera; hated the climate, constantly harped on about going somewhere warm."

Aela filled in the gaps as he revealed details. "Ruaridh had his boatyard business here?"

"Ruaridh wasn't a man to compromise when it came to the boatyard. And he doesn't compromise on his lifestyle now either."

At his intent stare, she wondered if he was highlighting what he regarded as his father's negative qualities on purpose.

"My father, Miss Cameron, wouldn't budge his ass from

Lanera even if a tsunami hit – not for my mother and not for any woman now."

"That bad?" She joked, though was curious since she didn't feel she'd had a real answer to her question. "But you still felt you had to be so far away?"

"They separated when I first went to University. Before the divorce papers were even drawn up my mother had taken up with an obscenely rich Spanish lover, a man she married at first opportunity." Nairn sounded so bitter Aela swallowed at his tone. "With future money no object, Caitlinn never lowered herself to haggle with Ruaridh over assets on Lanera during the divorce proceedings." He scrubbed his hair back before massaging his neck, a trait Aela realised highlighted his tension. "But she haggled constantly over me."

"But you were…what?" She was dumbstruck. "Nearly twenty?"

"Caitlinn had existed for years being jealous of any time I spent with my father, and after the divorce she wanted me to spend every vacation at her new home near Barcelona." Nairn appeared to shrug off unpleasant memories as he looked askance. "I wanted to be on Lanera to be at my own fledgling business. So, if I was on the island, it always appeared Ruaridh won the battle."

"Do you ever see her now?"

Nairn's eyes lightened a little as he dredged up a smile of sorts. "Sometimes…though still not as often as she'd like. But that's enough of my history for one session. Time for a break, Miss Cameron."

Aela was confused. Nairn's friendly attitude was what she wanted, what she'd suggested in the pool suite. Yet she should also be glad he was demonstrating he could maintain a control which kept them within the bounds of employer and employee. Somehow, though, she was disappointed.

"I'm going back to work, though I won't need you. If the weather improves by midday, and conditions are favourable, maybe you'd like to take out the floatplane?"

"Yay! How do I learn a Scottish version of a reverse rain

102

dance? Got Shamans-R-Us in your local directory?"

Nairn's chuckle was her only answer as he hobbled off.

After a solitary lunch the weather had improved. An occasional cloud shadowed the sky, but high enough not to be an issue for handling a floatplane. Heading to the key-safe she collided with Nairn coming out of the bedroom.

"Sorry. Wasn't paying attention," he laughed, looking so glad to see her the day seemed to get brighter.

Aela wasn't so sure of his apology, though, for it seemed he'd just barrelled himself out into the corridor, yet she wasn't quibbling because he'd just wrapped himself around her and held her tight. Pity she didn't want the contact.

Crap. What a liar she was!

"I'm heading down to the floatplane now." She mumbled at his shoulder, the peculiar smell one she was getting used to. Reluctantly extracting her arms from their tangle she was pretty sure Nairn appeared as unwilling to break free as she was. She wanted to slide back into his embrace...and maybe...do a bit more than clutch?

It wasn't really a surprise when he told her taking out the floatplane was a great idea, but she could only do it if she took him too. Aela bristled like a porcupine. Was he checking up on her flying skills? Her tone likely came over sharper than intended, but she didn't care to be an object of doubt as she took a deliberate step away from him.

"Listen, you silly cretin. Those ribs of yours are not nearly well enough for a trip in a tight little floatplane. And there will be no room for that stiff cast of yours."

To her total surprise Nairn's laugh was hearty...and didn't look too pained. Just a little squint showed his discomfort.

"Don't you worry about my stiff leg. Somehow I am going to...fit." His deliberate hesitation didn't faze Aela as his laugh rumbled even more. "I'm going stir crazy. I've checked the weather and everything's favourable."

There was no impediment to them taking out the floatplane.

Well, actually there was, but it was overcome with ease.

No way could Nairn negotiate the cliff staircase, so Aela deposited him at the boatyard, left him there to do a bit of catch-up while she nipped back to the castle and garaged the range-rover. Afterwards she taxied the floatplane around the headland to the quayside slip having done an even more thorough check than normal of the floatplane, to ensure no messy tampering problems. Nairn was totally happy to agree with that strategy.

As she rounded the headland, handling airplane controls again was so thrilling. Travelling had been a fun experience, but she'd missed flying so much.

Under guidance from Nairn, Aela flew the floatplane over the Isle of Mull, the birthplace of her grandfather, and further north over the Isle of Skye. Banking to the west took them over the Outer Hebrides, the flatter, more barren lands of North and South Uist a huge contrast to the mountainous Skye. Fabulous. Her questions had been incessant but Nairn had seemed happy to satisfy every curiosity.

A few hours later she felt she had proved to Nairn that she could fly his beloved floatplane.

"Okay! I'm now convinced your knowledge of flying floatplanes – and no doubt jets – is superior to mine. The jets you can prove another day, but it's time for me to give in and head home. It's time for more of those damned painkillers Sir Smash-Em-Up macho-me is taking regularly."

Aela grinned at the faces he was pulling knowing the ribs he'd claimed earlier were fine were anything but fine.

"Did you really call me that?" Though Nairn was laughing he seemed incredulous.

"Well, what was I supposed to think? Who the hell would interview looking like a battered train wreck? A re-enactment seemed to fit so well." Her hearty laugh echoed around them.

Back at the boat slip they were lucky to catch Jamie who'd just completed an overtime shift. It was no trouble for him to organise Nairn's transport back to the castle.

Knowing her boss was in good hands she taxied the

floatplane back around the headland. It gave her the opportunity to check out his catamaran, the small dinghy and the kayaks in the cove boatshed. There was no way she was going to be taking out any of Nairn's transport without making thorough checks. One great advantage from having worked in her Uncle Harris's company meant she'd learned plenty about engines and working parts of many kinds of vehicles before she'd even been allowed to fly or drive them. By the time she locked up the boatshed she was happy all was in order with the assembled craft – but she was almost late for dinner.

Her backpack didn't run to elegant evening wear though she did have a couple of tops of good quality she'd bought in Italy. The one she wore to dine was already a firm favourite of hers; deep purple with sequins and overstitching.

"Miss Cameron," Kirsty exclaimed when she arrived at the dining room. "You look so pretty in that colour. Doesn't she look fine, Mr. Malcolm?"

The whisper of sound passing Nairn's lips as Kirsty bustled out of the room was probably an assent. After a long pause he met her gaze. Sheer frustration mirrored back at her.

"Gorgeous," he rasped. "But then you look stunning in everything."

"Thank you, sir. You're likely to see it often, since I don't have many alternatives."

They picked up their casual banter of the afternoon, yet one of his tiny glances, or the merest brush of their fingers when she helped him cut awkward parts of his pasta, set up an awkward strain.

"I know you're having your meal, Miss Cameron, but someone called Jed was on the castle's phone line," Kirsty informed her as she brought their next course. "When I said you were eating he told me it was fine if you phone him back later. Says he's missed you so bad."

"I'm missing him too, Kirsty. Thanks for the message. I'll call back as soon as I can."

Aela's smile was reciprocated by Kirsty but not by her employer. Nairn, it seemed, wasn't happy about interruptions to his food, or maybe he was just annoyed Jed had used the castle phone. He regressed to grumpy curmudgeon for the rest of the meal.

"I don't need you any more tonight. Take the time off to do whatever you like."

Aela watched his tense back muscles as he leaned on his crutch and stomped off as much as one can with a leg cast.

Bloody chameleon.

The temptation was high to go back down to Mariskay, it being Saturday evening. Instead, in the office apartment, she decided to research official government records of births, marriages and deaths, in an attempt to find her great-grandfather's relatives. But before that…

"Jed!" Aela clucked. "You were checking up on me again." Her cousin Jed always cheered her up even if his tendency to be overprotective sometimes annoyed her.

***

Nairn succumbed. He'd forced himself to work but his concentration was shattered. He needed to know if Aela had gone out. Like the night before. Jealousy of Ruaridh; this Jed person; and maybe other unknown men, ate at his gut.

Frustration crippled him almost as much as his leg cast. Full attention from a woman he was dating was what he liked when they were together, but he'd never bothered about what they were doing when they were apart. What did his urges mean now? Was he jealous because he'd got used to Aela's proximity? Was it because they weren't just sharing a work space but, almost, their living quarters? Regardless of those answers he missed her. Missed looking over at her; missed hearing her sexy, husky voice even when her laughter was overt, or berating his stupidity regarding his health.

At the apartment he found the sitting room door wide open and a loud throbbing beat playing on the music system. Sitting with her back to him she seemed intent, working on the computer. She was home, and he felt like a louse for checking up on her. Relieved, but still a louse. He turned and hobbled to his lonely office.

He wanted her at her desk across the room, but he was the one who'd chased her away. He was, even now, begrudging giving her time off to do what she wanted in the apartment. As his employee she deserved some time off... but he wanted to get to know her.

He looked down at his casts and in a miserable temper tossed his crutch away.

Chapter Twelve

"Aela!"

The loud plea shocked Aela as she rinsed her hair in the shower. Punching off the water she grabbed a towel wondering what on earth the matter was. The day before Nairn had seemed so much better – give or take his bad moods. No symptoms of concussion had returned, his ribs were causing fewer problems, and even walking with his crutch was less awkward. Rushing out, tucking the towel in place into her cleavage, she found him entering the bedroom in search of her.

"What's wrong?" She took in the sight of his naked torso at once, because the sad fact was he'd managed to cover himself far too well the last few days.

"Sorry." Nairn's gaze fixed on her face as he stared at the rivulets of water she felt trickling from her hair. He looked ill-at-ease as though it was a great effort to keep his eyes north of her shoulders. "I didn't think before I barged in. I'll…leave you to get dressed. Talk to you later."

Turning around too swiftly he hobbled out, a grunt escaping.

"No! Nairn. Wait. Mmm…sir." Aela found her voice. "What did you want?"

His throat sounded rough when he turned back. "I can't get the new dressing back on. I wondered if you could help me."

Aela found her own voice hoarse. "Give me a couple of minutes, and I'll be along to help you."

His beam of thanks floored her. She stared as he lurched out of the room: it was the first time he'd asked her for help regarding his injuries. She was finding the man lethal.

When she taped on the new dressing, her fingers trembled so much she thought she wouldn't be able to smooth it into place. His whole ribcage was now a myriad of lighter purples, green-yellows, greyish-blacks; still bruised but pulsing with a need to be soothed. Fearful of hurting him further she smoothed the edges of the tape with great care, Nairn's unique male scent mingling with the balm-sweet smell emanating around him.

Under her fingers, she could feel Nairn's minute trembles. His face dipped down. She couldn't fail to hear the sniff when his nose drew deep of the scent of her washed hair. His hand reached up and stroked her still-wet locks.

"Miss Cameron…Aela?" Nairn sounded strangled.

"Am I hurting you?"

Nairn clutched her chin and enclosed her mouth with his as though he couldn't stop himself.

Aela was unable to do anything but respond, the insanity of it escaping her till she felt Nairn's agonised gasp against her lips. She felt the sheer ache of his ribs because her grip around his torso was too tight. His face leeched colour; his breathing erratic and troubled. Breaking free, her embarrassment was as heated as her voice.

"Sir." His torso wasn't ready for more stress. She had to suppress her own desire because she was going to make him need another hospital visit if she didn't back away. The lie she produced was so hard to voice; nearly crumpling her to her knees. "I don't do passing flings. And you don't date employees."

Pulling free from his grip, she retreated out of the room and flew down the corridor like a bat out of hell.

She heard his faint cry echo along the corridor. "I'm sorry, Aela."

Clothes a haphazard throw on she bolted for the stables unable to be near Nairn for one more second without jumping his battered body. Her feverish mind perfected the best approach to make love to a body with two plaster casts and extreme sensitivity around the torso. How perverted did that make her?

It was regrettable Lanera had no huge prairie to gallop out her demons. On the positive side, there was a horse available she could use: the others already out to the locals, mainly kids Nairn allowed to ride free of charge. She learned Nairn's sole stipulation was if someone rode one of his horses, they had to spend some time mucking out, or doing other stable chores.

After her ride and some light tack cleaning – all she was permitted to do – she headed down to Mariskay for lunch to avoid Nairn, having made her apologies to Kirsty. Her meal had just arrived at the outside table of her harbour restaurant when Ruaridh's appearance was so timely Kirsty must have phoned him.

"So, how come you're here and my son isn't? What's he up to today?" His inquisitive nature came to the fore.

"No idea. Left him to his own devices."

"So, Nairn's giving you the cold shoulder?" Ruaridh's question was serious.

"We're being polite and businesslike, Ruaridh, which is how it should be." Her retort was firm knowing full well she lied through her teeth, for how on earth could Nairn's kiss of the morning be called businesslike?

After her snapping she was amazed when Ruaridh invited her to go out in his catamaran, his smile cajoling. How could she refuse, desperate as she was to learn how to navigate them, to do her transporting jobs well? It was much easier than the learning curve in becoming a detached PA to Nairn Malcolm.

Nairn was asleep on one of the huge couches in the great room, his full length stretched out, on her return to Garvald Castle. She'd missed him all afternoon and how stupid was that? Give or take a bruise or two, he was so handsome in repose. There were none of those ugly frowns marring his attractive face; no lines fanning out from his lips indicating disapproval. The residual bruising had faded to a faint yellowish tinge. She wanted to capture his curving lips and taste them. Prudence won, though, as she crept out instead.

110

"I'm not quite asleep," Nairn called out to her, but she could tell she'd just wakened him by the sleepy pitch of his voice.

"Sorry, I tried not to wake you," she whispered, warmed not just by his tone, but by his intense scrutiny of her skimpy shorts and camisole since the afternoon had been warm.

Nairn's movements were sinuous as he worked himself upright. A pair of swim shorts was all he wore, though she was sure he hadn't been so rash as to use the pool. "Had a nice relaxing day?" His enquiry was casual, but his eyes were hooded.

"Lovely." She didn't quite know how to respond to him: he was being so nice.

"I told you the day was yours but, if you don't have any evening plans, would you mind driving us both down to Mariskay for a meal?" He sounded apologetic, and followed it with the admission that he'd told Kirsty she'd not need to cook that evening.

"I'm happy to drive you down, though you don't have to include me in your dinner plans."

"The truth, Aela?" The rise to his feet awkward in front of her, he dominated her airspace once he was standing. "If you're with me I'll not be accosted by well-wishers every two seconds. You could save me from such a fate, surely?"

The teasing grin accompanying his request was a deal breaker. How could she resist? "Your ego wouldn't need polishing a little would it?" She jested, amazed at his arrogance, yet having learned how well-thought of he was she didn't doubt there would be people who'd stop by asking after his health.

She wasn't wrong.

The meal was convivial even though there was a constant interruption of people asking after him. Everything was extremely pleasant till Ruaridh arrived, just as they began their desserts.

"Aela! I'm so glad to see you." Ruaridh swallowed her up in a big bear hug. The light kiss to her cheek surprised

111

her, but with Ruaridh she didn't know what to expect, or how to interpret his enthusiastic welcome. "So you've given up the chariot already, Nairn?" Ruaridh launched in without preamble when he straightened back up. "Feeling much better?"

Nairn didn't answer right away, continuing to fork his chocolate pistachio mousse with determined precision. "Thought I was." His reply was cryptical since he didn't look at Ruaridh. "Now, maybe less so."

All Ruaridh did was grin.

"Aela? Got personal things to talk to you about that I forgot to tell you this afternoon," Ruaridh declared after a few minutes of general chitchat. "Maybe we could meet tomorrow night after work?"

With startling speed their waitress was signalled, the bill paid and in double quick time Aela found herself heading out of the restaurant. No coffee. No further chat to Ruaridh. Not even a proper goodbye because as soon as Nairn had tossed down some banknotes on the table he'd limped off for the door. She made her apologetic goodbyes to a grinning Ruaridh.

Nairn didn't speak at all on the way back. Blowing hot and cold with her seemed to be his favourite pastime. She fumed. He was so unbearably rude to his father. She hadn't a clue what'd caused it, but she couldn't condone his manner.

Unlocking the back door she preceded him inside, feeling around for the hall light switch. In her wake, Nairn declared he was heading for the office his eyes lingering on hers for much longer than ever before when she turned back to him, a question there she couldn't interpret before he bid her a clipped goodnight. He wasn't angry. His silent question was almost...disappointment?

Aela didn't want the evening to end on a sour note. She couldn't pretend she wasn't affected by the blasted man. Yet what he wanted she couldn't seem to give him – at least she didn't think so because he kept walking away.

Aela experienced the full force of Nairn's dynamic personality when she presented herself in the office just after eight a.m. Monday, the beginning of the traditional working week. Traditional for some – Nairn's week proved to be a little different.

"Miss Cameron."

She'd begun to dread the formality of her surname because she knew it firmed her in her place.

"We're leaving by nine o'clock. I need to do a day trip to my London headquarters. Weather and landing conditions are already checked and maintenance in Glasgow has the jet on standby."

Aela almost blew a gasket. They had planned this but later in the week when he might be a little more fit to do it. "Are you loco? You could barely manage a few hours in the floatplane on Saturday, Nairn Malcolm, so what the friggin' heck makes you think you're ready for a trip to London and back?" Nairn's one-eyebrow lift was impressive, but she wasn't fazed by it. "All the healing you've done to date will be for nothing, you stupid prat."

The silence was telling.

Since Nairn wasn't put off in the least by her censure, she stomped to her computer and powered up, muttering dire warnings.

Quite unperturbed Nairn detailed his usual flying procedures, Aela making hasty notes for future reference. His mood was light, yet she didn't quite trust it somehow. Why, or what, would make him so changed from the angry man of the evening before?

"For this first trip would you prefer a chartered pilot to take us from Glasgow to London? Now, don't get your hackles up! I'm asking because I also need you in the capacity of my PA immediately after the flight."

She wasn't sure how to interpret his inquiry. On the one hand he could doubt her expertise, yet on the other he could be thinking about her energy reserves as she juggled the different jobs. Either way she knew this was a first test of her stamina and of her capabilities. "I'll be fine with all the

113

transportation, sir, and with my role as PA."

"Glad to hear it."

Nairn nodded, then detailed the calls they each had to make before they left, and the correspondence which needed completion before leaving.

Around eight forty-five Nairn declared he was off to get dressed. She hadn't even noticed he was wearing the ubiquitous towelling dressing robe since she'd become so inured to it. Scooting off herself, she changed into her one and only suit.

Ten minutes later he was at the office door wearing a short sleeved white shirt, unbuttoned, and a pair of black cargo pants, one leg unzipped to the knee, baring the stark white plaster cast she'd become so accustomed to. A striped tie lay across his arm on top of a formal suit jacket of soft black cashmere. She heard an irritated exhalation of breath as he lurched into the office.

"I'm going to have to call up that extra clause on your contract already."

Her eyebrows rose in inquiry since she hadn't a clue what he was talking about.

"Those extras during my incapacity? It's too difficult to fasten all these small buttons, and there's no way in hell I can tie my tie."

Her surprised chortle couldn't be suppressed. "You expect me to tie your tie? How do you know I can?"

"I've every confidence in you."

The twinkle in his gaze she disregarded. "Do you need to be so formal?" In his present circumstances, she was amazed formal clothing was necessary.

Nairn's reply was definite. "I always wear a tie at the London office, and I'm not going to change that because of a blip in my health." His eyes strayed down to the cargo pants. "This is as close as I can get at the moment to cover my legs, though I assure you I do need the tie."

Aela spent the next few minutes deftly fastening his buttons, and re-zipping the leg of his pants as far as it would go over his leg cast. Tying a tie was easy because she'd

114

worn a tie at formal pilot events and knew how to do it – except tying it for Nairn meant very close proximity to her heavily breathing boss.

Nairn reached forward to hold onto her shoulders while she concentrated on knotting the tie. Ignoring the pressure of his gentle squeezing she continued with her task. When his lips got closer to her hair as she bent her head, she imagined a whispering kiss.

Nairn drew in a pained breath because she was firm in pulling the knot up into place, her fingers caressing his neck before she smoothed down his collar. The breath she huffed on purpose onto his stretched up Adam's apple made his skin erupt into little goose pimples.

Nairn's fingers curled on her shoulders as he put her away from him, his sigh loud, so close to her ear.

"Thank you, Miss Cameron."

Were his ribs paining him again? She somehow didn't think that was what the sigh was about.

Chapter Thirteen

"Almost in Glasgow," Aela shouted to Nairn. "So, was that spectacular...or what?"

Nairn's dry answer blasted her ear. "Not down yet, so I guess a nine and three quarters."

A little after ten o'clock found them moving from the hangar where the floatplane was berthed. Her laugh rang out as they sat atop one of the powered baggage carts as it chugged them along to Nairn's jet. Aela had warned the ground crew that this time Nairn might just need a little shunt between planes. Glasgow to London was the next leg of the journey, and she just couldn't wait to get her hands on the jet controls. She'd been conscious of the way her skirt rode up her thighs as she'd used the foot controls in the floatplane but decided not to make an issue of it since Nairn had mostly been looking out of the side window.

Nairn's jet was a delight to fly, a slightly newer version than any she'd flown before, yet not so different. Too soon, she followed instructions from air traffic control in London for descent and after that handed the plane over to the maintenance crew.

Her next challenge presented itself, the greatest to date because flying had been familiar. Another Range Rover awaited, Aela expected to drive it to the London office. Driving the vehicle wasn't the issue. She'd spent five days as a tourist in London when she'd made landfall in the UK and knew London traffic was vastly different from Lanera.

Profound swearing burst free as Nairn hobbled down the jet ramp, followed by an apology. "Sorry. Didn't think ahead enough to ask if you'd rather have had a driver get us to the office." When both of his feet were on *terra firma* he smiled at her then explained, "I'm so used to doing all this myself I haven't broken it down to individual transportations."

She made sure her grin looked confident. "My driver's license allows me to drive in the UK, and we've sorted out insurance details. With directions I'll get us where you want us to be…so long as you don't expect me to scoot around like a London cabbie, because there's no way I could do that."

Nairn's answer was good-humoured. "I don't expect you to be familiar with London streets. Soon, though?"

His smile wasn't just around his mouth, his blue eyes twinkled and the day seemed to get brighter.

Their relaxed attitude was a boon, since the drive was daunting. Thank heavens for satellite navigation systems. The posh voice was very clear and helped her negotiate the route. All she'd to do was concentrate on driving on the left and wend her way through the traffic throng. Soon she parked in a dedicated bay at an impressive waterfront development which housed Nairn's main office building and two warehouses. His glance settled on her as she engaged the handbrake and turned off the ignition.

"Not too late to back out, Miss Cameron."

Aela knew very well what he was doing, but she wouldn't change her mind anytime soon. Their eyes clashed as she shook her head. "Nice offer, thank you, but I'm here for the duration and in this quest just as much as you are now, sir. Shall we get to work?"

Stepping out of the car she slung their laptop case straps across her shoulder, fisted his walking aid, and toed her door closed before she went round to hand Nairn the metal cane.

"Don't say you didn't have your chance." His jaw was set, a steel glint in his eye as he manoeuvred himself out of the car. "If you're sure about not deserting, then let's get on with it."

"I don't feel like abandoning you today, sir." She zinged the automatic locking device and opened the entrance door to the offices. "A problem shared is a problem halved? Isn't that what they say?"

Nairn's look wasn't convincing. He still appeared uncomfortable. "So I've heard, but my problems shouldn't be your problems."

Their entering the building created quite a stir.

"Mr. Malcolm! You'll need the lift today." The entrance level receptionist gushed as she hastened over the tiled foyer to summon it. "I didn't know you'd had an accident."

Her inquiries regarding Nairn's health were brushed over, Nairn's terse and impatient manner indicating he wasn't having any truck with gossip. "Sandra, this is my new PA, Aela Cameron. She needs a security pass. Organise it, please. Field all my calls through her direct line, and send Robert up to my office right away."

Aela barely had time to note the doors with clear insignias for Nairn's different companies. Lanwater – Traders; Dry Gear; and Whitecaps.

"Personnel and Payroll Departments on this side," he barked at her. "The link door leading to the warehouses is the one at the far end of that corridor beyond the Security office."

A bleached-blonde head popped out of one of the offices, noted Nairn's injuries and made a hasty retreat. "Mr. Malcolm's here."

The comment was discernible by them although it was no doubt intended to be a stage whisper. Aela could well imagine the flutter inside the office. She guessed as soon as the lift was in motion that his health issues would spread like wildfire before they even reached his top floor office suite. Nairn ushered her into the Gale Breakers office and made introductions. She'd already spoken with the woman on the phone so there was marginal familiarity.

Nairn spent no more time than necessary on updates from Lanera then led her into his small Technical Division. It housed a computer department and a room serving as a base for his small team of technicians.

"Nairn Malcolm, what the hell have you done to

yourself?"

Aela was surprised by the informality of the chirped question being asked by a female seated at a large bank of computer monitors. She watched the woman's head bobbing as she tut-tutted, appearing highly amused by Nairn's state of health.

"Good morning is all the greeting I need today, Miss Faulds!"

Nairn smiled at the woman who was still chuckling and muttering to herself about idiots who should only sell and not try out all the products.

"Ginny Faulds, meet Aela Cameron, my new PA."

"Glad to see you got lucky about something, Mr. Malcolm," Ginny chortled, the stare she sent Aela's way quite blatant.

Nairn looked from woman to woman, his grin wide. "You know something? I believe I did, Ginny."

Aela had no idea of the relationship between the two people next to her, but they were very comfortable with each other as Nairn got a brief update on her departmental progress.

Robert, the security guard, was already waiting in Nairn's office by the time they entered.

"There's nothing at all, Robert?" Nairn sounded frustrated, the lack of evidence a disappointment he couldn't seem to mask.

Robert confirmed he'd looked at the security tapes, along with police officers. Nothing from the previous Thursday, when the tank problem was discovered, appeared suspect. He clarified the tapes from the previous two weeks were still being checked, the police matching up movements with personnel who were legitimate around the area. "The warehouse staff has been interviewed but nothing has transpired from that either, Mr. Malcolm."

With no new information to process they set down to work. In some ways Aela found the office situation easier. As PA she had her own front office, Nairn occupying a spacious corner office overlooking the Thames. Now, she wasn't aware of his dominating presence every second on the opposite side of the room, but it did mean buzzing him often before transferring some of the constant calls coming up from the main switchboard.

A couple of hours later she buzzed him yet again. "Warehousing just rang about the new two-clip buoyancy aids for kayaking." She checked her notes. "They think you should assess them before they're dispatched to Adrenalinn Adventuring, Tallinn, Estonia. Someone in warehousing doesn't sound happy about them."

Almost before she'd finished speaking Nairn hobbled towards her. "Let's go. It's time for you to meet Adrenalinn Adventuring staff and visit the stockrooms."

She'd been quite surprised nobody from the floor below had made any kind of excuse to come and talk to him but then again, with a grin she had difficulty suppressing, she guessed why no-one had bearded the grouchy ogre in his den.

They exited the lift on the floor below, Aela trekking behind as Nairn got into a good lurching rhythm and entered a large office with a dozen littered desks, manned by clicking staff in communication with customers.

Nairn stopped at the desk of Robin Ellesmere, the Manager of Adrenalinn Adventuring, introduced her and asked for an update on the buoyancy aids in question.

"The spring clips are harder to operate than those from our last manufacturer. In extreme conditions they might be too difficult to deal with, but I don't have the practical kayaking experience you have, Nairn, to be sure about them."

"When did you place the order?"

"Stella organised it about a month ago. Remember you requested a bigger front pocket than those on the previous design?"

Aela watched Nairn nod at the memory of it. "Sure, but I don't remember okaying this manufacturer."

"I'd need to check, but I'm pretty sure Stella got a better deal on this batch, so long as it was a bulk order, and that's why it went through."

As Robin answered Nairn's question he pointed out an example for her on a brochure, to bring her up to speed.

Nairn nodded acceptance of Robin's reservations over the goods in question. They were going to climes where extreme cold was common and deficiencies in them couldn't be contemplated. "I'm taking Miss Cameron on a tour of the warehouses, so I'll look at them when I'm there."

Nairn lurched away from Robin, passed the next desk which was empty, and moved on. She was quite used by then to his terse announcements as he introduced her to the rest of the staff, but she detected a tension that didn't seem related to his injuries or to the staff's concern for his welfare. Nairn scanned around as though looking for something…or someone.

"Stella isn't here today?" Nairn asked Robin.

Aela knew from personnel lists Stella Grainger had joined the company some months before as Assistant Manager of Adrenalinn Adventuring.

"She's down at Payroll. There was an issue about the wages and conditions for the staff at our bungee site in Perthshire."

"I've heard nothing of it."

Nairn's brow was creased. She had already realised he hated to be out of the loop about anything, though delegation meant he was only informed about the larger issues.

"Want me to send her up to you later, Nairn? Stella's not been to visit you for a while." Robin's chuckling request was accompanied by twitching of his eyebrows, a suggestive twitching she wasn't meant to miss. Robin's hearty laugh accompanied Nairn's silent exit.

Aela wouldn't pry: it was none of her business. Nairn had told her he didn't date employees, and even if he'd forgotten, or lied, it was still nothing to do with her.

A slow tour of the rest of the premises followed, where she was introduced to the employees, Nairn familiar with everyone. She could tell Nairn knew his business intimately and had a good rapport with his employees. They were respectful; no animosity towards him – in fact there was a general camaraderie. So who on earth had been sticking knives in Nairn Malcolm? She got no bad vibes from her tour at all.

The slow progress around the warehouses exhausted Nairn. His brow furrows deepened with every move forward, although she knew him well enough now to recognise he was unwilling that his employees should see his debilitation. But if he was as well liked, as it seemed, why were the incidents happening?

Nairn interrupted her slight distraction. "Miss Cameron. We'll take a sample up to my office. I'd like to have another think about it, John."

John Reid, the warehouse manager, passed a floatation vest over for her to carry.

"Maybe someday I'll get a chance to try one of these out." She winked as she hitched the buoyancy aid over one shoulder. "I fancied kayaking in Estonia, but I never made it so far north in Europe."

John's friendly replies were cut short by Nairn's declaration that they were done and were returning to his office. As they headed back along to the lift, she sighed. An incommunicative Nairn occupied the lift alongside her.

His voice buzzed through the intercom a while later. "I'm through with the buoyancy aid. Could you take it back to the stockroom, please?"

Another jaunt was very welcome. She was aware Nairn was exhausted; an earlier blatant inquiry if he'd remembered his pain killers had been received with one of his condescending black glowers. Time to make a strategic exit, but first she went in to collect the vest.

"Call in to the Adrenalinn office, please, and give Robin this file for counter-signature." Nairn's request was accompanied by a suppressed grunt when he stretched his arm a little too far, his last words gagged.

"Not a problem." Her answer was blithe, amazed at his

stamina but bugged by his determination to act normal when he clearly wasn't. "It's way past time for you to chew down some more happy pills and take a break, sir, but I don't suppose you're going to listen to little ol'me?" Another black glower was the answer she expected as she picked up the buoyancy aid and slung it across her shoulder.

There was no way she was going to wait for the lift when Nairn wasn't with her. She skipped down the narrow staircase and elbowed her way in the Adrenalinn Adventuring office door. A blur of russet hair flashed past her, almost knocking her down as she made an awkward negotiation of the buoyancy aid in one hand and the now cascading file of papers in the other. Someone was in a hurry! But she wasn't and she was going to take some time out from Nairn.

Using Robin as a fount of knowledge she spent some time clarifying issues she was still unclear about.

Returning the buoyancy aid was her next priority as she stepped onto the lower staircase leading to the ground floor. A few skips down her foot slipped off the step; her whole body launched itself clear into the air, feet first, and she landed with a spectacular whoosh on the bottom step, right on top of the buoyancy aid which had somehow managed to end up under the small of her back. The air was punched right out of her lungs, her head whacked back like a whiplash on the concrete step behind it, and her legs sprawled out in an ungainly loll.

All within sight of anyone and everyone who was, at present, in the entrance foyer.

"Miss Cameron!" Sandra's shriek as she ran across from the front desk penetrated the haze around Aela as she felt her faculties flip back into place again. "What on earth happened?"

A flurry of people appeared in an instant to help her. Once the adrenaline stopped pumping so hard she realised short of having a bump on the back of her head she was otherwise unhurt. Assuring them everything really was in good working order had no effect – their concern for her was overpowering. There was no doubt she'd have her own bruises appearing to match Nairn's, but they'd be in places he wouldn't be seeing. Thank goodness for the buoyancy aid. It hadn't exactly floated her to the bottom, but it had saved her lower back from being pulverised by the bottom step.

"Sandra!" Robert's gruff tones hissed in her ear as he helped her to stand. "Don't let anyone go up that staircase, and get Miss Cameron to a seat right now."

All Aela wanted was to be up in the office she'd been having a little escape from. Embarrassed by her tumble she hated the solicitous fuss.

"Someone take this back to the warehouse now, please." Robert indicated Aela's burden as he bent to examine the bottom step of the staircase.

Margaret, Head of Payroll, prised the buoyancy aid from Aela's tight grip and assigned it to one of her staff before she helped her towards the soft seating near the front door.

"I'm fine, really…I'm okay. I'll just get back up to my office and have a seat there," she assured Margaret, summoning up a hearty laugh to minimise the tense concern.

Margaret insisted on escorting her into the lift and up to Nairn's office suite.

"I'm fine, Margaret," she persevered, dredging up a reassuring smile for the woman as she went and sat at her desk. "Look…I'm sitting down."

Nairn appeared in the doorway as she entreated Margaret to go back down to her own work. "Is there a problem, Miss Cameron?"

"She took a bad tumble on the bottom staircase, Mr. Malcolm. Claims she's fine but I think someone should be getting a doctor to look her over." Margaret clucked like a mother hen.

"No doctor!" Aela was adamant.

"Thanks, Margaret. I'll deal with Miss Cameron."

Nairn's abrupt dismissal was final, waiting till Margaret was out of sight before he wrapped his good arm around her. Aela felt him urge her up before he hobbled her into his office. He let rip as soon as he closed his office door.

Chapter Fourteen

"Bloody hell, Aela! What happened? Are you really all right?"

Aela winced as she gingerly lowered herself onto the chair at his desk. "I guess you could say I found an unusual method of descending your staircase."

"Jacket off."

"What?"

"Take off your jacket, pull up your top and let me see your back."

Ignoring his high handed way of asking she complied knowing his concern was justified. She slid around in the seat as she hauled up her top, baring her back for his examination. The phone buzzed alongside them, but Nairn ignored it.

His voice came out muffled as he twisted himself around to see the damage. "Thank God, there's no actual bleeding, but it's grazed and quite bruised." His fingers were gentle as he probed the area around her lower spine. "Feel that?"

"Sure, but it isn't so bad. Honestly."

She was much more conscious of the fact that his fingers were a gentle caress on her. Her skin prickled in awareness. As she pulled down her blouse again, she shivered – not caused by any draught.

"How the hell did it happen?"

She told him about slipping, landing on the buoyancy aid and how it bore the brunt of the impact with the bottom step.

Nairn's swearing was vehement; no surprise there. The phone buzzed again.

"Will you answer, or shall I?" Her inquiry was calm since

she realised just how upset Nairn was by her tumble.

As she put her jacket back on he picked up the phone and dragged around his plaster-cast leg till he seemed to remember how awkward that was. She had a hunch his words to Robert were not the ones he really wanted to vent. "Yes. Call the police now."

The phone thumped down on its cradle. He groped his way back to his chair and sat down with a struggle, his breathing back to being laboured again. She knew he'd overdone some of the moves in ensuring she was in his office and checked out. "Robert wants to talk to me."

"Okay, I'll be out in my office." Moving to rise, Nairn's bark stopped her.

"Sit right there. It concerns you, Aela."

"Things are just getting better by the minute," she huffed, knowing she wasn't annoyed with him – far from it. Although he was very angry, he wasn't angry with her, and the concern in his gaze swamped her.

Robert's update wasn't a good one. "Grease of some kind. I'm guessing something simple like Vaseline, but it was slathered thickly enough on the edge of the step to make it effective. I've cordoned off the staircase till the police arrive."

"Shoes!"

Nairn's request was a bark, though Aela knew what prompted it. Slipping her heels off, Robert – the healthiest of them – bent down and lifted them up. All three had a look together at their undersides. She'd walked off the grease from the sole, however, there was still a solid smear of it on the arch of her left shoe.

"Could it have got on the stair by accident, by someone dropping something?"

Nairn wouldn't be convinced about the accidental theory. Neither would Robert as his phone bleeped.

"The Police are in reception, Mr. Malcolm. I'm going down to meet them, but Detective Woods is on his way up to interview Miss Cameron. I suggest you leave your shoes off; he should take a look like we've just done."

Having taken a statement from her, Detective Woods would have liked to take her shoes in for evidence but, since they were her only footwear, he took a sample of the grease after recording the shoes on his phone camera. The detective then went off with his uniformed colleagues to interview every staff member in the building. She wasn't sure she wanted to wear the damned pink shoes again but they were all she had, and being realistic…the shoes were not to blame.

Nairn hobbled to the window as she sat down again, a tad cautious. He turned back and stopped by her chair, his hand thumping the desk, the violence of it startling her. His blue eyes implored, his voice determined. She could sense the anger held in check by the twitching of his neck muscles. "You've got to go now, Aela. You've not even been here in London one day, and the bastard's hurt you, too."

"Nairn Malcolm." Fury consumed her, as indignant as he was when she stood up to match his height. "You're not listening to me. I'm not leaving you." Grasping the hand pumping a deadly rhythm on the desk beside her she drew it to her front, flattening his fingers across her heart with her own. "This person will be found. And this will all stop, but believe me now…" She dropped his fingers and took his face between her two hands, her eyes scant inches from his, seeking his endorsement. "Look at my lips, Nairn. No friggin' way will I give in to threats!"

His eyes closed, Nairn's forehead dipped to rest on hers. He was exhausted, distressed and so angry she felt he was going to combust. With careful movements she supported his strung out body, her arms sliding round his back to banish some of his tension, her fingers a light caress over bowstrung muscles. After long minutes she felt him relax, only a very little.

The kiss she started was gentle at first, a confirmation of sorts of her decision to stick with him, but it soon escalated. When the end came their foreheads touched once more for long moments while Nairn's breath eased, then he slid out of her grasp, his gaze unlike any they'd shared before.

Anxious? Yes. Concerned? Also yes.

But so full of guilt.

"I should be comforting you, Aela. You're the one in the firing line today." The blue of his irises darkened, regret changing to a much deeper emotion. "I can't let you be hurt again."

She slipped from his arms. It wasn't going to be easy to make him believe her so she was deft in changing tack, forcing a brisk tone. "Nairn. The police are still downstairs making their enquiries. There's nothing I can do about leaving you right this minute. I'd have to get myself back to Lanera anyway, in case you've forgotten that little fact, so sit down, please. We're going to carry on doing your business till the police come back in here to give us their updates."

She knew Nairn wasn't happy with her decision. It wasn't simple to continue to work, yet she drove the pace. While the detectives were questioning the staff, nobody was able to leave the building.

The police authorised a doctor's examination for her as soon as they declared the incident a malicious attempt to harm. X-rays were not thought to be needed, but the assertion was she should go to an A&E unit should any change occur in her mobility, or should she have any tingling, or changes to the feeling in her legs.

Nairn wasn't convinced about the doctor's decision.

"Nairn Malcolm. Would you just listen to yourself? You're neither my mother...nor my father, but you are one helluva big pain in the ass. I do not need to go to a hospital."

The tender kiss they'd shared faded into memory, as though it had never occurred, discord a poor replacement.

The grease was dispatched for lab testing, the police in accordance with Robert: it likely was some kind of petroleum jelly, the kind found in medical kits. There were loads of those kits at strategic places around the buildings, accessible to the whole staff. Not exactly good news for pin-pointing the exact source.

The conjecture over why it happened took less time to establish. If she was injured, unable to ferry Nairn around, then Nairn would be confined to base – and back to square one.

Too many people, it would seem, had been party to the information that she had flown his jet, and had driven him to the office.

Way past nine p.m. they were still in the London office though everyone else had long since exited the building – apart from security and those working night duty. The return trip Nairn had planned had not transpired, but nothing had been mentioned yet about a stay-over in London. He hadn't rested at all: relations between them still glacial. She'd refused to leave him so many times he'd stopped asking – he'd also stopped speaking to her except when absolutely necessary.

Aela knew she'd have to get herself booked into a hotel and get Nairn to his London apartment. Thinking about the effort required made her groan. Wincing as she rose from her chair she knew her back was fine, but her butt cheeks had not got off so lightly.

A determined grin spread as she met Nairn coming through the connecting door, her inquiry clashing with his.

"I'm booking myself a…"

"Bring round the car, please. I'll wait in the downstairs lobby."

He tottered past her to the lift without giving her a chance to say any more. Knowing he was back to almost passing out again she gathered up their laptops. Chiding him for neglecting himself seemed such a waste of energy…and now it smacked maybe just a bit too much like the pot calling the kettle black.

After she plotted the route to his London apartment, he reeled off a telephone number, his eyes already closed.

"Tell Richard we'll need a meal as soon as we arrive."

The classy block of apartments wasn't far away, thank heavens. She had been dreading a long drive.

"We're here, Nairn."

His sleepy eyes met hers and he smiled a genuine smile just for her, a smile which rocked her bones before he looked around and acknowledged his surroundings.

Nairn's housekeeper, a dapper white-haired man of around sixty, ushered them inside the apartment. Much to her surprise she was shown into a bedroom for her use and in no time at all Richard had them seated at the dining room table, a meal in front of them. Almost too tired to eat she was conscious of how fatigued Nairn must be. The limited amount of bruising she had made her empathise more acutely with his extensive injuries.

They ate in silence because Nairn was distracted. Not morose: disturbed. She sensed guilt sat heavy on his shoulders, but she'd had more than enough of it. Her tone was harsh, intended to break through his abstraction.

"Nairn. Would you cut the bloody guilt trip? I'm fine."

"Are you sure?"

Again, convincing him wasn't going to be easy. "The doctor checked me thoroughly. My butt feels like a friggin' punch bag, but I've enough padding to take it. My injuries will heal long before yours."

"I guess I'll have to take your word for it." A weak smile accompanied his next quip. "I suppose I'm not getting to see all your bruises up close?"

"No way!"

Nairn declared he was going to bed, instructing her to be ready for breakfast at eight a.m. after which they'd return to the office. "Will you still be here, Miss Cameron?" The formal name put her back in her place.

"You can bet your life on it, sir." Her mock salute gained her a sleepy grin from him. "I keep my promises."

She was annoyed by his neglect of his recovering body, yet was in awe of his stamina. All she wanted to do was drop into bed and sleep the sleep of the dead, but she still had a predicament. Nairn had clothes, and basic necessities, stored in the London apartment. She had nothing apart from what she was wearing, since he'd categorically declared they were making a short day trip.

131

Asking Richard for directions to the nearest store operating twenty-four-hour trading she was told anything could be acquired by placing a few phone calls, even at such a late hour. For some reason his assured answer disturbed Aela; it smacked too much of him kitting out Nairn's lady friends on previous occasions. Not appealing at all.

"Good heavens, that's not necessary." She tried not to sound judgmental. "Could you just direct me to a store which can provide basic supplies?"

Richard mentioned a large supermarket nearby stocking almost everything, his scathing tone indicating they didn't cater to anyone of quality, but he relented sufficiently to say he would arrange for a porter to accompany her. Only a short walk away, using local pathways, was quicker than going by car.

"You have porters downstairs?" Aela's eyebrows shot up since it wasn't a hotel.

"Of course, Miss Cameron. These serviced apartments can organise anything our owners might require, and that requires twenty-four hour porter services."

Before she left, Aela ensured Nairn could get properly undressed before bed. "Mr. Malcolm might need assistance with fiddly buttons because he's totally exhausted right now. Could you help him without awakening the ogre?"

Richard glided towards Nairn's bedroom. A discreet knock on the door came before he declared he'd sorted out alterations to Nairn's suit trousers as requested, and could he lay out a suitable choice for the morning? True valet style.

She smiled at the panache, but Nairn's problems weren't hers – she had enough of her own to sort out.

Chris, the porter she found downstairs, couldn't be more than sixteen. Delighted to help, he accompanied her to the store.

"If you don't mind, Miss, it'll be best if I wheel your purchases for you," he declared, grabbing a shopping cart.

The purchases she intended to make were going to be items of a very personal nature. However, the cheeky grin on the porter's face said it all, as did his next words.

"I've shopped with my older sisters. I know how to turn the other cheek. No worries there, Miss."

Aela hated shopping, knew she'd be out of the store as soon as she found the basic necessities, but found the clothing racks and lingerie section displayed plenty of choices. Though low budget items they would do well enough, and since her backpack back at the castle only held casual items she kitted herself out with a selection of business attire. Having gained the help of the fitting room assistant, her shopping cart filled up quickly. In a record twenty minutes, they were approaching checkout, and she was brandishing her credit card.

"Chris? I need a suitcase. Do you think there might be such a thing here?"

Chris beamed since he knew exactly where the luggage was situated.

Much as she'd wanted to drop into bed earlier she enjoyed the little sojourn with Chris who was a well-informed young man about the neighbourhood.

***

Nairn blinked in admiration of the woman who stepped into his dining room. Leaving aside the newspaper he'd spread open at the side of his breakfast plate, he gave her his full attention. Aela was indeed still here. She was a woman who did live up to her promises…and how.

The day before she'd been wearing the flirty little suit she'd interviewed in and now she looked so elegant, clad in a suit of black pin-striped with cream. The yellow silky-knit top she wore hugged her curves. A pair of black court shoes were suitably business-like. She was so beautiful, he ached. All his pains intensified.

Where had she acquired the clothes? They'd brought no luggage with them the day before.

Although he'd had previous lovers stay the night in his apartment, he was certain none of them had ever left a work suit like the one Aela was now wearing. In fact, no previous lover had ever left anything personal since they'd been fleeting contacts, their clothing never remotely like business attire.

The day before had been so fraught with anxiety it hadn't occurred to him a stopover might present problems and Aela hadn't quibbled at all when it'd become obvious they'd have to stay in London. His London wardrobe was better equipped for business clothes than the castle, so he'd not considered any inconvenience to Aela.

Yet, somehow, she'd managed to kit herself out very proficiently. He wasn't sure how he felt about this capable woman – apart from finding her far too tempting.

"Good morning." Aela's breezy greeting warmed as much as her beaming smile.

He belatedly realised he'd been gaping without returning a dickey-bird. It was Richard who greeted Aela with a smile as he held out the chair, and seated her at the table.

"Good morning, Miss Cameron. I see your evening stroll went well," Richard said.

A stroll? Last night? Nairn flicked open his newspaper to the next page, his ears perking up. In London? His apartment wasn't in the suburbs, and it was always busy around his neighbourhood.

Richard continued. "Please permit me to say I was too scathing, since your choices look superb. May I assist you with some coffee or tea, Miss Cameron?"

After a solicitous flapping of her napkin into place Richard smiled again, a smile Nairn had rarely seen during the five years the man had been in his employ.

He watched the exchange with mixed feelings. It appeared Aela could charm any male over the age of puberty. He'd never seen Richard so attentive to any of his previous guests' comfort female or male. Although Aela was clearly the most beautiful woman he'd ever brought to the apartment, previous girlfriends had also been attractive.

"Coffee please, and thanks for your help last night. Chris was a wonderful escort."

Aela's warm recognition earned a little smile from Richard who excused himself to go to the kitchen.

"Chris?" He made his inquiry sound casual as he noisily turned another page, one-handed, but the sudden churning in his gut unsettled the breakfast he'd just finished.

How was it possible for her to have met someone last night after the stressful day they'd put in? Someone had maliciously harmed her. Was the woman bionic or something? She'd gone out on the town without him, seeing how incapacitated he was? Even after her own accident? What the hell else had she done with this Chris? Her escort for the night? While he'd been sleeping the sleep of the dead? In the next room?

He was beginning to be sick of all the questions spinning around his bothered brain.

Aela had said she was afraid of nothing. And it seemed she was. Capable, very capable. He told himself he could shed the guilt and not even think about putting her in harm's way again. Quiet seething consumed him; a totally different kind of fuming from the day before. Retreating into his paper, he didn't see a single word in front of him. That stubborn trait of his shut his mind down. Analysis of this sort wasn't his style.

"Mmm…Chris."

Aela's expression looked quite dreamy when he chanced a glance. Only the one.

Chapter Fifteen

"What a nice man."

Aela felt her grin spreading. She'd noticed the tightening of Nairn's fingers on the paper he was gripping like grim death and realised how he'd misconstrued her statement.

"Very skilled Chris was: made my evening so memorable."

A vein pulsed at Nairn's neck indicating just how tense he was; demonstrating just how much he was trying to control his temper. But perhaps it was something else? She wasn't entirely sure.

"And I'm fine today, just in case you were about to inquire, sir."

Nairn's preoccupation with a particular article seemed intense so she judiciously tucked into her breakfast. The short exchange served its purpose, though. He mentioned nothing about her leaving his employment.

A tense silence reigned all the way to the office which suited her just fine. Navigating the traffic was enough to think about in the morning rush hour.

Later that morning she was glad she'd splurged on a range of new clothing since plans changed yet again.

"Miss Cameron!" Nairn's bellow through the open office doors rivalled the chiming of Big Ben. "In here, please."

Count to ten…and then again.

Drawing in a deep breath, she summoned a polite smile and picked up a sharpened pencil. Fingering the point she mentally assessed which part of Nairn's already bruised torso could take a nice little jab. He was being a pig again. He'd taken to hollering her into his office, disregarding the indicator on the telephone system.

She decided not to challenge why he was dispensing with it in favour of bawling her name and focused instead on ignoring his bad temper. Since breakfast, it hadn't diminished. When he didn't even bother to look away from his current work she refused to get riled as she walked up to his desk. The fingers of his left hand stabbed away at his keyboard, his abrupt instruction drifting up to her from his bent head.

"Book a hotel in Muscat for two nights, Wednesday and Thursday."

Aela couldn't help her enthusiastic response. "Muscat, Oman? How lovely. Another place I've never been to."

Her attempt to lighten their interaction went down like a kite without wind, his acerbic rejoinder distinctly unfriendly when his expressionless mask faced her.

"Did I say you would be going too, Miss Cameron?"

Professional *faux pas*! Her throat was suddenly dry, her face hot, a weak smile pursed her lips, but she'd not be baited any further by his continued blank stare. "Got it. Book for how many? Just one room...or a suite for your... harem?"

Nairn flashed a dark sardonic glance before dipping back to his keyboard. "I do prefer a suite, Miss Cameron."

"We're talking Wednesday of next week?" When Nairn made no move to give further information she persisted. "The date, please?"

Not as polite as it should be but Nairn's attitude wasn't well-mannered either, barely making eye-contact for more than a nano-second. And horrible at that.

"I'm talking tomorrow, Miss Cameron. For possibly two nights. Which part of that didn't you understand?"

"Tomorrow? You're joking!" Scepticism tumbled out. "Come on, Nairn. You're not fit for such a long-haul flight."

One look at Nairn's tight jaws was more than enough; she knew a little backtracking might just be the order of the day. "Okay! If you say you're friggin' fit, you're fit. It's your broken ribs that'll be on that seat for hours."

His intent focus was on the desk in front of him; a pen

slid around and around the fingers of his left hand as though he was about to blow a fuse…or maybe he was just readying the pen for a direct hit at her? She knew not to expect any kind of agreement, but wouldn't be cowed by his attitude.

Less than four weeks to work. A furious mental count was done…only three weeks and one day? She could manage to keep going for such a short time, but her lip wouldn't stay buttoned for the duration. Far too much to expect. "Know any good hotels in Muscat, with palatial rooms and multiple beds, sir?"

Nairn's head rose slowly as he rattled off the hotel where the business meeting was taking place: a hotel he'd used before.

"Any other details I should know about, sir? Anything else I need to organise for your trip?"

Nairn's reply was toneless; devoid of eye contact since he stared out of the window.

Prince Hasson, a potentate who was developing a coastal resort area in his Arabian Gulf state, intended to order a fleet of two-seater jet-skis, and had heard of the new version Gale Breakers had recently brought onto the market. Prince Khalid – their current customer – had recommended Gale Breakers. It was far too good an opportunity to defer till later, Nairn declared, no matter what his present health requirements might be. He was going regardless.

Aela jotted notes during his monologue, her concentration jolted when his phone rang.

"I must see what John Reid is talking about, Miss Cameron. Let's go."

She trailed after Nairn like the proverbial collie dog. What wasn't part of the job were the collisions he created, caused by his inability to stride properly, though that hadn't happened the previous day. She'd bumped into his back too often when his abrupt halts to reposition the walking aid had startled her. It seemed he expected her to have some sixth sense about his hitches…but she didn't. "For cripes sake, sir. Give me some more warning, please, or I'll be mowing

138

you down like a bloody combine-harvester."

She was tight as a drum as she shouldered her body free of his to punch the lift button.

He'd set up an embargo: neither of them would go anywhere around the building without the presence of the other. At first hearing, she had balked at the infringement to her autonomy but had then relented when she realised just how fearful he was over her safety. Her use of the staircase had been categorically banned.

She forced the day to get better knowing she had to do something about their frosty relations or she'd burst a blood vessel. Nairn mellowed a little when she enthused about Chris's fabulous porter-cum-escort services, but the news from the stockroom was disconcerting.

Stock control had taken delivery of breathable drysuits for diving activities at the newest Lanwater Whitecap site in Ireland, due to begin operating the following week. John Reid showed them all one hundred drysuits were of the same XXL size, instead of a range of sizes.

"I'm going to throttle the bastard who tampered with this order!" Nairn's anger blasted off him, as surging and violent as the waves could be in the Northern Atlantic at his dive site.

Again a petty mistake…but who had changed the order at the last minute, by telephone, was unclear. The manufacturer had been used before so they'd had no problem with changes made to the original order. Nairn seethed, and grumped as they returned to his office suite, Aela finding a hasty retreat her best option. Minimising physical contact with him for the next few hours, her office desk was a haven.

Late in the afternoon he surprised her. Buzzing her through, his tone was affable. "Do you need time to go shopping, Miss Cameron?" Mmm…Suspicious. Her immediate reaction was to be on her guard.

"Shopping?" She was mystified. "Why would I need to shop?"

"For going to Oman. Perhaps you need…toothpaste…or

something." Nairn's tone sounded laid-back.

"I'm going to Oman? With you?" Her questions were cautious, her mind reeling, replaying their earlier conversation.

"Yes, of course, I'll need my PA."

"But you…" His enigmatic smile made her decide not to complete the sentence, realising that he'd been winding her up. However, she wouldn't be trapped again. "Should I book myself a room at your hotel, sir?"

"You booked a two-bedroom suite, didn't you?" At her nod he continued, "You'll use one of them, Miss Cameron, and I'll make good use of the other."

She felt he was being obtuse, still not giving a proper answer. She remained dogged about their travel arrangements. "Do I need to pick up anyone else for the flight? Maybe a female friend to tide you over, till you meet up with your ever-so-ready-harem?"

Her face was as innocent as she could make it, though that wasn't saying much since subterfuge wasn't really in her make up. Subtlety wasn't either.

One eyebrow raised itself just a hint as Nairn met her gaze, neither of them giving an inch. Eventually he spoke, a low hum purring around her ears, the merest hint of a grin escaping him. A cheeky twinkle lightened the blue of his irises. "No, Miss Cameron. It will be just the two of us, and, of course, my discreet flight staff. Since you're determined to stay employed by me, you'll come too."

The frost melted. A little. No surprise, though, when he got in the last word. "Naturally we'll be busy on the flight."

His attitude for the rest of the afternoon and evening was professional. He was polite, yet under the surface tension simmered again, a bubbling and brooding combustible heat that Aela found more and more difficult to suppress. She avoided glances, avoided unnecessary touches. Sort-of. Nairn didn't. Collisions seemed to have become part of his norm.

She didn't think he was trying hard enough. The deliberate clash in the hallway of his apartment as they were headed to their own bedrooms later that night was too coincidental. He lost his balance and was tipping over. Her frantic clutch got him upright, but his yelp of agony was again alarming.

Nope. Nairn wasn't healthy enough yet. She went to bed feeling a bit confused about his strategies. While she was increasingly frustrated as hell.

Drawn up in the mercurial tornado that was Nairn, they were flying to Muscat a little after seven a.m. the next morning.

In her role as PA they worked through the first four hours, during which Nairn's fear for her welfare seemed to have diminished. Aela guessed this was because the perpetrator of the incidents was unable to do anything personally to them. Adamant on being present during extremely thorough flight checks, the flight staff was miffed, but Nairn was a good customer.

She relaxed, because although she'd been brave enough the day before, she, too, was concerned over their joint wellbeing. After lunch, a pained looking Nairn prepared to spread out the laptops and business papers again. "Not going to happen, Nairn Malcolm." Insistent as she reached for his pain-killers, she shook two into her palm. "Rest time."

Nairn grumbled through a mouthful of pills. "I never rest on flights, Miss Cameron."

Her reply was sweetness and light. "No, but you're not normally sporting all these injuries. I've already rubbed my sore little butt down with anti-inflammatory gel, so I'm doing fine." Firm tones brought his wandering gaze back to her face, the sexy groan she ignored. "My face is up here, sir. I can't conduct the business talks myself, so, if you don't want it to turn into a fiasco, a little rest might be in order."

Little resistance from her workaholic employer surprised her, beyond muttering for the first few minutes after his chair was reclined. The jet didn't have a dinky little bedroom – a disappointment on embarking- but Nairn had cheered her up with a sexy twinkle, and by saying that he tended to charter longer flights with little bedrooms on board.

Aela's dream was wonderful. Lips feathered around her mouth, captured her lower lip and nuzzled it, caught her too rapid breaths and absorbed them. The kiss deepened. She moaned. Fingers slid over her neck. She felt herself quiver and shudder. Delicious.

An arm gently nudged her awake. Her reluctant eyes opened to focus as she squelched the lingering tingles. The table in front of her was spread with paperwork.

"You've had your rest, Aela." She heard Nairn crow. "Back to work now." Her eyes took time to adjust as he moved back out of her vicinity and booted up his laptop.

Jittery. That's how she felt because the sensations in her dream had been so real. She stole a glance at Nairn's lips. Glistening? Had he been kissing her? Nairn smirked like a horny teenager who'd got laid for the first time. Mmm...

Another couple of hours sped past. Satellite communications were a delight – usually – but she wondered if maybe reading a dull in-flight magazine would have been a better bet. Business was the order of the day. Unremitting business. Yet contrarily their interaction was enjoyable.

Towards the end of the flight Nairn turned to her, his face warped into to a tight mask, their comfortable mood totally zapped. "Miss Cameron?"

Looking up from the information she was scanning, she found him staring at his cell phone as if it had just bitten him.

"My father wants you to get in touch with him since you haven't returned his calls."

"Pardon me?" She was confused. Why was he so upset over Ruaridh trying to reach her?

Nairn's tone was contemptuous. "Ruaridh's sent text messages you've not responded to, so he's requested I ask you to call him."

He pocketed his cell and proceeded to ignore her, indicating he didn't want anything further to do with the communication.

She'd switched her phone off before takeoff. A quick call to Ruaridh confirmed he'd managed to track down the son of her great-grandfather's sister on a nearby island. "Oh, lovely, Ruaridh. Yes, I'll meet you the minute we're back on Lanera."

The rest of the flight was almost silent, Nairn in a black mood she decided not to encroach on. She couldn't understand his attitude at all. Ruaridh was a lovely man.

Aela was moderately familiar with high class hotels but the one they'd booked into stole her breath. It had been built as a palace for an Arabian Prince but now functioned as a regular hotel, except during special conference times once or twice a year, when important dignitaries descended there to thrash out political and international issues.

Arriving at dusk was the absolute best way to appreciate the initial impact of the splendid building; a startling white against huge dark and craggy mountains soaring up behind. Strategic floodlighting created an incredible setting; romantic and enthralling. Huge palms were planted in columns like majestic sentinels guarding the entrance, swaying in the soft breeze beside the fountains and shallow ponds which fronted the whole exterior. Magical.

The heart of the hexagonal tiered block was a huge marble atrium with areas discreetly sectioned off by lush planting and Moorish screens. The upper floor walkways circled around the heights of the atrium and led to the accommodation areas behind. Many floors up the domed ceiling was made of delicate stained glass, the star-lit sky just visible, twinkling here and there in places – but she had no time to peruse it further than a cursory glance.

She checked them in since Nairn was in serious flag mode, still by her side, but in an awkward prop against the marble desk. In minutes, they were whisked up to their luxury suite by an efficient desk clerk, a bellhop trailing behind with their luggage on the most ornate gilded cart she'd ever seen.

"Just time for a quick clean up before the initial meeting downstairs at nine p.m." Nairn prompted her as he negotiated his way behind the desk clerk who displayed the first bedroom, the décor redolent of traditional Omani architecture with its fret-worked panels and patterning on the blue and white walls. "This one has your name on it."

An attempt at levity? She thought maybe, but Nairn's voice sounded so tired.

"Do you need me tonight?" she asked, not sure what was expected of her since it was eight-twenty p.m. local time.

"Of course, I do!" Nairn looked perplexed by her question. She could read his expressions quite well now: he most likely had intended to brief her earlier but their communication breakdown had put the scuppers on that. "We're having an initial drink in the Piano Bar where we'll begin the consultation before eating in the main dining room. I'll expect you to take any necessary details."

"Then business attire will be suitable for me?"

Having seen the hotel patrons in the foyer, business attire was not the order of the day for the women she'd glimpsed.

Nairn's eyebrows rose as though he'd never even considered what she should be dressed in. "I suppose it will have to do, unless you happen to have a little black number in the suitcase you magically filled last night?"

Her thoughts were pretty mutinous in view of the fact that her spending spree had been on business related apparel. Nairn followed the bellhop into the second bedroom where his bag, packed by Richard and full of altered clothing to accommodate his casts, was deposited. Clearing her throat and beckoning the desk clerk, she pressed a discreet tip into his hand, saving Nairn the embarrassment of fumbling around. She did likewise with the bellhop who beamed at her.

Excusing herself she declared she'd be ready in half an hour, but not before. Slipping out of the suite she rode the lift back down to the mezzanine shopping level. The tinkling sounds of a soft harp being plucked down in the foyer filled the interior and created a peaceful ambience, soothing and unhurried, but Aela had no time at all to appreciate the excellence of it as she sped into the small corridor housing several expensive boutiques. Pulling out her credit card she swooped along the racks.

Ten minutes later she was back up in the suite and into the shower in record time. At one minute past the expected time to meet Nairn she was in their elegant salon: he wasn't there but his vehement cursing informed her he was having difficulty getting dressed.

"Aela," he bellowed. "Get in here, please, and help me with this bloody tie!"

Her eyes were met with a horrendous mess when she opened his bedroom door. The expertly packed case had been raided. Clothing was strewn all over the bed, or was cascading onto the floor. Nairn was standing in front of a mirror wearing a partially buttoned formal shirt, a tie drooping around his neck. Dark suit trousers were sliding down his legs, his good hand fumbling to hang onto them as he failed to zip and hook them.

"Got a little problem here, sir?" She responded as serenely as she could, stifling a full blown grin as she sped to help him recover his dignity. Not meeting his eye she ignored his blasted tirade of profanities. Obviously Richard had worked wonders in organising new trousers, sufficiently wide to pull over the cast, but the hooked fastening at the waist needed more than a one-handed approach.

She couldn't deny the rush of feelings engendered by Nairn's closeness; neither could she remain unaware of his clenched jaw as her deft fingers pulled his trousers up and into place. Touching him was inevitable as she fastened the clip. His breathing was ruffled though she knew very well it had nothing to do with rib pain. His head was bent towards her as she completed the process. Heat emanated from him in waves as she straightened up, her head bumping against his chin as she fixed the tie.

Looking him squarely in the eye, she calmly berated him,

steeling herself not to drown in the blue depths glistening there.

"Next time, Nairn, just ask. Let's call daily business dressing part of my job description. Remember the little clause about during your incapacity? It includes cuff links."

She watched the sexy glint soften to an even deeper blue yet couldn't quite gauge what he was thinking as the twitch at his mouth deepened. His lips swooped onto hers in a brief yet satisfying kiss before she could evade it.

"Nairn. I'm here to help you with those little things you can't do yourself, that's all," she chided, no longer able to deny the inevitability of a closer connection between them.

"Exactly." Nairn's gaze twinkled with mirth.

Seconds later she was slipping his widened jacket sleeve over his arm cast – though how she did it at speed was a miracle, an unaccustomed jitteriness making her feel clumsy. What she really wanted to do was rip the clothes off him and take full advantage of his partial incapacity. Having straightened the front of his jacket in place she faced him, handing him the walking aid.

"I think you'll do, sir."

Nairn's gaze was relentless as one finger tilted her chin up. "My name is Nairn. Call me that when we're alone." He cleared his throat, his head shaking as though to dispel a dream.

"Let's go, Miss Cameron."

Business took priority.

As they waited for the lift she heard Nairn's indrawn breath as he took in her dress. "Once again you surprise me, Miss Cameron. Not a little black number, but a sexy dark red one. So, you did have something in your suitcase?"

The merriment wouldn't be contained as she took his compliment in her stride. "I didn't. The hotel happens to have some very well-stocked boutiques."

"If you bought that here then I definitely must reimburse you. Your salary package obviously needs to include an evening wardrobe as well as a day one. Give me any clothing bills you incur for our business needs."

"For exceptions, maybe, sir. Otherwise I'll seem like a kept woman, and we wouldn't want your accountants to think that, would we?"

Before she hastily repaired her lip gloss in the copper mirror of the lift, she feathered her fingers across Nairn's mouth. The twinkle in her eye she wouldn't repress. "Just a little still there, sir. Wouldn't want you to be embarrassed."

Nairn's hearty chuckle vibrated around the small compartment.

Chapter Sixteen

"Good evening!"

As Aela preceded Nairn into the intimate Piano Bar she heard a voice ring out from a nearby alcove seating arrangement. Two men sat there, the only occupants of the whole area. One of them, lounging wide on the curved banquette, Aela reckoned to be Prince Hasson – his headgear indication of his rank. The prince's aide sat to his side, on a separate stool, his laptop resting on the table. As soon as the prince's greeting rang out the aide jumped to his feet and gestured them forward.

"You have to be Nairn Malcolm. There can't be too many men of your description here tonight." Prince Hasson's English was excellent as he spoke from the couch. His words addressed Nairn, yet his focus was elsewhere.

She was conscious that the prince's gaze lingered far too long on her chest, and was immediately put on her guard. A gut-feeling sparked, something told her a professional approach to her wasn't what he had in mind.

Introductions completed she sat as requested by the prince in the middle of the u-shaped couch, large enough to seat eight people though Nairn needed to remain at the edge to extend his leg cast. Prince Hasson, seated opposite Nairn, had not risen during the formal greetings, his dark looks handsome…yet he exuded a false charm she detested on sight as he muttered something to his assistant. A waiter appeared at the flick of a long finger.

"Miss Cameron. What would you like? To drink?" His smooth tones, she realised, were meant to seduce for his eyes had not removed themselves from her discreet cleavage. She was to all intents and purposes maybe fair game to him, since her introduction was as Nairn's PA, not his girlfriend…or wife.

Masking her feelings, she avoided direct eye contact, believing it wasn't the done thing. "Sparkling water, please."

She needed to keep her wits about her given that she'd a hunch the man would take liberties. Efficiently powering up her laptop she settled to take notes.

As they discussed the possibilities Nairn could provide, Aela was aware of Nairn's increasing tension. He had to be exhausted, of course, for they'd already put in a long day, the strain of travel an additional factor. The fingers of his good hand clenched around the table edge, his jaw progressively more rigid as though it was a strain to even talk. There was a bit of teeth clenching going on she didn't understand since the conversation was urbane; business-like as Prince Hasson inquired about small changes to specifications.

Her own role was purely secretarial. She wasn't familiar enough with the nuances of the newest jet-ski designs, although she remembered seeing an example during her whirlwind tour of the boatyard.

Her own tension increased as her hunch proved to be true. Little by little Prince Hasson slid alongside her…and remained close by. The urge to shake him off was immense, but, her teeth set, she ignored him without being impolite. She wanted to whack him when his wandering arm curved around her shoulder to rest on the seat back. Sliding closer to the table she sat so erect she felt her back would surely break with the rigidity. The shivers rippling her frame had nothing to do with temperature…or excitement at his proximity. Loathing was too trite a word for how she felt. Her natural instinct was to use some choice words and tell him to take a hike. Of course she wasn't expected to make any eye contact with the prince so she couldn't even give him the back-off eye she'd perfected over the years.

Protocol was a bitch!

Nairn was furious. Why hadn't he thought about the scenario that was being enacted right in front of him? Why hadn't he factored in the implications of bringing Aela down to this late evening meeting? He cursed himself blind for being so short-sighted and stupid.

He detested it when the prince slid along the seating towards Aela and settled within touching distance of her – ostensibly to see the display on her laptop better – even though his own secretary had the same screen for his perusal. It had been impossible not to note how the prince's eyes had lingered on Aela far too long on their arrival: impossible not to note the predatory gleam in the potentate's eye as he appreciated Aela's beauty. Impossible not to realise how easy it was for the prince to have his wishes... and likely whims...fulfilled at the flick of a finger. A woman like Aela was a tasty morsel for the man. Nairn had heard, through the grapevine, of the prince's predilections for picking up beautiful women for the night.

Aela was beautiful. But she wasn't for the prince.

It mattered that she was uncomfortable: he'd put her in such a vulnerable position. For years he'd not had to be aware of any such thing when Brian was his assistant, but it was no excuse for not thinking ahead. Her restless resettling on the couch warned him she wasn't happy about the prince's changes of position either.

When his potentially lucrative client's fingers strayed again to brush against her hand, as she moved on the touchpad, protective instincts Nairn didn't know he had rose to the fore. Even worse, when Prince Hasson's arm crept over the back of her body and all but caressed her hair, his insides roiled.

Nobody should be touching Aela in such blatant fashion. His temper spiked when she recoiled, the prince's drifting fingers a fleeting touch at her neck. He had no wish to offend an important client, but he wouldn't sit there any longer and watch Aela being pawed.

On the verge of abandoning the prince's business, they were informed their table awaited them. No announcement could have come at a better time. Moving through to the dining room, he was unsurprised to find a whole section had been cordoned off, the prince's security detail a discreet hover around them.

The hotel was not only a business venue. The live music quartet was a charming and lulling backdrop to the low-lit romantic ambience. Other patrons, just visible, were mainly couples in splendid attire, enjoying a meal at leisure. He was glad to see Aela wasn't out of place in her purchase from the boutique. It almost matched the gowns of the women present, yet was subtle enough in its simplicity to double for business. He just wished, again, he'd had the foresight to have thought of the need beforehand.

Between mouthfuls of food Aela made pencilled notes as he directed, but Prince Hasson's leering of her continued – no matter how much he deflected his royal highness's attention. The arrangement of the seats at table meant Prince Hasson wasn't right up close to her, but his examination of her person was so overt Nairn's hackles remained roused.

Every now and then when Aela had to look at him for confirmation on something, he sensed her rising resentment. Determined to end the discussions as soon as possible, he set a furious pace in the negotiations. By the time their coffee arrived Aela looked as strung out as he was feeling. He felt beyond exhaustion, emotionally tattered in a way he'd never before experienced, so much so he wondered if he'd be able to manoeuvre himself into the lift and up to bed.

A deft winding up of negotiations completed, he was relieved when Prince Hasson agreed to an eight a.m. breakfast meeting to finalise the last few details. But he fumed as the prince bid them goodnight, lifting each of Aela's hands in turn and kissing her knuckles, holding onto her fingers too long and seeking eye contact with her. Thankfully Aela neatly fielded that. The invitation to continue personal relations with her was so barefaced.

Prince or not, he'd had enough truck with polite protocol.

"Summon the lift, please, Miss Cameron!"

It galled him to do it, but he managed a curt goodnight to his client. Inside the lift, he again cursed the maniac who had caused his body to be in such a state. Fatigue warred with every kind of frustration. He was so damned pathetic that dragging himself to his room looked too much of a challenge.

***

Aela buttoned her lip, disgusted with the prince's sleazy moves and annoyed at Nairn's presumption she should blindly obey his curt orders. She hadn't flirted with Prince Hasson, not once. Riding in the lift was an excruciating affair: Nairn draped over the walking aid – the grim ogre definitely back.

Inside their suite he snapped. "Breakfast at seven. We've a lot to discuss. Goodnight, Miss Cameron."

She was glad to escape; dog-tired and furious. She had no idea why he was so angry as she'd tried hard to be competent and professional. Hanging her dress up with some care, in case it was needed again soon, she removed her bra and shrugged into the thin silky robe she'd bought in the London store. Her minimal makeup had just been removed when a deafening curse accompanied a loud crash.

Good God, what had happened to him?

Nairn was flat on the floor at the side of the bed, his trousers a tangle round his feet, his plastered leg lying at a horrifying angle. She didn't really mean her screech to be so loud. But it was. "You stupid man! All you needed to do was ask for help. You can't be so annoyed at my incompetence you'd endanger your own health."

Disentangling the trousers and wrenching them behind her she straightened his leg. Biting her lip in sheer frustration at her outburst, and with the heart-beating concern that he might be hurt even more, her hands cradled his face, her eyes beseeching. "Do I need to call a doctor,

Nairn?"

Pained blue irises reflected up at her, darkening to the deepest, softest blue as she sniffed, the merest tweak at his lip calming her frantic heartbeats. "No, Aela. Just my pride, but I would appreciate help to get off the floor."

Her arms cradled as she helped him sit on the edge of the bed where she loosened the tie and unbuttoned his shirt. Kneeling between his legs to remove his gold cufflinks his head was so close the exhalations of his breathing ruffled her hair. It was a torment to peel the shirt down his arms and off at the wrists, unable as she was to look at him since she knew he traced her every movement. Her shaking palms hovered over the waistband of his boxer shorts, incapable of proceeding further.

Her bent head felt the whisper of his fingers as he gently combed the strands covering her cheek before he urged her head up. His lips found hers in an urgent collision of teeth and soft flesh. An agonised groan escaped as their kiss deepened.

"Nairn?"

"Let me…"

"You need to get into bed, Nairn. You're knackered."

"I just wish…"

She couldn't help her gurgle. "Save it for another day, sir."

When Aela surfaced the next day her conscience bothered her. She shouldn't have allowed Nairn to kiss her. She wasn't sure she'd be able to walk away in three weeks with her heart and soul intact. He was coming to mean far too much to her…and no man had ever done that.

She had to distance herself. It had to stop now.

Business only.

Showering and dressing was on automatic pilot.

"Aela?" Nairn's light-hearted plea reached her as she walked past his bedroom door. "Can you help me, please?"

Hells bells and baubles. It was going to be much harder than she thought. Mentally bracing herself for the inevitable she drew deep breaths before walking into his bedroom.

"Good morning, sir."

"Sir?"

Nairn's eyes lost their happy welcome as he took in her expression, his tie outstretched for her assistance. Pretending nothing had happened between them, without meeting his eye, she silently helped him fasten his trousers, touching at an absolute minimum. When he was properly dressed she faced him, forcing her tone to be even, and impersonal. "I don't want to talk about last night except to say it was my fault, and it won't happen again. It was a mistake. We need to get back to our professional only relationship. Friends maybe, but definitely nothing else."

Eye contact was no longer possible to maintain when she watched his jaw firm, and a vein start pulsing at his neck. Far from blushing this time she felt blood drain from her face as his eyes grew antagonistic, shutters slamming into place. He viewed his neatly sorted appearance; lips tightening to a slit his words were clipped. "I hear you. Thanks for helping me dress. I'll not ask too often."

When she bent to gather discarded clothing he stopped her, his hand a zinging brand on her arm, his hiss urging her upright again. "No need! A valet will pack during our breakfast meeting." He held her shoulders, his fingers trembling with tension, his anger seeping into her. "Aela, I can see you're regretting last night, but we need to work around this."

Shrugging out of his grasp she turned away unable to face his pleading. "No. We don't. I'm sorry." Taking a shaky breath a whisper was her best. "I may have responded to you last night, but it can't happen again. I'm sorry to disappoint you, I'm going back to Canada soon, and I don't want a fleeting relationship."

Rushing off to her room, unchecked tears dripped down her cheeks while she ensured her case was ready for collection.

The strain was horrendous as they rode the lift down to meet with Prince Hasson. When the prince was called away, soon after their meeting started, she was barely able to contain her delight. Morning had changed the potentate's inappropriate attentions.

They departed after the aborted breakfast meeting and headed for the airport, their charter jet having been quickly readied, polite professionalism in place again. She had work to keep her going during the flight back to London and typical of Nairn – she knew him well enough already – they even had time for a short visit to the office on their return.

"Too late to head back to Lanera tonight," Nairn declared around eight-fifteen that evening. "Alert Richard, please, that we'll be staying over."

By then she hadn't expected anything different. Controlled attitudes had been maintained by both. It was what she told herself she wanted...

Indifferent interaction between them was detestable, but it was how they played it the next day as well. Into the office early, she slogged on till around two p.m. when Nairn buzzed her, both of them having had a working sandwich lunch.

"I've a client meeting in half an hour. Bring the Range Rover to the door for me, please."

"You don't have anything on your diary, sir." Her tone was snippy as she'd heard nothing about this plan.

"Change of tense, Miss Cameron. I didn't, but since I just made the appointment I now do have a meeting. Do you have a problem with that?"

Stony silence accompanied them on the short journey – apart from the posh voice of the navigation system – till she pulled up in the car park of the office building he had requested.

"Do I need to be prepped for this meeting, sir?" Determination to be professional reeked from her, maybe a little too much because she hated the impenetrable wall between them.

"You'll cope. I'm here to negotiate a better deal for the newest advertising campaign for Adrenalinn Adventuring.

Robin Ellesmere was primed to attend, but he's gone off for emergency dental treatment – having broken a tooth, or something. That's why this meeting wasn't on my diary."

Aela refused to apologise for her manner. Their cool relations were his fault, just as much as hers, but she was careful not to allow her feelings to be noticed by the advertising executives. As she was coming to expect, the meeting was successful from Nairn's perspective though it took a couple of hours. By the time they were through, some of their antipathy had melted: not totally relaxed, but not at odds either.

Nairn was describing an earlier ad campaign as she drove along the slow lane of a busy motorway on their return to the office. "What the shit...?" Nairn broke off when his butt began juddering on the seat.

"Brace yourself!" she yelled as her finger flicked on the left indicator, the nearside of the car shuddering even more, right underneath a yelping Nairn.

She yanked her foot off the accelerator. Defensive driving techniques she'd learned years before got their first proper airing. She was wrapped in traffic. Car in front; one behind; another in the next lane alongside. A glimpse at the rear-view mirror told her the car behind was too close for sudden deceleration. Harsh braking was no option anyway.

"Hazards!" she yelled at Nairn.

Nairn angled forward and punched on the hazard button set in the middle of the console since Aela needed both hands to control the jouncing and slewing of the car. Before sliding back in his seat again, he flipped down the visor at his side of the car, the mirror giving him a rear view.

"He's too bloody close, Aela," he warned.

"No. Look. He's slowing down."

Adrenalin pumped fiercely as she guided the convulsing car over onto the hard shoulder, thanking the almighty the driver behind had got the message as soon as the hazards flashed – but he was still a hairsbreadth from her bumper.

Struggling to keep on a straight course her grip was indomitable till the car eventually grated to a halt. Yanking on the hand brake, she braced her forearms on the steering wheel. Her whole body was still vibrating – though thankfully the car wasn't any more. Her head twisted around to look at Nairn before she collapsed back in her seat.

"You okay?" she muttered, a nervous smile erupting. "Bejeezuz! Thought we were done for, there."

His eyes flickered, his mouth twitching before he groaned. "You sure are a cool customer under pressure. What the hell just happened?"

Aela didn't care to analyse. The adrenaline was still pumping high and all she wanted was to devour Nairn. Unclipping her seat restraint she grabbed his face and took his lips in a kiss robbing both of them of their senses. Still on a roll she snatched another. Nairn needed no prompting to control the next as his good arm crushed her to him.

Sanity slowly returned. They were not in the safest of places to be conducting any kind of lovemaking...or affirmation of life. For in a way that's what it was. Slipping free of his grip, her chest heaving, she grinned. "We are still alive, aren't we?"

His answering smile was not constrained. Admiration, gratitude...and something else, really intense, radiated back to her. When he eventually spoke his voice was the deepest whisper. "Yeah. My...oh...so competent PA. More alive than you know." His knuckles stroked her cheek, the merest soft touch.

For an aeon she stared; Nairn stared back. Neither of them moved. But the car did from the buffeting blast of other vehicles whizzing past them.

"Don't you dare move yet, Nairn Malcolm. Not till I make sure it's safe," she ordered as her pulse settled, just a little.

A swift check of the side mirror told her when it was clear to open her door. Staggering her way round to Nairn's side she checked the state of the car.

The front wheel under Nairn was in place though only barely, and was pitched at a precarious angle. Exactly what was wrong with it, she hadn't a clue. The tyre seemed to be intact, no air leak as far as she could tell. Nairn wasn't sure either when he gingerly removed himself from the car and stood alongside her. Both, however, thought it much too coincidental to be just one of those things. The Range Rover, Nairn explained, was less than a year old and had never had any malfunctions before.

Vehicles gusted past them as they gaped at the wheel, but since the Range Rover displayed no appearance of an accident on the road side, other cars passed by on their merry way.

"I get the impression that a change to the spare tyre is not what this needs." She waited for Nairn's response to her question as he pulled out his cell phone.

"We're not touching this at all. It would be normal to call the emergency road services, but I'm thinking a bit of advice from Detective Woods won't go amiss on this one. What's your opinion, Aela?"

Easy to concur.

Detective Woods was categorical. They should sit tight and await the breakdown services he would send out. The Range Rover would be towed away for a thorough inspection; the garage services being authorised ones used regularly by the local police. He would send transportation to get them to wherever they wanted to go – back to the office, or to Nairn's apartment. Detective Woods wasn't treating the incident lightly, even if it was a false alarm.

The hard shoulder wasn't the most comfortable place for Nairn to wait but there was no choice; remaining inside the vehicle wasn't the best place to be either. After what seemed like a very long fifteen minutes a bright yellow breakdown truck drew up behind them.

"Looks like a problem with two of the wheel nuts," the mechanic muttered after he had squatted down and had a first inspection of the wheel. "We'll know better after it gets a good investigation back at the shop."

Aela stood back as the man got to his feet and brushed off his fingers on his already greasy coveralls.

"I'll just take some shots of this, sir. Standard procedure now."

The mechanic disappeared inside the cabin of his truck, returning with a camera. After taking some general shots Aela watched him take detailed ones of the wheel area. The Range Rover was just onto the tow-truck ramp when Detective Woods arrived in an official squad car. He didn't look too impressed at first when he came alongside them and squinted at the car up on the ramp.

"I'm getting the feeling you need a minder, Mr. Malcolm." His words were softened by a small smile.

Aela wasn't sure whether to be miffed by his statement, or to ask who he recommended.

"I don't think a bodyguard could have done any better than my competent Miss Cameron," Nairn grunted as Detective Woods went off to confer with the mechanic.

The look Nairn sent her way scalded her nerve ends, much more than any complimentary words could ever do.

On Detective Woods return, he confirmed the mechanic's preliminary diagnosis. Something had likely caused damage to the wheel nuts.

"More paperwork for me to shunt around, Mr. Malcolm, but don't worry, I'm sure you're not on a suicide pact with this new PA of yours."

It appeared as though it was yet another botched attempt to ground Nairn. Aela as well.

After helping Nairn to fold himself into the rear seat of the squad car, she squeezed in alongside. By then sanity had fully returned, their frantic affirmation of life past history.

"My apartment, please, if it's not too much trouble?" Nairn requested of the police driver, his voice dispirited more than exhausted.

Six-thirty was really early to be home, but she agreed a return to the office wasn't worth it – they could just as easily continue in Nairn's study.

Richard produced another tasty meal for them a few hours later. Her grin was wide since she now knew who might have been dispatched to the nearest restaurant for it.

Richard, she'd learned, did not do all the fantastic cooking himself.

Strung out with the events of the day – and the day before – it wasn't too difficult a decision to hit the sack early, her resolve to resist Nairn having strengthened again. Business only.

Nairn was far too exhausted anyway.

"My sore bits need a little TLC, Aela. How good are you at body massage?" Nairn's weak grin followed her as she turned for her room.

"Useless, sir," she quipped.

She'd walked back and had given him a swift peck before she realised her resolve hadn't even lasted seconds. She evaded another kiss since he hadn't even the strength to reach out his good arm and catch her. "But I'm pretty sure Richard could arrange a real masseuse in a blink for you. Want me to ask?"

Nairn's genial laugh echoed in the hallway, though it was a weak one.

Aela was stumped by Nairn's bold statement on entering the dining room the next morning. Saturday.

"Breakfast quickly, please. A taxi's on the way to take us to the airport."

Told nothing the night before, she wasn't too surprised when Nairn declared she was flying him to Estonia to check the setup at the Adrenalinn Adventuring base.

A few hours later, she had them landed at the airport in Tallinn and straight on to meetings at the base. Routine stuff – not boring, but time consuming.

"I won't need you for the rest of the afternoon, Miss Cameron. I've arranged to meet with a representative of the Tourist Board." Nairn's declaration after their lunch at the centre floored her. He was far too good at arranging things without giving her information, or consultation. The atmosphere between them had been congenial during the morning, yet now he didn't want her?

"You won't need me for notes…or something?"

Nairn's voice was unequivocal. "No. But I do need you to go to the check-in desk out front. There's something waiting there that you need to pick up."

Like the good little PA she was, she trotted to reception to find he'd surprised her again. Nairn had arranged for her to be included in the afternoon kayaking tour around the waters of Tallinn.

Fabulous.

The ancient marine castle of Tallinn was astounding as Aela paddled her way around the bay in a two-person kayak, an instructor from the centre seated behind her. Strong sunshine reflected off the water, the old medieval town a fascinating backdrop for it. The stone fortifications, turreted walls and parapets made such an impact from the water her smile seemed never ending. The old prison buildings were just as fascinating as they paddled by. The whole tour was exhilarating.

Four hours later, she was struggling out of her buoyancy aid just as Nairn hobbled up to her, the clip taking more than a few tries before she could undo it.

"Impressed?" Nairn's midnight blue eyes twinkled.

She could barely answer, so fired up with the pleasure she'd just had. "Totally incredible, and I must come back, sometime, and do the two-day kayak tour to the island of Saaremaa that your guide just told me about."

She dropped the buoyancy aid onto the counter top as the assistants hung the returned suits on the racks and stowed the other gear in behind. Peeling off her sticky neoprene-sided boots, she dumped them too before she turned to Nairn and gave him an unconscious hug of thanks, her eyes latching onto his. "You've no idea how so at home I felt paddling out there on the water. Peter the Great's walled city is incredible, unlike anything I've experienced and to see it from out on the bay like that was…heaven."

Nairn's arms clasped around her. Even more heaven, but his next words shattered her comfort zone.

"Sorry to burst your euphoric bubble, Aela." He grinned down at her, those eyes of his a teasing glimmer. "I need you to tell me right now: how easy was it to unclip?"

Aela knew her eyes hit the ceiling. "You used me as a guinea pig?"

Nairn's answering laugh said it all.

She couldn't believe it. Nairn had given her such a fabulous experience...yet had used her at the same time! Still, she couldn't stop the mirth rising. "You watched me, didn't you? So you know just exactly how much I fumbled, Nairn Malcolm. And it's only the month of June...not September, or October, when it's much colder!"

On their way back to London that evening Nairn confessed to wanting to give her a taste of northern Europe, since it was all new to her. And he had to have someone reliable give him the low-down on the clips on the buoyancy aid. A firm glow settled around her. She loved it that he thought her reliable, and that he had virtually engineered the trip for her enjoyment gave her such a buzz. She wasn't sure she'd ever meet anyone like him again. Heaviness crept over her...nothing to do with the exertion of the afternoon.

She forgave his subterfuge but resisted his playful advances when they got back to his London apartment, shrugging off his straying hand as she rose from the dining table. The atmosphere between them had been light. The fact that no suspect incidents had occurred that day had made her fear less for their safety; no doubt it had lightened Nairn's mood as well.

Placing his hand carefully down on the table and giving it a little pat – since she needed just a hint of contact – her avowal was firm. "A couple more weeks of being your employee. Let's just focus on that, sir."

"What if I don't want to focus on that, Aela?"

Her laugh echoed in the hallway as she closed her bedroom door. Fourteen, maybe fifteen days tops, still to go. The old prison at Tallinn flashed up before her. A prison sentence, indeed. Difficult to go to her lonely bed.

Aela's dreams were full of...

A confined, happy prisoner.

Chapter Seventeen

"Two short hops to organise for tomorrow."

Nairn was, as usual, succinct.

Well, they had stayed put in the London office for a couple of days, Aela reckoning it was par for the course that they were off again – and truth be told she was excited by the prospect of being on the move. Nothing untoward had happened yet it seemed the whole office, and warehouse staff, were walking on eggshells since knowledge of the earlier incidents had affected everyone. Unfortunately, no evidence had been uncovered.

"The Netherlands first for a meeting in Rotterdam with a hot air ballooning company representative. I'm negotiating to add ballooning to our repertoire of European activities. Ever done any balloon trips?"

Her smile was huge. "Just one. Floated over Ayers Rock and the Australian desert for a bit out at Alice Springs. It was one of the highlights of my Australian leg of the world trip. I splurged out a heap of dollars, but it was so worth it! Can you imagine drifting up in the hazy grey-blue alongside the MacDonnell ranges? Then, when the muted colours of pre-dawn seep into the oranges of sunrise, the kangaroos start bouncing across the rugged landscape." She sighed dramatically with the recall of it. "The birds were pretty fabulous too."

"I've got to say that in Europe ballooning is more at the vagaries of weather conditions, but I'd like to get my fingers in that particular pie, as well."

She shared Nairn's amusement since he was showing he remembered lots of things she had said or done when she'd first met him. "You've done some ballooning?"

"A bit like you. A totally memorable trip over the Kalahari in Africa, but I've ballooned in other places, too."

Her pencil was poised ready for details. "Ah...the joys. But back to organising. Rotterdam then fly back to London?"

"Not quite." Nairn was back to an enigmatic expression and mischievous tone. "When the Rotterdam meeting is over we're moving south to Paris, to meet with a guy who is looking for investors to support a new facility he wants to build."

"Paris?" Her squeal of excitement could probably have been heard all the way to L'Arc de Triomphe. Nairn grinned at her enthusiasm.

"Ever heard of Bun-J-Ride?"

"Can't say I have."

"It's a cross between a bungee jump and skiing- or cycling – off a ramp over a valley, or a canyon."

"Wow! Sounds scary." Her eyes goggled at the vision: her one and only bungee jump had been a bit daunting. "And then back to London tomorrow night?"

Disappointment probably peppered her gaze but she couldn't help it because Paris was such an exciting prospect to visit.

"No. We'll stay over in Paris since the second meeting isn't till four p.m. and I've no idea how long I might want to thrash that one out."

She'd spent three days in the Netherlands, mainly around Amsterdam and Den Haag, managing to zip through quite a number of the tourist attractions, adoring the quaint style, including the canals. She'd love to see more, though, and another fleeting visit appealed a lot.

But Paris? That was even more attractive.

The flight from London to the Netherlands was short, the airspace extremely busy. Vigilant concentration was required as she followed landing procedures at Vliegveld Zestienhoven, near Rotterdam. Their first meeting was conducted effectively, Nairn ecstatic that ballooning looked on the cards within a couple of months.

Flying to Paris was much the same as the earlier flight. Busy European airspace again. After landing at Le Bourget Airport, an arranged car sped them to their destination. She was delighted about that since driving Nairn around Paris didn't appeal, even if they did drive on her customary side. Everything enthralled as they whisked past numerous landmarks and she could drink her fill.

The meeting went on till around eight-thirty, Nairn only concluding when he'd negotiated the best deal. She'd taken notes, referencing when required, Nairn's grasp of French impressing her. Although the talks were largely in English, at times the client couldn't find the words to describe the experience he wanted to set up. Nairn's French filled the gaps, ensuring translation for her when needed.

What a guy!

Exhaustion had crept in by the time they were ushered into their hotel suite. She could only imagine Nairn was hanging on to his last energy by the thinnest of threads. Opening the door to their small balcony her gasp went uncontained. "Oh, friggin' heck! Would you look at that?"

Directly in front of her was the Eiffel Tower. Since dusk was only just falling, the view over the city was incredible. So incredible it brought a lump to her throat. "You've done it again. You've stayed here before haven't you? You knew we'd have a view like this?"

Nairn hobbled out onto the flagstones to join her at the railing, his arm draping her shoulder, his fingertips tingling her skin. "Never stayed in these suites before, but I've been on a lower floor, so yes, Aela, I did expect to get a good view when I told you to book this place."

The balcony was the perfect spot as dusk fell, the temperature still pleasant to be out in, so tempting to flop down and savour the view for hours. Showering and gearing up to go downstairs, or out to another restaurant, seemed too exhausting for words, Nairn looking even worse than she felt she must do. Again Nairn took her breath away.

The dinner he'd ordered to be delivered to the small balcony table was…something else.

165

Enchanting. The setting was so magical she seriously struggled to keep her distance from the charm of Nairn Malcolm. Though shattered, he gave her a verbal guided tour of what they could see as they ate.

Room Service discreetly cleared away leaving them with the fascination of a perfect Paris evening. Aela didn't want it to end, but Nairn was beyond whacked. He hadn't complained yet she could tell his chair, though normally comfortable for most people, wasn't supportive enough. He'd already taken his pre-sleep dose of pain-killers and they were kicking in with gusto.

"This is too beautiful for words, Nairn. I don't think I can tell you how much I appreciate what you've done."

Nairn's reply was sleepy. "Glad to be able to provide, Aela."

"Come on, Mr. Masochist, time for bed." Dropping a tiny kiss on his forehead she grasped his hand. Nairn's tired eyes glowed in the semi-darkness. Her arms cradled him as she ushered him through the doors and on towards his room.

"Have I wasted money on this suite, Aela?" Expectation, tinged with a dose of resignation, was in both tone and heated glance.

"Naughty, naughty of you, sir. Told you before. Friends, Nairn. I'll help get you to bed…but that's it. No extras. Remember?"

It was so hard to keep to the infernal resolution she'd made; impossible not to respond when he stole a fleeting kiss but it had little oomph in it. Nairn swayed in her arms and it wasn't due to the excellent wine he'd had.

"You need rest or I'll be flying you onto some hospital helipad for emergency resuscitation."

"Bet you can give me all the emergency resuscitation I'll ever need."

"Not even going to take a rain check, sir. PA only, remember?"

Two mornings after the Paris trip, Aela walked through to Nairn's office and switched on the speakerphone. The

Glasgow City Centre Police Office was on the other end. Security tapes from the hotel car park had been examined, and they had evidence Nairn needed to view whenever he was next in Glasgow, though it wasn't urgent. On its own, it wasn't conclusive enough evidence but might prove helpful. She listened in, hearing a clearly disappointed Nairn agreeing to meet with them as soon as possible though business would keep him in London for another few days.

Later on the phone chirped again.

"Who's calling, please?"

She maintained a professional tone even though she felt anything but gracious since she and her workaholic boss were at loggerheads again. Just short of four-thirty p.m. it had already been a long day. That 24-hour-a-day contract had been no joke, the frosty relations with Nairn so draining.

"It's taken me ages to track him down. Put me through now."

She winced and waited for a name. It was another of Nairn's bloody women.

"You must be a new hire from the filing floor so I'll excuse your ignorance. My name's Thaliana."

Through the open office door she could see Nairn popping his next pain killers into his mouth, swallowing them down with a swig of water.

"One moment, please." Punching the call on hold, she walked over to Nairn's office door, her voice like treacle, the false smile just as sickly sweet. "I'm transferring a personal call, sir. Don't ask me who because she's not enamoured about speaking with new hires." She deliberately returned to her desk loudly informing him over her shoulder, "By the way, your caller doesn't like to be kept waiting."

Smacking the appropriate button to transfer she then set about her next task, scolding herself for getting annoyed; reminding herself the woman was no concern of hers. She was only going to be Nairn's employee for a getting-smaller number of days, and she personally wasn't going within ten feet of him again. Even as she thought the words she knew how much of a lie they were. Her mood darkened as the afternoon waned.

Just short of six p.m. her irritability infuriated her. She needed to lay down the law or she'd surely combust. Broaching Nairn her tread was determined, a Nairn who'd been grouchy for hours as well.

"I'd like to finish soon, sir." She forced her tone to be impersonal, yet decisive. "If you don't want to return to the apartment now, I could organise a taxi for you if you want to wait longer?"

Nairn's glare could have stripped varnish. "Ten minutes. Then we'll go."

Their drive to the apartment was totally silent, but she wasn't prepared to ask him if it was because she'd had the temerity to prompt their early exit from the office. Whatever caused it Nairn's mood was as murky as her own.

He seemed on edge when they entered the apartment, his eyes hedging as he spoke. "Have the evening off. I've made my own plans. I don't need you till after breakfast when we'll leave for Lanera."

Though he didn't specify, it appeared he'd made a date with Thaliana. Aela knew she only had herself to blame if he turned his attentions to another woman, but she didn't have to like her decision.

Determined not to be distressed by Nairn's nasty dismissal she donned her best semi-casual clothes and made her way downstairs where the concierge ordered a taxi to take her to a Greek restaurant she'd seen advertised just weeks before, during her brief stay in London. At the time, she and her backpacking friends had avoided the expensive restaurant, but now it was the perfect boost to her spirits.

After her solitary meal she lingered in the restaurant over coffee and ouzo, enjoying the traditional Greek dancing on the small dance floor. It was noisy, friendly and energetic – just right to lift her spirits. Advances by some handsome young men she rebuffed easily: she wasn't in the mood for anyone else's company, but did allow herself to be persuaded by her server to join in when snaking lines danced together. It was fun enough to pull her out of her gloomy disposition over deliberating what Nairn might, or might not, be doing with the sultry-sounding Thaliana.

Just past midnight she returned to the apartment and buzzed for entry, surprised Nairn answered himself instead of Richard, although he was clearly dressed for bed. On opening the door his intense scrutiny was accompanied by a Neanderthal grunt, his words not fit for polite company. He'd not seen her change of clothes earlier, had not seen the sparkling orange vest top and black satin trousers she was wearing.

"Been painting the town red, or should I accurately say, orange, Miss Cameron?"

"Yes sir, probably just like you have." Her reply was tinged with jealousy she couldn't subdue. "I've had a lovely evening, thank you, but I'll be ready whenever you want me in the morning to make our way back to Scotland."

"That was the plan, Miss Cameron, though if you hadn't been out partying all night," he unfairly stated, "you'd already know we're heading to Barcelona instead. I've appointments there tomorrow." He looked at the clock hanging on the wall. "Today. Later today."

Aela refused to feel irresponsible since he was the one who'd insisted she have the evening off – which although she'd enjoyed – had been solitary. He could easily have called her cell to give her the update, so why hadn't he? "I'll be ready whenever you want me." Her voice was efficiently clipped as she bid him goodnight. The man made her so mad.

***

Nairn cursed quietly to quell the rising torment. "Breakfast at half past four. It'll take at least forty-five minutes to drive to the airport. The plane will be readied for your six o'clock take off slot which I've already organised, myself, this evening."

169

Aela's swearing was unpleasant as she closed her door with a definite thump. His door thump was even better, but he was swearing at himself – not Aela.

The fact she was safely back at his apartment didn't cancel out the anxiety he'd felt during her absence. Alone and wandering about in London. He'd expected her to have Richard get her a meal; had expected her to remain in his apartment. Had expected, hell, he didn't know quite what he'd expected her to do, but it certainly hadn't been go out and enjoy herself looking the way she did.

He'd had a bloody awful evening. He'd agreed to meet Thaliana for dinner, a stupid gut reaction to Aela's rejection, but as a diversion it hadn't worked. On three past occasions Thaliana had been amusingly sexy and temporarily available, the way he liked women. Short-term fun.

Thaliana had been sympathetic to his injuries, in some ways touchingly concerned, yet it had taken only a few minutes with the woman for Nairn to realise he didn't want to be with her. He wanted Aela. Except Aela wanted nothing to do with him.

Riled over his wasted evening he yanked off his dressing gown. The need for Aela gnawed and he was no longer thinking short-term. What about her though? When he forced recall of her actual statements all she'd said was she didn't do flings. He was sure now a short fling wouldn't do it for him either. Could she have meant she would want him long-term, like maybe even very long term?

His feelings stunned him. Did it mean he more than just liked feisty Aela Cameron? He wasn't sure if he was in love with her but he did know he'd never felt such yearning.

Chapter Eighteen

"No more coffee, thanks, I'm done." Nairn plonked his cup down and made to rise from the stool in the kitchen.

Four-thirty a.m. had found them snatching a quick breakfast. A few hours of sleep had done very little to bolster Aela's confidence in confronting Nairn, yet she determined to be competent as she drove them to the airport. He was pleasantness personified. The infuriating man got her back up so easily, but she was being paid well to be on call twenty-four-hours-a-day.

Confidently flying Nairn's jet, she was pleased she hadn't had to talk to him since he stayed outside the cockpit. After handing over to ground crew in Barcelona they climbed into the waiting taxi, Nairn orchestrating the conversation as he organised the day's meetings, his attitude so positive it made her sick. He was a bloody android. How else could the unfeeling tyrant seem so smug? He didn't need to rub his conquest with another woman in her face.

She had visited Toledo and Madrid but hadn't gone anywhere near the coastal cities of Spain during her backpacking trek, and she'd not stayed in anything like the stylish hotel he'd had her book them into. Again top of the range, it had every comfort they would require and many that they would never use.

After an early check-in to their suite, Nairn declared some rest time before their eleven a.m. meeting. Too strung out to relax, their tense interaction almost suffocating, she took the opportunity to go on a short walkabout close to the hotel.

The buildings around her were utterly amazing. Some were incredibly fanciful concoctions with pink checkered facades and magical balconies which just had to be for show only, since they seemed too impractical to be otherwise. Other buildings appeared just plain weird in their architectural style. Many had strong Islamic overtones in the turrets and long narrow windows, the streets a mish-mash of whimsical styles. The balconies of one particular building reminded her of face masks, the kind worn at regency masked balls, though she was unsure of why she thought that. The Casa Batllo…according to the sign. She resolved to pick up a guide book for more information.

The sun shone, and the air was pleasantly warm. Her grin widened as she moved on and found something just as exciting at the next corner. What an incredible city and she was only in one tiny part of it.

The last working days had been so fraught with tension it was a relief to be free of Nairn's overpowering presence for a while. And free from the spectre of sabotage. Focusing on the views, she pushed aside gloomy thoughts.

Fabulous little tapas bars and small boutiques peppered the streets as she whisked around at warp speed to make the most of her short break. She wasn't normally impulsive, but there was a dazzling gown displayed in one window that she couldn't resist. Feeling reckless, buying it was a huge confidence boost. The sheath was a deep, sensuous petrel blue-green. One shouldered it had delicate beading around the moulded bust line. The back was non-existent with the exception of one slender cross strap.

Not long after, she was back in their suite clutching the cellophane-wrapped garment, contrasting ankle-strapped heels and a tiny clutch bag hung from her other hand. Her credit card had another serious dent in it though her savings account in Vancouver would cover the purchases till her generous salary was paid by Nairn.

Flopping down on her bed she exhaled, excitement still tingling. Who was this new woman? She'd existed for more than six months with a backpack full of inexpensive practical clothes and for no logical reason she'd just blown hundreds of euros on a dream dress she might never wear.

Being in Nairn Malcolm's orbit was turning her head, but she'd needed an outlet for the intense frustration consuming her.

She decided later that the mad spending-spree had been worth it since they spent hour after hour in tight negotiations with two different sets of clients. Their eleven a.m. meeting lingered through a late lunch, concluding around two. By then it was Spanish siesta time, though they didn't have one. Up in their suite Nairn prepared her for the next client meeting starting at four. After the second round of talks, they stepped in to a small tapas bar next to the hotel. Over a quick glass of local wine and a selection of mouth-watering tapas Nairn declared another rest time as, Spanish-style, their dinner meeting wasn't going to start till ten p.m.

Though the appointments had been hard work, the tension had dissipated and a more relaxed atmosphere had been the state of affairs. Swings and roundabouts.

"It's only just after six. If you're not too tired we could maybe do a tour of Barcelona for the next couple of hours?"

"If I'm not too tired? You're the one who must be shattered, Nairn Malcolm, but it's a very tempting suggestion."

She told Nairn about the buildings she'd had a brief glimpse of.

"You're talking about the Antoni Gaudi buildings." Nairn laughed at her expressions of delight. "Pretty impressive, huh?"

At her nodded agreement he insisted she must see more of the architecture because she'd only seen the tiniest bit. It wasn't too difficult to persuade Nairn that touring around in a taxi wouldn't be nearly as exciting as going around on an open-topped City Tour bus, even if they could only go inside. "They're tremendous value, Nairn, and the commentaries are packed with great information."

An official tourist bus stop was right alongside their prestigious hotel, since it was situated in one of the main plazas.

Nairn manoeuvred himself into the empty back seat where he could stretch out his leg cast. Although they didn't take advantage of the hop-on hop-off facility, she loved the couple of hours spent around the city and even allowed herself to be persuaded to go on the top of the bus at strategic points during the tour, egged on by Nairn who promised she'd get a better view of the fanciful Gaudi buildings, and the multitude of church spires adorning the skyline. His claim of being content to ride the lower deck she was happy to accept because she could see the break from work was rest enough for Nairn.

They were leaving the restaurant after their late dinner meeting when Nairn read a text on his cell. He flagged a taxi, the grim ogre back again. "My mother is meeting us at our hotel for breakfast before we head back tomorrow."

When she suggested she'd breakfast alone and meet him afterwards Nairn's refusal was categorical.

"You'll be there, Aela." His tone brooked no options.

"Why?" She looked at the line of his tense mouth, and the anger flashing in his eyes.

"Ruaridh has, apparently, been singing your praises." His teeth looked almost glued together. "My mother has insisted she meet you."

Again Ruaridh's name was enough to send him into that thunderous black pit. Caitlinn had learned Nairn was going to be in Barcelona, and she must have learned the information from Ruaridh, because all day they'd been conducting Gale Breakers business.

Caitlinn was a chic woman in her mid-fifties, superbly well-presented for eight a.m. From first introduction she was unfailing in her manner, and friendly. She asked Aela interested questions about her background, her world travels, and her current status as Nairn's PA. Then Caitlinn asked about her intentions to visit her Scottish relatives with Ruaridh. Nairn looked confused as well he might because, as far as Aela knew, he'd been told nothing of those intentions.

"When I can arrange an afternoon off I'll organise a visit," she told Caitlinn. "I've got family photographs on a USB stick that I intend to print out when I need them. I'm hoping someone will recognise my grand-father and family."

She found Nairn's interaction with his mother difficult to judge. They were comfortable with one another in a strange, detached way. His mother rebuked him for not meeting up with her often enough and he in turn berated her for not visiting Garvald Castle either. Caitlinn then retorted he was never there long enough for her to visit.

"You have to know Ruaridh is very taken with you," Caitlinn gushed as they said their goodbyes. "I'm sure I'll be hearing more about you in the near future."

Aela was mystified that Ruaridh had talked about her during a conversation with his ex-wife. Caitlin's devastating last comment was meant to be a whisper for Aela alone, but was loud enough for the whole restaurant to hear. "Ruaridh looks forward to you joining the family. Now, I believe I can see why."

Aela felt a blood-rush fierce across her cheeks.

It was a huge relief when they bid Caitlinn farewell and headed to the airport to return to London, communication between her and Nairn sparse.

It was as well that the days were passing quickly.

Early next morning, Aela drove Nairn to the office for a quick visit before their return to Lanera. She couldn't say why, but he seemed a different kind of edgy.

"I don't need you to come in with me." Nairn's statement was a surprise when they arrived at the car park. "Take time off. Go walkabout. I'll text you when I'm ready to head for the airport. No longer than an hour; two at most."

When she asked if something was wrong Nairn barked at her so vehemently she backed off, hurt by his rejection.

Although she felt redundant and quite cast off, accepting his bald dictates she sped off to visit a street market she'd heard was close by. It was an intriguing mixture of flea market, world-trade food stalls and stalls with new products.

After spending a pleasant hour browsing around, she found a seat at an outside café for a coffee. There was just time enough to appreciate it before Nairn sent her a text message. She couldn't explain the flood of relief, happy her role had shifted to being his chauffeur once again. It had nothing at all to do with being needed by him.

Scolding herself was easy. Self-delusion was the pits.

***

Nairn's heart shifted when Aela arrived for him, glad he'd made the decision to keep her out of the office, out of harm's way. Gut instinct had unsettled him earlier, alerted him in some weird way that she'd once again be in danger if she entered the building. During his short time in the office he'd found absolutely nothing to confirm those feelings, yet was convinced his decision had been the correct one. Temporarily pissing her off was better than her being dead.

There'd been too many people solicitous of her health. Most he knew were genuine, but he was now so suspicious it was hard to decide who was trustworthy. A few ill-judged comments about Aela having an easy job with extra time off he quashed, with no mercy spared. Especially the semi-ribald comment Robin Ellesmere made about him having ridden his new work-horse so hard he'd exhausted her. Robin had been joking, he knew it, but his comment had been heard by the whole Adrenalinn Adventuring office. He hadn't appreciated the acid look on Stella Grainger's face when he asked her how a particular work issue was progressing.

Now Aela was in the car waiting for him, safe and well as far as he could determine, though her neutral look wasn't inspiring. Next, he had to face the prickly problem over their return to Lanera. It couldn't be postponed any longer. He remained irked by his mother's parting comment of the day before, yet couldn't bear to have a bust up with his father over any woman.

The flight from London to Glasgow Aela accomplished

with her usual competence, her sheer delight evident to Nairn since this time he squeezed onto the co-pilots seat. Handing the plane over to maintenance crew in Glasgow, he bid Aela organise a taxi to a nearby hotel where they could lunch, too hungry to wait till they arrived on Lanera. He ensured the conversation during their meal was pleasant. He really, really liked competent, gorgeous Aela though she remained civil, with that artificial friendship thing she had going, making him even more determined.

The floatplane trip to Lanera wasn't accomplished so textbook-easy. No sooner had Aela checked in with air traffic control than she was apprised of a potential problem that Nairn listened in to on his earpiece.

A raging inferno in a disused Victorian warehousing block on the outskirts of the city, close to the airport, was causing major flight traffic problems. Many commercial and domestic flights in and out of the passenger and freight airport had been cancelled, others rerouted where possible, since a huge pall of dense black smoke was drifting up and over a wide area. Aela was given clearance, though only if she took a huge southwards detour. The detour itself wasn't a problem, but the weather update for later wasn't good. A storm front approached from the Atlantic and would affect their flight by the time they got closer to Lanera. Nairn watched her chew her bottom lip as the information was relayed to them. He could see her concern wasn't about flying the plane; rather more about how he would cope with the ride.

"I've every confidence in you, Aela, but if you don't want to do it we'll stay in Glasgow." He tossed responsibility in her court.

"I've had many a scary flight in British Columbia when the weather has suddenly gone down the toilet. I'll be fine piloting, so long as you think you'll cope?"

The much longer detour had definite moments as Aela evaded the drifting black clouds sweeping up from the south-west, hitting severe turbulence as the weather front made its mark. "I'm making another wide sweep, Nairn, to avoid this low drift. Brace again," she shouted over the growing noise of the battering rain.

Even in his extreme discomfort, since seating in the cockpit was tight, Nairn sensed the adrenaline pumping through her body. Her concentration never faltered as she controlled the floatplane. By the time they got closer to Lanera they were being well-buffeted by Atlantic winds, Aela relying on her experience to keep the little floatplane level, adjusting the height more often than during a normal flight and balancing it constantly.

"Nairn!" He heard her, though her cry was faint over the noise of the howling wind and pelting rain. "I'm going to have to go down on the other side of Lanera, then I'll taxi round to Mariskay, but it'll be rough."

She bawled over the clamour rocking them; the vibration juddering up her arms to her locked in place shoulders as she clutched the controls. Her expression looked as tortured as he was feeling, her sympathy radiating out to him in waves. If he'd wondered before if she was concerned for him, he definitely knew it now. Concern for his health was in her eyes, yes, but he hoped the rest he could see meant what he wanted it to mean. Something stronger like affection.

"Can you bear it, or should I try landing on Mull instead?"

His good arm braced against the dash as buffeting turbulence jolted them. For a healthy person the instability would have been a wild tremor but with his condition it was something else. As pilot, Aela would have been concerned for any passenger in his state, but he knew her concern for him was doubled as she flicked her gaze his way more often than she should have, yet without endangering them both. He was in agony, he just wanted the damned flight over, but he didn't want to make it any harder than it was already for Aela. He wanted to be home safely, able take her in his arms and kiss the hell out of her.

"Land on Lanera waters." His teeth were grinding together, but he couldn't stop it happening. He attempted a smile, knew it was weak as dishwater. "I'm fine."

One thing he wasn't lying to himself about was the fact that very soon he was going to tell this woman exactly how he felt about her. He loved everything about her. Her looks. Her generous spirit. Her courage. Her empathy. Her competence. Right at that moment he really, really loved her competence.

With incredible skill, Aela landed on the far side of the island in heaving waters so high at times that the waves sloshed over the wings, on breakers he wasn't convinced he'd tackle himself. Although only late afternoon the summer sky was so slate-dark it was like night; the angry grey-caps surging up and around them, their height dangerously close to submerging them. The rain battered the glass fronting them, sheeting Aela's vision, a momentary blocking of the way ahead till the wipers did their job.

"Brace again, Nairn!" she yelled over the horrendous noise around them. "This isn't going to be smooth." Her words were no sooner uttered than he felt the floatplane lurch, a dangerous list in the high winds. "No worries. I've got it under control."

How Aela managed to keep it steady he hadn't a clue, but he knew it would have been beyond his own experience. The whole craft vibrated, a violent and relentless buffeting, as she taxied round the headland to Mariskay harbour. The storm lamented, the rain bombarding them with even more force from that direction. Having radioed ahead, the automatic roller doors of the boatyard opened for them as Aela made the harbour entrance where she bumpily-bounced the little plane up the slip and inside out of the weather.

"You still with me, Nairn?" Aela grinned. He knew her adrenaline was raging, still pumping wild around her because his adrenaline surge was no different.

"My God! You're a horrible woman." His smile was weak, his pain-wracked body having given in to the relief they were home. Not dry by any means…but home. And Aela was safe. "Jeez! That beat the hell out of a boring ride,

Aela."

His words gained strength as she drove the floatplane into an empty bay. When she killed the engine he grasped her one-handed and kissed her soundly before she could evade him. His first greedy kiss led to another…and another…before a noisy knocking on the side of the door jolted him from his absorbance. His release of Aela was reluctant; curses flew at the interruption.

"Someone's trying to tell us something," she chuckled in his ear as she unbuckled and prepared to exit, then waved merrily to the bystanders who had watched their entry, and their ardent embraces.

"Just get me home without any more delay, woman." His impassioned plea was matched by the eagerness he could see in her sparkling eyes. "We're not done, yet."

"Mm…sounds delicious. But don't worry, Nairn Malcolm, you're in good hands. I'll get you home in one piece."

He waited while Aela saw to the plane checks before leaving the boatyard, since in the current weather the floatplane would remain there till conditions improved. Keeping his eyes off her proved impossible as Grant, one of the boatyard employees, drove them the couple of miles back to the castle. If her expression was anything to go by he knew Aela was just as keen to get back as he was.

"You go on in, Nairn, and get the kettle on right now," she chided as he got out at the back door. "Grant will help me with the bags."

Chapter Nineteen

The minute Aela opened the castle door it was obvious something major had been happening inside.

"Nairn!" She heard the woman's delighted greeting well before she saw a tiny blonde vision do a jaunty skip down the nearby spiral staircase and rush forward to hug him.

"I've got those bedroom needs sorted out for you," the woman trilled.

"Mhari."

Aela inwardly groaned. So, this was Mhari. Side-stepping their enthusiastic hugging she moved along the corridor, wishing she'd got well out of range since Nairn's soft greeting to his visitor cut her to the quick.

"You lovely woman. Get me to the bedroom without delay."

She didn't want to hear any more as she sped to the office apartment where she dropped her case and flopped, with no ceremony, onto her bed. The words bedroom needs repeated till she was ready to scream. She even surprised herself by drumming her hands on the mattress, a fevered beat that lost control. He'd been with Thaliana nights ago; he'd just kissed her senseless on the floatplane, and now here was some ditzy blonde called Mhari? How many more females would crawl out of the woodwork?

Eventually, she raised herself off the bed knowing she needed an alternative diversion to pull her out of the fug she was in. Latent adrenaline from the extremely difficult plane ride warred with emotional frustration. Nairn Malcolm was a temporary boss and not a long-term player. Some splendid oaths followed.

A half hour later the pool suite Jacuzzi bubbled around

her, her furious swim having re-energised her rather than exhausted her – because she was still so buzzed. The pulsating gushes had only a marginal effect in warding off the horrible images she was creating; images of Nairn with the bubbly blonde up in the master bedroom. She wiped his navy and grey decor out of her mind and tried to focus on the gurgling noises around her.

Gastown bloops.

In a deliberate attempt to banish Nairn Malcolm, she thought of the famous gas-driven street clock in Gastown, her favourite street in Vancouver, even though it was a tourist haven. Home. She'd see it soon. She should have been buoyed up by that thought but it was…weirdly depressing.

Having swum at least another twenty furious laps she was exhausted and savouring a second soak in the Jacuzzi. A prune wouldn't look any more wrinkled, but by then she had resigned herself to her role as PA, chauffeur and whatever else. Except the 'whatever else' would never be diminutive blond bunny: not without a serious doze of chlorine, and some leg chopping. It was amazing how difficult it was to huff under the bubbles of a Jacuzzi.

"Aela?"

She was astounded to hear Nairn enter the pool suite.

"Sorry to disturb you."

He didn't look sorry to disturb her. He was staring as she dipped in and out of sight in the bubbling foam. She wasn't naked; she wore a bikini, but he looked agitated. His arm lifted as he checked his watch, and then groaned. Loudly. "Just came to tell you we need to leave at seven-fifteen for Mariskay. I've booked a table at the Ship's Inn for seven-thirty."

Having given his information, she watched him drag his gaze away. There was a momentary closure of his eyes and then he whirled away.

Instinct told her his first reaction to her almost naked body had been hunger. Now he was at the door, using the walking aid so well he seemed hardly incapacitated at all.

182

She lay back and closed her eyes, willing herself to stop yearning. Who was eating with him in Mariskay? It crushed her to ask his retreating back but her professional conscience had kicked in and she felt she had no choice.

"Nairn?" She watched his slow turn, noting his eyes darting askance, avoiding her. "When will you want me to come back and collect you?"

His eyes whipped back in her direction. "Come back? Why would I want you to do that, Aela? You'll be eating there with me." His mouth formed a grim slash as she rose from the froth and walked towards him. He looked angry, his brows drawn into a frown as though something had just occurred to him. "Unless you've managed to make alternative arrangements already?"

"No, I haven't, but I thought perhaps you meant your visitor, Mhari, would be eating with you."

"Mhari?" Nairn looked genuinely perplexed. "Why would Mhari want to eat with me when she has a husband and child at home to eat with? Aela, if you'd waited long enough to be introduced you'd have found out Mhari was the architect I employed to reconstruct Garvald Castle four years ago."

Aela dipped her head onto her chest. The significance of his words kicked in. She was so embarrassed. "I'm sorry. That was so friggin' rude of me."

The words were broken off as Nairn lifted her chin. His searching look into her eyes made her even more embarrassed. Oh piffle! That darned rush of blood scalded her cheeks. She felt on fire again, powerless to prevent it happening. This man made her so…mad.

"Aela? Were you jealous of Mhari?"

He didn't wait for her answer, or a denial. A whispering kiss followed. She wanted it to go on, and on.

"Mhari's original plans for the reconstruction of the castle included a small service lift. The construction work and mechanics were already done when I came back from one of my trips. I was an arrogant shit. I pulled the plug on it, deeming it would be unnecessary."

She thought Nairn looked a bit sheepish. He wasn't a man to admit to any kind of bad judgment.

"I didn't like the anachronistic look of its metal door in the corridor. As you can see, we've tried hard to give the castle a feeling of age, even though it's all a facsimile. I thought the shiny steel door spoiled the continuity in the corridor and made the place look like a hotel."

"A hotel?"

He cuddled her close, his fingers tracing a light pathway up and down her spine. "I was being bloody-minded and unreasonable, as recent events have proved. At the time, I was living out of a suitcase, sometimes in bijou hotels with dinky little lifts, and I didn't want that here in my home. Even though Mhari put up some resistance, I insisted she had the doors removed and false walls put in place, instead of removing the interior structure entirely."

She squirmed even closer. "So, all the innards were hidden and uncovered without too much bother?"

"Yes. But let me finish my story, woman." He nudged her hips back just the tiniest bit. "In view of my recent incapacity I realised how wrong I'd been and asked Mhari to get it operational as soon as possible."

She found herself whispering, "What time is it?"

"Doesn't matter, because it's never going to be enough for this." He drew her in for another, longer kiss. A few moments later Nairn disentangled himself. "Now I wish I hadn't made the dinner arrangement."

"You'd rather stay here?" She knew her own answer to that one.

"Yes, I would, but I must talk with my father. Can't postpone it any longer."

At seven-fifteen she was at the back door. Nairn wasn't in the bedroom on the ground floor because she'd checked. It had been cleared of his presence, the room starkly bare and tidy. The subtle new developments had just been worked out when she heard a soft hiss, the deep bronze door not looking too out of place with the décor in the corridor.

Nairn exited his grin exultant, his kiss a fierce plunder.

"I'm not often wrong, Aela, but I was about this little beauty. It's small, though I did specify Mhari had to make sure it could take a proper wheelchair. There's no way I will be so ill-prepared again."

Her enquiry lacked punch when he ushered her towards the door. "Food?"

"Got to go, Aela. Can't wait over this one."

She was unclear of what couldn't be postponed, but got on with her job.

Dinner was marvellous although Ruaridh had cancelled. Nairn seemed annoyed about it but Aela wasn't fussed since there was a strumming tension building between them. She couldn't wait to get back to the castle, though it was no great surprise when Ruaridh joined them in the bar as they were having a nightcap before returning home.

"Aela!" Ruaridh's bear hug of welcome almost crushed her. "It's good to see you back."

"You too." She gave him a little peck on the cheek.

"Don't even think of hugging me, Father." Nairn's sarcastic quip blasted, phoney emphasis being put on their relationship as he glowered at Ruaridh. "I've a bone to pick with you."

Ruaridh's answering grin gained the laugh he'd intended from Aela. "Only one? You must be slipping, my lad!"

"What was in your mind, old man, foisting your ex-wife on me in Barcelona?"

Ruaridh's grin was even wider. "That's no way to refer to your dear mother, Nairn."

She accepted Ruaridh's hand-patting before he continued. "I hope it wasn't too much of an ordeal, Aela, meeting Caitlinn?"

She polished her tact. "Caitlinn was very nice and very keen to find out lots about me. Thank you very much, Ruaridh."

"Nosy, was she?" Ruaridh's chuckle reverberated across the room.

"Mother was her usual domineering self, driving the conversation where she wanted it to go." Nairn's gaze

185

remained on her as he added, "It was very enlightening, Aela, to find out both my parents seem to know much more about you than I do."

Ruaridh shook his head. "You just don't ask the right questions, lad. When you learn to do that you won't be left behind."

"Well, tell me, then?" Nairn pinned her gaze, seemingly refusing to rise to Ruaridh's bait. "Have you got lots of family skeletons you're hiding from me?"

"I don't think so, but I won't know till I meet them." She truly found the situation amusing though the dissent between father and son was still unfathomable.

"Fancy coming out with me tomorrow, Aela, if Nairn can spare you for a while?" Ruaridh's tone was mirthful as he turned to include Nairn in his innocent gaze. "I've hunted down your great-grandfather's nephew on Mull. There's also a cousin of his still alive, and they'd both love to meet you." Ruaridh then quoted the names of the people he'd located.

"I found records for those names on the internet," Aela cried, now sure they were the correct Camerons, since Cameron was a fairly common name in the surrounding area.

***

Nairn couldn't refuse to give her the time off to go sailing with his father; how could he deny her anything when she was so enthusiastic?

He felt such an idiot.

He'd been blind jealous of Ruaridh, but the phone calls and meetings made good sense now. Ruaridh definitely liked Aela, but now the jealous haze had cleared a little – just a little – he could see that his father's regard for Aela was that of a concerned friend, and nothing more. Relief washed through him because he no longer had to suppress the concept of alienating his father over a relationship with her. Of course, he still had to make her stay longer than the four weeks of their contract.

They spent another while chatting to people who came by to get an update on his health, though at the same time it was clear that Aela was being checked out.

To his total chagrin she told everyone that her visit to Lanera was temporary, emphasising her short-term contract, and was so enthusiastic when relating her plans to do her Masters course back in Vancouver. An added bonus, she said, was Ruaridh helping her contact long lost relatives.

Though she wasn't ignoring him, he found sitting beside her unbearable.

As Aela drove him back to the castle, he reviewed his own plans. Her contract was still extant, but for how long? Rapid calculations made, there was a handful of days left to convince her she could be his lover for more than a fling.

Light and friendly, putting no immediate pressure on her was the tactic he decided on. Definitely for the best since he wasn't fit enough yet.

When they reached the castle hallway, he kept his invitation cajoling. "Would you care to try out my new lift with me, to make sure I reach my huge bed?"

Aela knew how to parry teasing. "Not happening tonight, thank you, sir. How about I take a rain check...this time?" Before he could kiss her again, she sped away to her own quarters.

Running after her was not yet in his repertoire. Cheeky wench! The reference to a rain check he filed away as a very positive step forward.

***

Aela found the next day dawning clear and hot, perfect for the floatplane flight to Glasgow for Nairn's early hospital appointment. Once again he was chameleon-like, back to being just friendly. She determined to be the same. What else could she do?

The consultant gave the green light for weight bearing on Nairn's broken leg as everything was healing nicely, and his cast was redone with a proper walking cradle. The new lighter-weight plaster stretched from below the knee to his toes since the patella hairline crack was not thought to be an issue any longer. Nairn needed to bend the knee again and gradually get the muscles flexing properly. A different lightweight walking aid replaced the heavy crutch he'd been using. Nairn was over the moon when he hobbled out to her, his limp fast and furious.

His arm cast had also been changed to a lighter weight support, freeing his fingers. When he reached her, regardless of the watching consultant, the kiss he gave her almost knocked her for six. A discreet cough behind them reminded her where they were.

She couldn't miss the twinkle in the doctor's eye when he, quite loudly, stated, "Give the ribs a chance, Mr. Malcolm. Or perhaps I should book you both into a recovery room?"

Nairn made a new appointment for a few weeks hence when the plaster casts would be removed and set off for the car at a jaunty pace.

An interview at Glasgow City Centre Police Office was their next venue. Minutes after their arrival she found herself sitting alongside Nairn in front of a bank of monitors – one of which displayed the hotel car park security tape the day of his motorbike accident. The detectives had included her in the showing explaining that although they'd no expectations of her recognising anyone they felt she should view since she'd also been targeted as a victim.

The grainy images were hard to discern; careful viewing being advised. Nairn concentrated on the freeze-framed images of a man and woman. They'd exited a car in the bay adjacent to his motorbike.

"Do you recognise either of these two people?"

She heard Nairn's breath exhale as he answered the detective. She recognised the tone already – Nairn was frustrated with himself. "The man I don't recognise at all, but there's something familiar about the woman, though I can't pin-point it."

Nairn was bothered even more when the footage was repeated because the man did seem to be tampering with the bike. The car had been parked cunningly close, the back passenger door left open deliberately. The woman partially obscured the view of the camera, but the opinion of the detectives was that the man was maliciously interfering with the bike front wheel.

Nairn's disappointment grew even more acute by the end of the interview. The woman, he'd repeated, was elusively familiar. The detectives concluded the tapes could be used as evidence later to prove malicious intent to harm, if further evidence was uncovered. Since no motive for the bike-tampering had been uncovered, the police warning them to continue to be on their guard sent shivers down her back.

It was easy for her to sympathise with Nairn's impatience since it was clear that the threats to both of them had been spitefully intended. Calming Nairn's rants was a challenge because he was again berating himself for putting her in the firing line.

Thorough checks were undertaken before the floatplane took off; there was no way she was going to fly an aircraft that had been fiddled with. Yet the extra time she took didn't seem to matter to Nairn since he was preoccupied, intensely frustrated and disappointed. At times during the flight his introspection was unbearable, and her advances to lighten his mood were either met with gruff answers or stony silences. What she knew she could do, however, was be a competent pilot and the short flight was accomplished smoothly with none of the drama of the previous day.

Ruaridh phoned after they ate a late lunch at Garvald Castle. Was she free go to Craignure, on the island of Mull, that afternoon? Nairn readily agreed. She felt too readily. She didn't know whether to be peeved or joyful about getting out of his range as he grunted his afternoon work could be done without her. She whipped out her USB stick and made print-outs of her collection of family photographs then fled. Her ancestry quest was what she'd come to

Scotland for, not to get embroiled with a moody man who ran hot and cold.

The visit was a revelation because she found the old man bore physical characteristics akin to her Uncle Harris. The tone of voice, and the deep rumble of his laugh were uncannily alike, but the man's lilting accent was a big difference. She was saddened to realise her own father might have looked just the same if he hadn't died while still a young man. On the positive side, her elderly relative was able to identify and name a few of the people in her photographs, telling her his female cousin on another small island nearby would be much better at remembering the family stuff. The visit ended with Aela promising to return soon to meet up with other family members. She hoped she'd be able to keep her promise, but her days as Nairn's general factotum were diminishing.

On their return journey Ruaridh relinquished the wheel for her to pilot them back to Lanera. Her spirits were buoyant by the time she reached the castle.

"Back down to London tomorrow," Nairn informed her as she entered the office. "Just a quick hop though. I'm going to my corporate lawyers to sign the agreements with Prince Hasson."

"Will he be there?" She wasn't sure she wanted to be there if he was.

"Don't expect so. His legal team should arrive with his signatures already in place."

The rest of their interaction was polite.

Except for the many times Nairn seemed to bump into her...or touch her hand. The looks were the worst before he turned away and hirpled off.

Chapter Twenty

"Can't do the floatplane today, Nairn."

The cloud levels and wind conditions the next morning weren't in their favour.

"How do you feel about piloting the catamaran?" Nairn didn't sound too confident but Aela was.

"It's no problem. Ruaridh let me have a shot of his. It'll be longer to get you to Glasgow, though, so we'd best get going right now if you're to make your meeting. I'll need to dump you down in Mariskay first."

Nairn muttered and mumbled as he picked up his briefcase – the cove staircase was still impossible for him.

It was an exhilarating sail even if the journey south took more time than flying by floatplane.

The day was successful, thankfully without the presence of Prince Hassan. Aela cherished transporting Nairn, and mentally patted herself on the back because she felt she'd been competent in her PA duties as well.

But for the rest she wasn't so sure. Their interaction wasn't unpleasant, merely tepid. Now, on their return journey she was desperate for some sort of compromise. There were hardly any days of her contract left.

As one colleague to another, Nairn coolly applauded her expertise on landing at Glasgow airport, having encountered some unexpected turbulence over the Scottish borders. During the sea trip back to Lanera he melted into a friendly companion, jabbering away like a bubbly jock. Aela could hardly credit him but wasn't going to literally rock the boat. She was coming to understand how Nairn's fevered brain worked. Problems were thrashed out in brooding silence; followed by some conclusion he personally could live with;

and then the sun appeared from behind his black clouds. His mercurial moods infuriated her, but at least she now felt she had an inkling of what drove him. The spectre of the sabotage still sat heavily on him as they discussed it, and she accordingly cut him some slack.

"We're here, Nairn." Her declaration came on arrival at Mariskay harbour in the almost dark. They couldn't possibly have made such a long day trip if it hadn't been the month of June. Daylight was at its longest, full dark not descending till well after eleven p.m.

Exhausted, she piled them into the awaiting Range Rover. Bed. What a lovely concept she thought as she switched on the car headlights, having berthed the catamaran next to the boatyard.

***

Nairn wasn't prepared to wait any longer to get closer to Aela, really close, but first he needed to touch base with developments. He'd not looked at his computer, or checked his phone for hours.

Deliberately.

The last hours of their travel time on the catamaran he'd spent asking Aela everything under the sun he could think about. Her childhood; living with her Uncle Harris after she'd been orphaned when her mother suddenly died when she was thirteen; her favourite things; her schooling; her time at university. Anything and everything that occurred to him. In turn, he'd fed her with any answers she'd requested. It had been a magical time of discovery. They'd laughed and shared, and bonded in a way they hadn't before.

He stopped at the office while Aela carried on to the apartment telling him she'd dump her jacket and make a bedtime drink for them. Minutes later he tracked her down in her bedroom to tell her they had to fly off to the Caribbean the following day. She was flopped down on the bed, her discarded jacket hanging off the edge.

"The Caribbean? Jeez, Nairn, you don't piss around, do

you?" Aela groaned as he watched her eyes open again.

"Hey! I'm paying you for twenty-four hours a day." Grabbing her hand he prised her off the duvet cover.

"Yeah! I know, body and bloody soul."

Nairn grinned at her phrasing since it really was what he wanted from her.

"Okay. You got me. Where should I book, and for how long?"

Guilt crept in as he heard the fatigue in her voice, struggling as she was to rise from the bed. "Is it so urgent you go tomorrow, Nairn?"

"Aela." He grasped her hand as she passed him and pulled her to him, loosely sliding his arms around her waist. "I know you're bushed but think about it. We've already worked out this possible contract is now the most likely reason my company – and both of us by the way – has been targeted for bleeding mayhem."

"Are you trying to flush them out?"

He meant his answer to be evasive. He didn't want to alarm Aela in any way. "You know I contacted the consortium last weekend for details of the meeting. They were the ones who postponed it, and now their confirmatory e-mail has come. The meeting is definitely on for this Friday." She'd pencilled in the consortium's two future possibilities. The first opportunity was for the Friday coming, now only two days away. "We are going to this meeting, and we aren't going to arrive too late for it. We leave tomorrow morning."

Aela slipped out of his arms to get things organised, yawning her head off. "Where do you suggest staying?"

He rattled off the hotel where the client meeting was being held, unable to suggest any others as he'd never been to the Caribbean before. He left the booking choice to her for a stay of three nights while he volunteered to make them their hot bedtime drink.

He appeared back at the office, two mugs precariously propped on his right cast, to find Aela flopped across her desk, her head cradled on her arms, her eyes closed. He only

193

just managed to decipher her mumble. "Okay. Weather's good. Leave early."

He closed down her computer, hobbled to the apartment where he placed the two mugs on the table in the small sitting room, then returned for her. "Come on wonder-woman-who-ain't-quite any more. Time for bed." He hauled her up from the seat in a one-arm hug and wobbled her unresisting body down the hall and into the apartment sitting room. Once there he gathered her into his arms and kissed her. "Thank you, Aela. You are one highly competent woman. All day long you've done my bidding and haven't complained once."

"I haven't?" Aela muttered into his shirt.

"Well, nothing that really mattered." He stretched for a mug and presented it to her. "Drink your hot chocolate."

Picking up his own drink he urged a salutation. "*Slainte*, Aela!"

Clanking their mugs together, eyes closing, she sipped.

"Come on," he declared a few silent minutes later, even before they had finished drinking. He stumbled Aela into her bedroom and started to unbutton her shirt, fumbling one-handed with the fiddly fastenings. "That clause again, Aela, my proficient woman? Get rid of these clothes for us."

"Nairn?"

She clearly wasn't going to deny him anything as she unbuttoned his shirt first and slid it off his shoulders.

"I can't wait any longer to lie next to you, Aela, even though we're not going to have mind blowing sex."

"We're not?" She looked ready to capitulate even though she was beyond shattered.

"No. Tonight we need to sleep together in the proper sense. Please don't say no because I need to wrap myself around you."

"I'm saying nothing, Nairn."

They crept into bed naked, Nairn cuddled around her, sort of, as much as his lighter leg cast would allow. "Aela?"

"Mmm…" Her sleepy response accompanied a directed wiggle.

"Not sure I can ignore that."

"Then don't."

***

Aela woke up before Nairn, just short of the six a.m. alarm chirp. There was no doubt at all in her mind now that she wanted to be with this incredible man on whatever terms he was willing to make, for as long as he wanted her. She denied it no longer. She loved him. Had for weeks; probably right from the very first stolen kiss. Or maybe even earlier.

Nairn snored a little whiff into her neck as she detached herself and slipped out of bed. She was showering when she heard him call out he was going up to his own room and would be ready to head out in fifteen minutes. Her tuneless whistling filled the shower cabinet as she rinsed the suds from her hair, thinking of the huge bed in the master bedroom suite and the fabulous shower stall, big enough for two.

A girl could dream.

Fifteen minutes later her suitcase was packed with a combination of business gear and casual items from her neglected backpack.

The burr of her cell phone stirred her from her introspection. Nairn.

I need you.

A grin broke free seeing the brief text message. Was he luring her up to his lair? Or was it just that sneaky little clause again? Didn't matter. He needed her. Didn't just want her – he needed her. Such a small change of word, but she put a wealth of meaning into it.

Clothes were strewn all over the bed, again, items he'd yanked from his dressing room rails, but packing them into his case had still proved a setback. Avoiding his straying fingers and lips she packed for him, telling him to behave.

"Heaven's above! Why am I such a workaholic? Why don't we just stay at home?"

"You're paying me to help you be one, Nairn Malcolm, so keep your clever fingers to yourself, and let me get us out of here."

Her laughs and smiles he reciprocated, but groaned at her bossiness as she swept up the case and made for the door. He caught her before she got very far. "You're a torture, woman. Why did I pick such a competent assistant? You should just agree with me and let me have my evil way with you."

Aela let his kiss deepen till she herself could stand it no longer, easing herself away and urging him to move on. "You're the one who made the decision about this trip. I'm going to do my bit now, sir, and get you there on time." She gently pushed him into the spanking new lift, softening her jokey chastising by dangling a neat little carrot. "Get your butt in there and keep your pants zipped. For the time being behave, and if you're a good boss man, I'll maybe give you a kiss tonight."

"Tonight?" Nairn's grimace told her what he thought about her plan before he snatched another kiss in the few seconds it took for the lift to descend. "You're a witch. Tonight is far too long away."

They were down to Glasgow and then on to London in good time for their long haul jet, piloted by Nairn's charter service. The connecting flights had been text book easy so it wasn't too arduous for her to launch straight into the arrangements for the coming business.

Any brushing of hands or eye contact wasn't inadvertent at all. It warmed her thoroughly for she craved even that small measure of contact. Sometimes it was more. Nairn couldn't seem to stop himself from taking lingering kisses in between explaining the details.

"Romala Hotels are building new complexes all over the Caribbean and doing corporate image refurbishing in most of the existing ones they've gathered into their portfolio. They'd heard about the package I put together for the first Malaysian deal, liked what I'd done and since they're looking for something similar their agent contacted me to suggest I put in this bid. It's a tight schedule for you to learn it all, but here's how we're going to do it..."

As Nairn continued she beamed at his use of 'we'. A figure of speech, but it bonded them even more as they worked on the presentation. His fingers often lingered on hers as he passed some documentation for her perusal. Or his eyes would seek her out and loiter when a question occurred. Or when she needed clarification on some particular point she, in turn, really just wanted to watch his lips explain it further.

"Go and lie down, Aela," Nairn cajoled when she felt her head droop for the third time. He was taking a call from Lanera and she was ostensibly ready to take any notes. "There's nothing I can't manage myself here."

It wasn't a curt dismissal: his smile was concerned about her welfare. Caving in she lay down on the neat little aeroplane bed.

The feel of Nairn's lips on her brow stirred her, her eyes fluttering open. So comfortable, pillowed in the crook of his good arm. When he'd joined her wasn't important; he was wrapped around her and that was all that mattered. Nairn's silent gaze warmed and rippled all the way through her; it spoke of fast and furious sex in the future but not right that moment. She let herself drift again knowing her smile was happy; more than a little bit smug.

It was a short hop from the airport on St.Vincent, to a nearby island, since she had booked them into the same hotel where the meeting was being held.

She was itching to have her fingers on the controls of the small plane. A little way below them the Caribbean glistened, the water taking on darker hues of blues and deep greys as dusk descended. The setting sun, almost vanished for the day, cast a strip of golden flame across the lightly rippling waves; a few ethereal cirrus clouds hovered alongside the blazing orb their edges backlit with white-hot fire. A deep excitement built as Nairn's thumb caressed lazy circles on her sensitive lifelines.

197

Their hotel complex was even more stunning than it had looked in the internet advertising, each villa having its own discreet butler service. She gulped at the decadence of their stone-built villa: the outside dining gazebo itself a fabulous structure. She hadn't realised just how much of a romantic getaway it was.

When the beaming porter introduced the accommodation it wasn't quite what she thought she'd reserved. There was only one bedroom with a super king-size bed and a convertible couch in the living area. Although they'd shared a bed the night before, and on the airplane, she didn't feel comfortable. No way did she want Nairn to think she'd set it up.

Nairn ushered the porter to the door, pressing a large tip into the man's hand, stating they'd need no further butler service at present.

"Aela, it's perfect." Nairn avowed when the porter's back retreated from view.

Quite a while later, his grin was as wide as it was exhausted. "You are the absolute best general factotum that I've ever had. You must have practised a lot."

"Twice."

"Only twice? I don't believe you."

A languorous Aela nudged his good arm. "Not literally twice, but I've only had a couple of lovers over the years."

"How come so few? You're so beautiful I can't believe lots of men haven't tempted you into the sack." His lips pecked at her neck.

"Oh, plenty tempted me, but Jed scared them off. Guess I chose badly, since the ones I had sex with were only interested in getting to home base with no detours, and weren't interested in the cheerleader getting a thrill." She laughed at the memories.

Nairn's fingers stiffened against hers.

"Jed?"

"My cousin, Jed." She was miffed he'd not been listening the night they'd made the sail back to Lanera since she was sure she'd spoken about Jed quite a lot.

Nairn seemed confused. "Jed's your cousin? The one you grew up with?"

She nodded back wondering what had led to the misunderstanding. "Yes, my Uncle Harris is Jed's dad. I told you."

Nairn captured her lips in an addictive kiss before he eventually broke off, a grin emphasising his relief. "No, actually you just kept referring to your cousin. You never named him Jed."

"Well, in a nutshell, Jed's my protective cousin who's only a year older than me. He takes the family thing too seriously, was the older brother I never had, scaring off wannabe adventurers he didn't like the look of. I wasn't too bothered since all through my teens I was happy being a tomboy. I wasn't pushing for a relationship with anyone."

"Aela!" Nairn gurgled, "Never in a million years could you be a tomboy!"

"I'll have you know I was a very successful tomboy. I told you I didn't do girly stuff with females. I grew up so tall I wasn't like them anyway. I was always mooching around the hangars. My mates, all boys of course, and I went around like a pack of jackals feeding on the older pilots and maintenance crew. Their knowledge was our quarry. They fed us well with know how till it was time for us to be trained up ourselves, when we were old enough."

"Okay, I believe you about that." Nairn's expression still didn't look too convinced about the rest.

"The guys made passes, but they knew I meant business when I rejected their overtures." Her laugh in his ear was a full blown guffaw as she deliberately held eye contact with him. "Jed taught me well, so you'd better watch out, Nairn Malcolm."

"You'd assault me?" His teasing query raised her eyebrows.

"I wouldn't kick a lame man when he's down..."

She didn't get to finish as his fingers tickled her ribs and set her squirming.

"Your pathetic story, woman. I really want to hear it."

"Okay, Okay. I was almost twenty before I launched myself onto the sex scene. I was tired of being the only virgin student around. I guess I felt it was time."

Nairn's grip tightened protectively around her. "It should only be time if it's what pushes your buttons."

"Yeah, well. In retrospect you're so damn right. My buttons weren't pushed in the slightest."

Chapter Twenty-One

Just short of noon, they headed to the lunchtime venue, Aela compensating for Nairn's cradle and walking like a three-legged race.

"Whoa! Did you see that woman?"

Nairn stopped at an intersection of pathways and whipped around so quickly her laptop case slipped from her grip. She hadn't a clue who he was talking about since there were plenty of scantily clad women around to claim his attention.

"The redhead skipping along there." Nairn pointed along a pathway to the side of them.

"No, I didn't see her, sir. I was far too busy supporting you."

She gave a playful punch at his good arm, but he was still staring at the pathway the woman had taken. Slipping from his hold, she stood right in front of him. "Nairn? Are you chasing another skirt already?"

Nairn came out of his reverie, his full focus on her. "Don't be daft, woman. I'm never ever going to get enough of you." He kissed her lingeringly then clutched her hand and shook his head as though to clear his thoughts. "It was nothing like that at all."

She forced full eye contact with a still mystified Nairn. "So, what then?"

"It looked like Stella Grainger."

"Stella? Assistant Manager of Adrenalinn Adventuring?"

Nairn nodded.

"Why on earth would she be here?" she queried, and then shushed his muttering. "She must just remind you of Stella."

"I hope to God it's true, Aela. Although you've yet to meet Stella, I regret ever employing her. The woman's a menace."

"A menace?" She was shocked since he usually had only good things to say about his workforce.

Nairn scraped back the hair from his brow and cursed. Loud enough to cause a flutter of birds to rise from the nearest tree and an older woman nearby to give him a non-verbal glaring reprimand. "Let's just say she came on to me almost from the first meeting after she was hired on. I made it clear at the time I wasn't interested in dating her, but the woman's a piranha. Every time she had to update me, she'd slink into my office and try some more."

Her giggle made him frown.

"You don't believe me?"

"I truly believe you. How could she not want to seduce you? You're a gorgeous man. That's what Robin Ellesmere was alluding to?"

He swatted her backside to move her on along the pathway. "Yep. On a business trip to some sites in Northern Europe she claimed her room had been double-booked and she'd need to share my suite, even though she knew the second room was already occupied by Brian."

Her smile was fit to break her jaw. "She never did. So unbelievable." A little niggle told her she'd done something similar with their present booking, but it was convenient to ignore it.

"Don't I know it? The stupid woman was miffed when I rebuffed her for the umpteenth time. Brian thought it the most hilarious thing ever." Nairn was exasperated even telling her the story.

"What happened then?" She could only imagine how awkward the trip had been.

"I got her a room in another hotel and only met up with her when strictly necessary. You can imagine how that went down like a gas-less balloon."

"Just forget the woman and concentrate on this bid."

She put his mind at rest by squirming under his shoulder

and set them off down the path to the designated meeting place in the central complex building.

**

Though Nairn felt his deal seemed favourable, the client made it clear no final decisions would be made till other personnel were consulted. A second meeting was called for the following morning at ten. He'd anticipated hitches; the reason he'd stipulated a hotel stay of three nights when Aela was booking. Using the hotel's business centre work sucked them in till dinner. His customary dogged dedication to business stretched him to the absolute limit but truth be told, he just wanted to relax with Aela and do…almost nothing.

The restaurant was just as excellent as the one the previous evening, a mariachi band entertaining them as they wended their way around the tables. He felt an unaccustomed feeling of utter contentment: good food, good wine, but best of all, Aela. In his mind there was no question. She mattered to him.

Conversation was spattered with questions about each others travels as they filled in details unknown about each other until they sipped the last of their wine on an outside terrace. They watched the water softly lap on the beach and listened to the sounds of the Caribbean, some manufactured and many of them the natural animal sounds around them. In the warm cocooning darkness, they didn't talk at all for a while. Feeling so at one with Aela his fingers caressed hers as she nestled into the crook of his good arm. Then, inspired by their surroundings, he related experiences he'd had at beach locations around the world, encouraging Aela to add her own.

Inevitably the narratives took on the proportions of angler's tales where they landed whoppers – except in both cases they had had the hair-raising experiences they related.

"I think I did a quadruple flip…"

"Whoa! Time for a respite, Nairn Malcolm, Adrenalinn Adventurer. Too much information for a wimp like me. You could have broken your neck. This wakeboarding sounds too scary for words."

Wakeboarding, he told her, wasn't provided for on their present island, the wave quality not generally available in that part of the Caribbean. He got the impression Aela was relieved to hear it.

"Stop! Toilet break before you go on any more." She slipped away from him.

***

Aela recapped Nairn's daring experiences as she wended her way to the nearest ladies room. Deep auburn hair joined her dark hair in the wide mirror as she approached the vanity basins. The woman glanced away, in the way total strangers often do, before she shook off her hands and scuttled for the nearby hand dryer, her head in profile.

Aela washed her hands, very slowly, as she observed the stranger. There was something she recognised, and it wasn't just that the woman had very eye-catching, long and curling deep red hair. Her profile was distinctive. She had a slightly hooked nose, wide plump lips and her eyebrows were plucked to the point of almost being non-existent, which made her eye sockets seem larger than they really were.

That was it!

Aela bent her head, squelching the bile-ridden anxiety rushing up from her gut. Stalling till the redhead exited the ladies, she then made her own slow departure. The woman had been glancing back towards the toilet door, she could tell from the angled bounce of the long hair, though the woman was now darting around the corner.

She needed to see the woman's face again, a full-front view. It might just be that she was imagining too much.

At the corner, her circumspect peek was just in time to see the woman enter the Piano Bar. She crept along to the nearest window. Though small, the bar was heaving as patrons sat or stood around conversing over the trill of soft piano playing.

The redhead approached a guy seated opposite the door, her lingering kiss an almost frantic clutching, the interaction indicating familiarity. Aela gasped when she glimpsed the man's face. Earnest talking and nodding to the entrance door of the bar followed as the woman squeezed down beside him. She surveyed their intent conversation for a few minutes. Both looked bothered: upset and angry.

What the hell was going on?

She sped back to Nairn, her mind in turmoil. "Back to the villa," she whispered all but dragging him away.

Laughing at her haste Nairn complied till he realised it wasn't because she was dragging him back to their villa to make mad passionate love to him. "What's wrong?"

"Not here!" She hauled him along the walkway.

By the time Nairn hobbled the short distance to the villa she knew he was spooked by the darting looks she'd been making over her shoulder.

"What's got you in such a tizzy, Aela?"

Standing between his spread legs she cuddled him, her words seeping into his shirt. "You were right. The redhead is Stella!"

"Stella Grainger? But you haven't met her, how can you know it's her?"

She lifted her head to face him. "A redheaded woman came into the ladies. She didn't recognise me. Though…" She reflected on how quickly the woman had turned away from her at the vanity, and then the darting looks the woman had made to the door of the Piano Bar. "Maybe she did? I'm not sure. But I recognised her."

"I'm too thick, Aela. You're not making sense."

"Nairn, she's the woman on the surveillance video in the Glasgow hotel car park. I'm sure of it."

"What?"

"It's the eyebrows. She's got very distinctive eyebrows, almost plucked to nothing, and she's got a very noticeable hooked nose."

When confronted with that information Nairn had to agree. "But the woman in the car park had short hair,

205

nothing like Stella's mane."

She grabbed his hand and linked fingers. "Had to be a wig. But that's not all. I followed her to the Piano Bar. Nairn. Her companion was the man we met today. She was all over him, and their kisses were familiar."

"Hold on. Which guy are we talking about?"

She knew her information was getting weirder by the second. "Remember when we finished the client meeting? We left the room and were still talking ten to the dozen when we rounded the corner?"

"Sure. The short guy you knocked over didn't appreciate his file folder being tipped out, didn't appreciate you being so pumped up with excitement over what we'd achieved."

"I'm sure he's the guy the redhead met in the bar."

"And?"

"Nairn. Think! Our meeting was in a private room hired by our client. Most people come here for leisure, and don't wear business suits, or carry business paraphernalia like that guy."

Nairn said he couldn't fault her logic.

"I helped pick up his papers then he went into the room we had just vacated."

"You're thinking he was a competitor who had an appointment after us?"

"Yes."

"Connected to Stella Grainger?"

Unfortunately, they both agreed the man seen at lunchtime was nothing like the one who had tampered with Nairn's bike. That guy had been a tall beanpole. The one at lunchtime, no more than five feet eight or nine, was stocky.

But, if she was correct, the implications were horrible. The culprit of Nairn's mishaps was right on their doorstep – Stella Grainger. What kind of trap were they in? Her head bent to his chest again, her palms making gentle circles round his spine.

Nairn had difficulty believing it could be Stella Grainger. "Too far fetched. Why would she be here?"

What did the woman have to gain by following Nairn to

the Caribbean? She herself had made the booking the night before they left, and no-one at his London office knew they were coming to the Caribbean. Prior knowledge of Nairn being on the island didn't seem plausible, or make any sense.

Or, she wondered, was it the man who'd lured Stella to the Caribbean?

"How can we find out if it really is Stella?"

"Mike Van Heyden might know who the guy is."

Their questions overlapped each other.

Aela let Nairn explain.

"Mike Van Heyden was initially bidding for this contract as well. He's snowed under with work. I heard he'd withdrawn, though he might be aware of who else is still bidding."

Nairn reached for his mobile.

Mike, a friendly rival of Nairn, told them two other companies were still in the running. Nairn knew one, though not the other.

Short of ten p.m. local Caribbean time, almost two a.m. in London, Nairn dialled his office, knowing someone was always on duty. He was delighted to find Ginny was working night shift. Aela hugged him tight to listen in. He had to stay safe. Even if she became the target again she was determined Nairn would not come to any more harm.

The news was disturbing. Stella Grainger had tendered her resignation three days previously, and hadn't appeared at work since then. Robin hadn't contacted Nairn about it since he'd guessed Nairn would be glad to see the back of the woman. Where she was now was anybody's guess.

She stopped Nairn's agitated pacing by the best method she knew. The kiss to soothe soon became one of desperation. Aela felt awed by the strength of her feelings for the man wrapped around her, a man of integrity she knew didn't deserve any of what had happened to him. Gradually frantic became calm, their foreheads nudging as her heartbeats regulated.

"Can we check Stella's whereabouts on the days of the

incidents?" she asked.

Stella hadn't been in the London office on the day of Nairn's motorbike accident, no real surprise since it was a Saturday, but she had been present when the other incidents had occurred.

"Where was she working before she came to Adrenalinn Adventuring?"

"It'll be on her file." Nairn vaguely remembered Stella telling him she'd worked as an events coordinator in a hotel.

"That's why she was hired, then? If she'd a background in the leisure industry?"

"Yes. She'd good experience organising events and activities."

"Did she worked for a British employer?"

Nairn couldn't recall, but he'd a feeling it was an international chain. Grabbing her hand he dragged her to their laptops. "We need to go back to the business centre."

Chapter Twenty-Two

A short delay ensued till the business centre was opened up for them. Once their connections were organised, Nairn's searches began. Typing one-handed on his laptop, the fingertips of his broken arm punched numbers into his mobile. Connection made he switched hands to lift his phone to his ear.

"Hello again, Ginny."

Nairn's smile broke the tension Aela hadn't realised was gripping them. Nairn requested Ginny access Stella's personnel records. Brief conversation. Succinct.

"Won't Ginny think it odd us asking for this information? Can you trust her?"

"Absolutely! Ginny's tight lipped about everything. She knows I'd only ask for something like this if it's really important."

Nairn declared he'd look up details of the other two competitors for the current Caribbean bid.

A short while later Ginny had emailed the information – a crushing disappointment since it seemed they'd gone down the wrong line of inquiry. Stella had never worked for either of Nairn's two competitors.

Her mood improved though when she looked at Nairn's information. "The outfit you'd never heard of before is based in Miami. I know Miami is huge, and it might be another red-herring, but it's the same location as Stella's last employer."

They passed on their hunches to Detective Woods, Ginny having been asked to locate a photograph of Stella and e-mail it to the police department. Till further investigations were made, they could do nothing else. She wasn't surprised when Nairn declared he would attend the next meeting with the client, regardless of the proximity of the maniac who'd put him in plaster, and who'd likely also harmed her. In spite of whatever machinations Stella Grainger and her accomplice were up to, Nairn told her he was going to win the contract fair and square…or not at all. She had no qualms about that, or with any of his plans.

Paranoid though it might seem Nairn insisted they breakfast on the fruit which was already in their villa. They drank the canned fruit juice from their mini fridge and used the coffee filter-machine provided. He wouldn't risk anything being tampered with if they ordered room service, and he'd no plans to leave their suite too early. They remained constantly vigilant till it was time to meet with the client at ten a.m.

At the meeting he clarified a few more points in his bid with the Marketing Director and reviewed the pricing structure. Again it seemed the meeting went well, though the results were not expected immediately.

"Shall I book the next available flight to St. Vincent?" Aela asked as they returned to their villa.

Nairn squeezed her arm, the arm he was already clamped onto. "No, my workaholic P.A. We're not budging our asses from this island. We both need rest. We're booked in for one more night, and we're staying one more night, regardless of Stella Grainger and her sabotage." He laughed at her raised eyebrows. "We'll still watch our backs."

Of course their rest period only started after they checked in with both police departments. No developments yet was a disappointment, but not unexpected. Contact with the London office was brief. Afterwards he surprised Aela by declaring an afternoon holiday, though their phones would remain switched on.

"I bet you've never taken a real holiday in ages, Nairn Malcolm."

She teased him as she whipped off her clothes, to his utter delight. Shrugging into a bikini, she skipped out to the pool leaving him shouting his frustration as he lounged on the bed.

Deciding to eat out that evening took some deliberation but since there was no way he was going to entertain anyone delivering poisoned food, he reckoned it safest to be random patrons at the first restaurant they came to. They walked along the widest and most well lit paths and took every care they could, seating themselves amongst the throng rather than being on the periphery. He didn't want to even glimpse Stella Grainger again…or her sidekick.

Back at their villa, he concluded if Stella had been maliciously trying to stop him from winning the present bid then the danger phase had to be over. It was incredulous to believe Stella would have gone to such devious lengths to prevent him from being successful with the Romala Corporation.

Nairn woke first, determined that the beautiful woman in his clutches would never be free of him. While Aela slept on, he contacted hotel reception and arranged a surprise for her.

"Get up, lazybones!" He greeted her from the side of the bed, bouncing a pillow at her head. "You are so beautiful, and you tempt me so much but…"

"You're dressed already? Why didn't you wait for me to wash your hair properly?" Her hands reached out and fingered his dripping locks since all he was able to do was dunk his head in the washbasin.

"No, Aela Cameron. I'm not going to be diverted by your fabulous hands. Get up. It's time to rise."

"Slave driver." She scrabbled to her feet and headed for the shower. "Who are we meeting now?"

"Nobody." He followed, unable to resist patting her bare behind. "Dress comfortable casual. Shorts would be good, bikini underneath and wear your soft sneakers, not flip flops."

"Such orders, sir. Going to brush and braid my hair too?"

The noise of the shower drowned his mumbled threats of

211

exactly what he'd be doing with her when his casts were gone.

"Promises! Promises!" Aela chirped, and reached for the soap.

A few minutes later she joined him at their Gazebo table, her glass of juice already poured, since he knew that was how she preferred to start her day. "Given the choice, what would you most like to do today, since we have six hours before we head back to Barbados for our London flight?"

As Aela pondered he hoped and prayed he'd read her correctly over the days he'd known her. Her pretended huff was spoiled by her big grin. "My first choice would be to jump back into bed and...."

The smirk he felt spreading across his face wasn't discouraged by her waving finger.

"No, no, not that. You made me get up, so my next choice would be to spend some time flying over these fabulous islands, over this sparkling sea and discover the delights of the landscape from a little way up. Absolute heaven and a total dream, I know, but you did ask."

Nairn pulled her onto his one good knee and put his arm around her. "How about we go for a limp on the beach instead."

Aela didn't look disappointed; she actually looked eager to join him in a lurching hobble. "Good plan. Let's hop the sands."

As they walked the length of their infinity pool he heard the approaching drone of a seaplane engine. It coasted to a halt in front of them.

Aela looked suspicious as she turned to confront him. "You didn't?"

Her glee was unmistakable when he simply replied, "I did."

Her answering whoop and bear hug almost toppled him but it had been worth it to see her delight.

A magical few hours were spent exploring the area, Aela having had a fast induction from the pilot who handed over to her, giving her details for local flying. Nairn itched to get at the controls himself but the next best thing ever was to have Aela fly him around. His competent woman of many talents. He now loved them all. He bided his time though. She wasn't quite ready yet for him to declare his intentions.

Nairn's cell phone chimed.

"Answer that for me, Aela?" he mumbled as he wielded his battery driven razor. Packing almost completed, they were readying to leave.

Aela popped her head inside the bathroom door and relayed the call was from New York. An established client of his on the Eastern seaboard wanted further water sports upgrades, an extension to the order of kayaks successfully supplied only six months previously.

"Great news. Tell him we'll detour to New York tonight and meet up with him tomorrow." He grinned at her.

"Excuse me a moment, please."

He heard Aela respond to his client before she put down his phone and scooted back to the bathroom door. Her next words were a stage whisper at him. "Nairn Malcolm! Do you ever stick to travel arrangements already made?"

"No sense in going all the way home to come back to the Big Apple in a couple of days." He repositioned the razor for a different angle of sweep to get under his raspy chin. "The order will be signed off after one meeting. Make it eleven a.m., at his New York office, if that's good for him."

He continued shaving, leaving her to arrange it, and was haphazardly packing up when she returned with an update.

"Client can't make eleven, asked for nine. I know it's early, but I agreed it since it's the only time he can make it tomorrow. Otherwise it would have to be three days from now as he's heading off somewhere."

"Good thinking." His good hand smoothed on his shaving cooler, the woodsy smell redolent of lime and cedar Aela seemed to love so much she couldn't resist a little sniff, followed by a peck at his cheek.

"Will you be staying at your New York apartment, or shall I book somewhere else for you?" She pulled away from him before he could start something they didn't now have time for.

"The apartment." He grabbed her and kissed her soundly. "Call my housekeeping service and have it made ready. Number's in my phone. They'll freshen it up and stock the refrigerator."

"Did I tell you I've never been to New York?"

Aela grinned as she bracketed her hands on his cheeks, forcing his attention. His blue eyes lingered on her lips.

"Are you going to tease me this time about whether or not I'm coming?"

"You're definitely coming. And you're sleeping in my bed."

This time their kiss lasted a lot longer. Aela's sensory system kicked up in anticipation, but practicality ruled as she teased herself away from his clutches. She felt the whispering touch of his hand trailing a pathway down her long hair, grasping it back to him, sniffing its fragrance.

"You're definitely my Snow White," he murmured, soft and sexily. "I love...your hair!"

Aela's heart blipped then slowly regained its rhythm. She thought he'd been going to say something else. They were having a fabulous affair but that's all it was. If she was lucky, for a few more days. Gulping down a difficult breath she sidled well away from him, her hair eventually dropping from his light grasp.

"We'll stay for three days. I've nothing really urgent on the calendar, have I?"

"You always have something urgent, Nairn Malcolm."

"I certainly do, but I don't want you driving me around New York. Order my usual limo service."

"Don't you trust my driving, Nairn Malcolm?"

"Aela, I don't even trust myself driving in New York. New York drivers scare the shenanigans out of me."

"I don't think anything ever scares you, Nairn."

"You'd be surprised." His look was...odd. Wistful... almost sad.

Chapter Twenty-Three

The insistent trill of the alarm startled both of them from deep slumber.

"Shall I book your ride now?" Aela mumbled a few minutes later as she slurped down a quick coffee from the drip machine that had been pre-programmed. Propped up against the countertop in her underwear, she'd had a really quick shower, but Nairn was still stumbling around naked in a sleepy daze. Yet even with plaster casts he was the most gorgeous hunk of man she'd ever clapped eyes on. It had taken such a short time for her to be comfortable with him. The coffee suddenly tasted vile.

His answer was dozy as he cradled his coffee mug. "Sure. So long as you come and help me button up quickly." He toddled off to the bathroom to wash and dress, yawning so widely Aela wanted to join in. He really didn't need her help anymore but still insisted on it.

As Nairn expected the client meeting was straightforward, brief. Her job was easy as Nairn negotiated a good price which would net a sizeable profit. His office was their next stop. Twenty-seven stories up in a huge tower block it was only one large room. Two out of five desks were currently being manned, the staff of five servicing the office on a 24-7 basis. She appropriated an empty desk opposite Nairn, and for the first time in days they had to be circumspect. Employer and employee.

Her glance strayed to the other two women, wondering if they could sense the attraction she constantly felt radiating between her and her boss. Nairn, she was glad to see, could compartmentalise because he didn't seem to find it too much of a strain as he caught up with a lot of USA news first, then he went global.

Around three-thirty p.m. he looked up from the pile of correspondence he'd been consistently working through. Catching her glance, he fingered a card on heavy vellum he'd just removed from an envelope. She wasn't sure how to interpret the little smirk sneaking around his mouth.

"Shania?" Nairn's enquiry sounded slothful as he turned to the woman who dealt with his Adrenalinn Adventuring business. "Is there anything in particular you need my physical input on tomorrow?"

"Nope." the young woman replied, shaking her neat bob of dark hair. "We've had no problems with any of our bookings recently, and since we didn't expect you to be here I've no appointments made for you."

"Great!"

Nairn's return smile looked decisive. Aela watched him close down his laptop then he added paperwork to his carry case. "Tomorrow, Miss Cameron and I are going to do some sightseeing."

"We're going sightseeing?" She wondered if his declaration had just catapulted her into some category which wasn't quite P.A., but since he was preparing to leave the office she packed up her own gear. "What do you think you'll be able to cope with, Mr. Malcolm?"

"Don't be so dismissive, Miss Cameron. I'm game for a lot of things I'll have you know."

She bit her lip to prevent the huge satisfied smirk she wanted to produce. Didn't she know what he was capable of? Squelching the truthful comment she answered, "Like what, sir?"

"How about we do New York by City Tour bus? Or maybe a boat on the Hudson? Something not involving a walk and I'll be fine."

He smirked as he shoved a pile of unwanted paperwork into the recycling bin beside him, and then turned to his employees.

"As these fine workers will tell you I've not often been to

the New York office, and I've not done much in the way of sightseeing myself."

"You're having me on," she quipped, preparing to leave. Her flashing eyes dared him to deny her words. "You spent a year at Harvard Business School. You're not going to tell me you didn't take a few little body swerves from Cambridge to New York."

"Ah, but way back then my priorities weren't sightseeing, Miss Cameron."

Nairn's cheeky answer and laughing eyes made her blush. He rose a bit clumsily, rebalanced his cradled foot, clutched the vellum card in his hand, and made his farewells short and sweet. "I'll see you two ladies next time I'm back this side of the Atlantic."

She gathered up their belongings and held the door open.

"Back to my apartment first, Miss Cameron. I've a dinner engagement tonight." His announcement was accompanied by a jaunty wave of the card.

"If that's what I think it is, Nairn, have fun!" Shania called to his retreating back as Aela made her rapid goodbyes.

At the bank of lifts she pressed the button to summon a car. "You have a dinner engagement tonight?" She hoped her reply didn't sound as unenthusiastic as she felt.

"Yes." Nairn's smile was inscrutable.

"A business dinner?"

"Not exactly." His appraisal of her mouth was becoming more interesting by the second.

"Nairn Malcolm, you are so maddening when you do that!" She gently nudged his good arm.

"Do what?" His question was innocent as he snuggled up close.

"Innocent you aren't!" Her tone chastised but also showed she loved his teasing. "Do I need to do anything for you?" She groaned at the thought of maybe having to be his chauffeur. He couldn't possibly be squiring around some beautiful woman he'd pre-invited? Could he?

"Just look your beautiful self, Aela."

The lift was full of crushed bodies. Their conversation halted till they reached the lobby of the building. She took up the threads again as they went out to flag a taxi. "That was no answer, Nairn. Is it business dress, or casual?" She waited but no answer followed. "Black tie?"

"Definitely black tie, Aela."

"How exactly am I supposed to produce that for you at such short notice?"

"I've a tuxedo at my apartment. Don't fuss about it." Nairn's chuckle deafened her ear as he leaned over to smooch at her neck. He refused to say more as they piled into a cab: seven New York blocks way too much for his hobbling.

"How long before you have to leave?" She stifled a sleepy yawn as she placed their laptops on the dining room table after reaching his apartment.

"Before we have to leave. You'll attend this event too, you lovely woman."

Nairn grabbed her round the waist and nestled into her neck. Pulling out the band securing her topknot he fingered her ebony soft hair.

"I've been dying to do that all day. And this..." he murmured, nuzzling behind her ear.

"How long, Nairn?"

Aela set her alarm for six p.m. knowing if she fell asleep they'd be snookered, and tumbled onto the bed. Nairn was already there.

***

Nairn looked up from the dress shirt he attempted to button. Aela was a vision in a barely there floaty gown of blue-green. The one shouldered creation was beaded here and there, emphasising her cleavage. It cinched in at her narrow waist then shimmered to her ankles, just above a pair of extremely high delicate shoes.

She was stunning.

"Aela." His voice croaked as he reached for her. "You're

218

so beautiful you steal my breath. I don't know how you do it but you surprise me every day. You are one hell of a competent woman."

His reverent kiss could have escalated into much more if Aela hadn't drawn back with a chuckle and stepped away from his reaching arms.

"Time to go, lover. You agreed to this dinner engagement so let's get on with it."

"Okay, but you're a selfish woman to deny me so. My fingers are worse than useless now. Look at them shaking with sexual frustration." He waved them laughingly in front of her, tendering his gold cufflinks. "You're going to have to satisfy that little clause again."

"Get on with you, Nairn Malcolm." She chided further as she buttoned him up, allowing him only the tiniest peck on her cheek as she yanked him into the tuxedo which was stretched to the limit over his casts.

He knew exactly what he wanted to get on with. Once again she absolutely floored him. He'd expected her to wear the little red dress she'd worn in the Middle East, but like a conjuror she'd produced the incredible gown she was now wearing. When had she had the opportunity to shop? His demands on her time had made it seem impossible.

"Where did you produce this sexy dress from?"

"I'll maybe tell you later." His bow tie was fastened in a blink.

***

Aela glanced around the New York venue: a room full of splendidly attired patrons. Nairn introduced her as his partner, followed with a by the way she's also my PA and chauffeur. A warm glow settled around her heart. It had more of a permanent ring to it since the word temporary didn't feature.

Her impulse purchases in Barcelona were perfect for the glittering occasion. Dinner was tasty if not ground-breaking exciting, Aela finding it easy to relax as she conversed with

219

people nearby. After the meal was cleared and the charity pledging over, soft music filled the room.

"Dance with me?" Nairn's head indicated the already jam-packed dance floor.

His request made her hoot as she pointed to his leg cast. "You can't dance, Nairn."

"Then let's shuffle." Dragging her from the seat he towed her onto the dance floor and held her tight. Swaying, just swaying, to the slow, sexy jazz throb. "I couldn't wait to feel your arms around me, Aela. You're driving me crazy, you lovely woman."

His lips hovered around her ear, close but not quite touching since it was a very formal event. Nairn's groan almost deafened her.

"This was a big mistake. I can't do it."

"I told you so! I knew it would be too much for you." Aela's scold was softened by her quick peck on his cheek.

"Sway-dancing's not the problem. Holding you like this is too much. Get me out of here, please."

Tourist pursuits were the order of the following day. The hop-on-hop-off City Tour bus was lazily perfect for more than four hours. This time they did a little bit of hopping. Stopped off to take in a few of the well known sites up close. Ate hot dogs from a street vendor. Lapped up rapidly dripping ices in the early July heat.

Much more exciting though was their speedboat ride on 'The Beast' which whizzed on the Hudson, Aela having had to work really hard and grease a few palms to convince the pilot Nairn really was capable of coping with the ride. She wondered what could top it after their trip was over, but Nairn wasn't yet done because they finished up with a tourist helicopter ride over the city at dusk.

Breathtaking.

They collapsed back into the apartment clutching a Chinese take out meal, since eating out at some fabulous New York restaurant had long since palled. All she wanted was to be on their own, away from the incredible crowds and the inevitable jostling Nairn had had to put up with.

Later, they were tucked up in bed and languidly watching a movie, a refreshingly cold dry white wine sitting in a cooler beside them. The peal of his phone was unwelcome, but it had to be important. Only on pain of death had the office been given leave to call. Reaching over for it, Nairn groaned when he glanced at caller ID. "Only a call from Detective Woods will make me answer right now."

Aela shifted out of his arms so that he could answer properly. Pouring some white wine, she watched his face as he received an update.

"You picked Stella up at Heathrow Immigration?"

One sided conversations were frustrating. She read between the lines as the call continued till Nairn slid his body up and sat with his back propped against the wall. Curving in alongside him, she listened when he flicked the volume higher.

Detective Woods explained further. "It appears she was so unnerved by bumping into Miss Cameron at the resort that she scurried back to London."

Nairn asked, "And the man was with her?"

"No, sir," Detective Woods answered. "Her fiancé went back to Miami, apparently very disappointed in Grainger. Claimed she'd bungled very badly since you'd made it to the interviews. Apparently, they'd been confident you weren't going to make it to the Caribbean."

"This guy, John Sanders, is her fiancé?"

"Correct, sir. Grainger and Sanders both worked for the same employer in Miami, till around nine months ago. Their relationship fizzled out when Sanders decided to strike out and create his own company. His aim was to acquire contracts for hotel water sports upgrades, much like you've been bidding for, sir."

"Stella Grainger returned to the UK?"

"So she informs us, sir."

"Not particularly supportive, was she?" Nairn's question was scathing.

Detective Woods sounded a derisive. "It appears from her

statement the lady in question was interested in having a financially sound future, Mr. Malcolm."

It was no surprise to Aela that she had targeted Nairn as her future well-heeled husband.

Detective Woods related that months passed before Sanders took up with her again while he was in London on business. By then Nairn had rejected Stella's advances many times and she'd thought she was on a hiding to nothing with him.

"Sanders managed to convince Grainger his company was thriving, and would soon be rolling in big money if he got the Romala contract," Detective Woods explained.

Nairn's voice was glacial. "What made the nasty bitch decide to take revenge on me?" Aela heard Detective Wood's voice catch a little at Nairn's vehemence.

"Sanders heard about the Romala Hotels possibility at the same time you did, and he regarded you as his only competition." The detective continued making a clear attempt not to sound judgmental. "It appears Miss Grainger liked the idea of Sanders making the profit, rather than you."

Again Detective Woods intentionally cleared his throat before continuing. "During her confession she was very happy to tell us you continually spurned her advances." Aela could almost hear admiration in Detective Woods voice. "A determined woman, sir."

Beside her Nairn grunted into the phone. "She's a bloody piranha!"

"Beautiful sir, but somewhat deadly I have to concur."

Aela could tell Detective Woods was quite enjoying the conversation though still careful to keep within the bounds of professional conduct.

"What about my bike accident? And the other incidents?"

"She has confessed to messing up orders; organising the computer virus; setting the fire; and later on paying someone to sabotage the electricity supply. She was most put out that those delaying tactics didn't have the effects she wanted, because she thought you would be too busy sorting them out to be on the move. Since you were still forging ahead with the Romala contract she decided something more drastic had to happen. Sanders was in Miami so she coerced her young brother to tamper with your bike, unquestionably malicious intent, but it seems it was designed to stall you rather than kill you."

"What about the accident to Miss Cameron?"

Nairn squeezed her fingers.

"A spur-of-the-moment tactic to put your chauffeur out of operation and thereby keep you from travelling around."

"And my Range Rover problem?"

There was a deep clearing of Detective Woods' throat before he continued. "Again, spur of the moment sabotage. She'd heard Robin Ellesmere organising his emergency dental treatment. It was easy enough for her to follow you to the Ad Exec car park."

"Bloody maniac! So what exactly did she do to my car?"

Aela retained Nairn's fingers before he yanked out all of his hair, and did a little bit of the finger massage she was getting very good at.

"Well, it seems her ingenuity and her bravado were a little bit thin by the time she got to your parked car. All she could think about was loosening the wheel nuts in the hope you might have a little problem when you drove off."

"We certainly did. She almost damned well killed us!"

Detective Woods was on a roll and wasn't finished.

"It appears the car park was busy and she only managed to loosen two of the nuts, a little bit. Since she was using the wrench from her own car it didn't fit properly. It was sufficient to mangle them, though, and they eventually loosened at the worst possible moment for you. The mechanic's opinion is they may not have slipped like they did if you'd been driving at thirty M.P.H. The fact you were doing sixty to seventy M.P.H. created enough vibration."

"So, with all of that, surely you have enough evidence to charge them?"

"Yes, sir, we do, for Grainger, her brother and the electrician friend. Sanders, unfortunately no, since he was not in the UK when the incidents occurred."

Sanders had left Stella, and her brother, carrying the can.

"Stupid friggin'…nincompoop!"

Nairn was so furious he had run out of suitable words for using when talking to a police detective. He was scathing beyond belief when the call ended.

"The deranged bitch thought she could put me off bidding with those unhinged tactics?"

"She obviously knew diddly squat about you and your relentless work drive, Nairn Malcolm. It's incredible she could have been so infatuated with you that she needed to take out her revenge in such fashion."

Startling her with his speed Nairn rolled her over and tickled her ribs. "Are you saying I'm not worthy of infatuating over?"

"Wanting your positive attention? Yes sir, that I can understand," she squealed as she batted out of his playful reach. "But infatuated? No. Who'd want to be so taken by you, Nairn Malcolm?"

"Are you saying you're not the tiniest bit infatuated by me? Or want to be taken by me?"

She remembered her initial thoughts on first seeing him at the castle wall. Taken by the sexy wild highlander? She'd achieved that…and never wanted it to stop.

Nairn pinned her to the bed and kissed her soundly. Then started to nibble and tickle again. "Don't I make you do passionately irrational things?"

"Hands off," she warned because he had indeed found her most vulnerable tickling spot. "Get back to your side of the bed!"

Nairn was now in a mischievous mood, declaring that no one was out there plotting to harm them or kill them. The relief was hard to believe. In turn, she no longer felt Nairn was under threat. He continued to tickle her along the bed till she cried, "Stop!"

He clamped her down again till out of breath he slumped over on the bedcover.

"I'm definitely infatuated by you. You make me do

passionately irrational things, all the time!"

Aela watched his eyes close as he regained his breath. Had he just declared more than a passing fancy for her? She dared not break the mood, and instead found an answer in glibness.

"Well, you'd better be nice to me or maybe I'll get crazy like Stella Grainger and do something ridiculously horrible."

Nairn knew her statement for what it was, and looked totally unfazed by her threat.

"I'll tickle you back." Her fingers theatrically reached for his ribs but knowing it was still difficult for him to laugh heartily, she aimed for a compromise.

"Okay. Let's see. I'll not scratch under your plaster when you itch...even if you beg. Or, I'll refuse to help you with fiddly buttons and stuff."

Their laughter echoed around for quite a while as they got creative.

The next day, when their return flight was an hour or so out of London, Nairn bid her pack up their work. Amazed at his request she complied readily, searching his face for signs of exhaustion yet found none. As par for the course, they'd been working all through the long flight. She sat back in her seat when all was cleared away and looked at him, just looked.

Locking her hand tightly in his the question came out of the blue.

"How much do you really want to do your course at UBC?"

She wished he'd said nothing because it seemed a complete slap in the face.

His eyes were earnest.

She was flustered. He'd just thrust reality right back on her doorstep. Only a few days of her contract were left. Her answer was slow in coming, and very guarded, as he threaded his fingers more tightly through hers. "I've been thinking about doing it for years. It's the sensible next step in my business career." She couldn't face his eyes, could only fixate on their linked hands.

"So, if there was a similar course in Glasgow, or London, would you consider doing it there?" Nairn sounded a little odd.

What was he asking? They'd had a fabulous few days, but although she knew in her heart he really liked her he had never indicated long-term.

"Full-time it would take at least a year," she answered, dropping his hand.

Could she have occasional contact with him knowing full-well the way business drove his life? She'd be busy studying, for sure, but she'd never see him.

No.

The price of not knowing where he was, and who he was with, was too high a price to pay. How could he ask her this? She'd heard people saying their heart had been hurting over a guy and thought they'd been exaggerating. They weren't. Her heart hurt so much she was surprised she was still sitting there. Turning to him, she met his eager regard.

Hope was in his eyes. She'd already capitulated and given in to him in their short-term fling, but she couldn't contemplate being discarded at a later date when it was no longer convenient for him.

***

Nairn knew he'd won when he saw the disillusionment in her gorgeous glistening brown eyes. He didn't want to ever cause her pain, but he had to be sure what they shared wasn't temporary for her. He had to be sure she wasn't just in the throes of a passionate end-of-world-trip fling.

"No, Nairn. I'm not going to stay on in Glasgow, or London, and do an MBA. I'm sorry I can't do it."

Tears hovered on Aela's beautiful eyelashes before the first one silently slid down her cheek. A cascade followed.

"Oh God, Aela, don't cry!" He crushed her to him. His finger gently forced her chin up and kissed her eyes clear of tears. "Do you love me then, as much as I love you?"

"You love me?" Her sobs became big huge gulps. "You can ask what you just did and then…you say you love me?"

"I love absolutely every single thing about you. You are the loveliest, sexiest, most desirable wonderful lover, even if I have to teach you everything." Their shared laughter shattered any tension. "You're also the most capable, clever, organising, sometimes cheeky, bossy woman I know – except for my mother. But in spite of all those faults…"

As Aela swatted him with her hands he saw her eyes fill up again.

"Nairn Malcolm, you are the most devious sod, ever. You come first in the scheming manipulator class, second only to…Stella Grainger!"

"Don't say my name and hers in the same sentence. Not ever. I didn't mean to make you cry, or hurt you Aela, but I had to be sure you weren't just using me for a few days' fling." Grabbing her, he held her close to his chest. "I want you by my side forever. As my lover, my PA, my sometimes chauffeur when I'm too tired to fly or drive myself…or when you're too bossy to let me have a go."

Aela climbed on top of him and pinned him to the airplane seat. "If that was a proposal, you insufferable man, I'm going to say no until you get down on your knees and beg. That was the worst proposal I could ever imagine."

To prove it, she kissed him till he was breathless so he had an idea of her real answer.

"Aela, you wouldn't do it to me in my incapacitated state, would you? I might not be able to bend both knees properly for at least another three weeks."

"How about you try?"

Nairn slid to the floor his leg cast at a precarious angle and held her head securely, well aware of where his arm cast was, knowing he wasn't in any way going to hurt her. "Aela, would you please be my wife, for ever and ever?"

The trilling noise of his mobile phone made Aela groan.

"Hells teeth!" She laughed. "Detective Woods again?"

It was.

"Detective Woods?" He flicked up the speaker. Aela made to sit on the other chair but he drew her close enough to share. "Yes. We wondered how they could possibly have known about it."

The policeman was referring to the fact Stella and her brother knew the whereabouts of Nairn's bike that memorable Saturday.

"Well, Mr. Malcolm, walls definitely have ears."

Detective Woods was in full flow again. The man obviously liked this denouement part of his job as he updated. Aela nibbled Nairn's neck as she listened in, making sweat bead on his forehead.

"Grainger was in Marsha Hilborne's office the Friday before your accident and heard of your plans to use your bike."

He felt Aela's clever little fingers travel down his torso. A little deliberate flick sent his voice spiralling. "Really!"

He brought the tenor of his speech down, swatting her persistent little hand away.

"While Brian Dalkin updated Marsha Hilborne on your travel plans, Grainger heard everything on the speakerphone."

Nairn turned the tables on Aela by catching her hand.

Detective Woods continued blithely unaware of their preoccupation. "Grainger ferreted out your hotel meeting place and time details."

Aela wriggled free, stood up and slowly pulled up her T-shirt.

"And?" he asked baldly, to rush the conversation on.

"Grainger gathered up her young brother and got them on the first available flight to Glasgow on the Friday evening. They were waiting in a hired car when you arrived at the car park on the Saturday."

There was a little silence, almost, as he watched Aela turn around and present her rear for him to ogle as she slid her jeans down her fabulous long legs.

The almost was a little squeal of throat clearing from Nairn.

Detective Woods added jauntily, "I'll let you get on with whatever pressing needs you and Miss Cameron have, sir, now you have those last details."

Nairn heard the clear laughter in the other man's tone. He thanked him profusely, switched off the phone, and threw it onto the nearest seat. "Fifteen minutes left, woman!"

"Fifteen for what?" Aela cried as he launched them onto the small bed, the sudden flip of turbulence not to blame, not to blame at all for his increased heart rate.

"Get these clothes off me."

"As you wish my very own Sir Smash-Em-Up!"

He grinned, a happy, contented...still a little bit pained grin as she flopped down on the cover alongside him.

"Do you think you'll ever stay put in one place for any length of time, Nairn Malcolm?" Aela's voice was satisfied and dreamy.

"Twenty-four-hours-a-day-for-a-lifetime forever is what I'm engaging you for, Aela Cameron. Why would I want to stay put anywhere?"

"Know any good doormat companies...?"

A happy sigh escaped them both.

THE END

Fantastic Books
Great Authors

CROOKED
CAT

Meet our authors and discover our exciting range:

- Gripping Thrillers
- Cosy Mysteries
- Romantic Chick-Lit
- Fascinating Historicals
- Exciting Fantasy
- Young Adult and Children's Adventures

Made in the USA
Charleston, SC
30 May 2016